THE PRINCE AND THE DRAGON

CAITLIN HODNEFIELD

Copyright © 2022 Caitlin Hodnefield

All rights reserved. This book or any portion thereof may not be reproduced or used in any manner whatsoever without the express permission of the publisher except for the use of brief quotations in a book review.

Printed in the United States of America

First Printing, 2022

ISBN 978-0-578-37810-7

Amazon Kindle Direct Publishing

To my family, friends, and all the readers who loved my first book—you gave me the much needed push to continue writing!

*To my Great Aunt Peggy (1952-2019),
your encouragement will be greatly missed.*

Land of ARDA

BLUE FIRE RANGE

CASCADE RANGE

Tiered Mtn.

Lonrach Lake

Arondale

Anapoth

Thraicin River

WILDS

Mirava

Sylvan Lake

ELF KINGDOM

Pronunciation Guide and Characters

Elestari: Say it fast! The "e" in the middle is short. The *Elestari* are a shapeshifting dragon people. They are fully dragon and fully human.

Saoirse: Sear+sha, magical Elestari woman

Aodhan: Ay+dan, half dwarf, half man, Prince of Amaroth and son of Avana and Killian

Avana: Pronounced like "Havana" without the "h," human Queen of Amaroth

Killian: Typical pronunciation, dwarf, husband of Avana

Fallon: Typical pronunciation, wild Northern wolf, family friend of the royals

Finris: Pronounced fin-ris, High Chief of the Northern wolves

Zellnar: Say it fast and you'll get it, common dragon and protector of Amaroth

Killkari: Pronounced kill-car-ee, said fast, evil common dragon

Valanter: Say it fast! Valant-er, elf king

Nedanael: Pronounced knee-daniel, elf smith

Nokoa: Pronounced na-koa, ancient dragon that lives in the elf kingdom

Halfor: Say it fast! Dwarf king and uncle of Killian

Table of Contents

Chapter 1	1
Chapter 2	11
Chapter 3	33
Chapter 4	40
Chapter 5	48
Chapter 6	54
Chapter 7	62
Chapter 8	69
Chapter 9	77
Chapter 10	87
Chapter 11	94
Chapter 12	104
Chapter 13	111
Chapter 14	119
Chapter 15	127
Chapter 16	140
Chapter 17	149
Chapter 18	157
Chapter 19	165
Chapter 20	172
Chapter 21	178
Chapter 22	185
Chapter 23	191
Chapter 24	202
Chapter 25	208
Chapter 26	213
Chapter 27	220
Chapter 28	226
Chapter 29	232
Chapter 30	237
Chapter 31	242
Chapter 32	247

Chapter 1

FIRE. DARKNESS. FEAR. WILD CRIES IN the night. She found herself tangled in a net of impenetrable webbing. She struggled and felt searing pain shoot up her arm. Thrashing wildly now she began to come to her senses. She was tangled in bed sheets, not the horrible net. Their softness brought her back to reality with a jolt. Where was she? Her mind raced frantically trying to remember how she had gotten there. Nothing. Everything was a gaping black hole. She realized with horrifying clarity that her memory was completely gone. She didn't even know her name. It was there but hidden behind a wall that she couldn't break.

With a frustrated sigh, she slowly opened her eyes and relaxed into the bed. She took in the room around her. White walls glowed from golden sunlight. The room was plainly furnished with a high-backed chair and nightstand. Through the simplicity there was a touch of unexpected elegance. The nightstand was intricately carved, and in the light, gave off a burnished gleam. The drapes were made of pleasant light green damask that were finer than she would have expected. They framed a large window letting in the light and gentle warmth of an early sun.

Deliberately, she began to untangle herself from the sheets, throwing back the dark wool coverlet. A sharp pain raced up her arm as she attempted to sit up. So that at least was real; she winced at her broken limb. Looking down, she realized that it had been skillfully bandaged. It was splinted with slender pieces of wood, bound tight with gray strips of cloth. More carefully this time, she eased herself into a sitting position.

As she sat up, she heard footsteps outside her door. Instinctively, she reached for her weapon but found nothing. Another fact to add to her slim knowledge of who she was. She was used to carrying a blade. She mulled this over as she watched the brass handle turn and the door swing open.

In walked a sable-haired man. His eyes widened in surprise to see her awake and sitting up. She was immediately struck by the color of his eyes. They were the brightest robin's egg blue she had ever seen. *Not that she remembered anyone else*, she thought wryly. Recovering quickly, the man smiled at her though she noted it didn't reach his eyes.

"You're awake. We've been wondering how long you would be out. You must be hungry. Let me bring you something, and then we can talk."

With that he turned and left the room, leaving the door partially open. She felt overwhelmed by his sudden appearance and departure. She closed her eyes again, picturing the man in her head. Who was he? And what did he want to talk about? A niggling feeling of worry wormed inside her. It told her that talking was not something she should do. But what could she tell him? She couldn't remember anything!

Again, she racked her brain hoping that somehow, she would overcome the block. She could hear the man in another part of the house clinking dishes together. Who was he? Did she know him? Soon she heard footsteps coming back toward her room. The man walked in again carrying a tray with a bowl of steaming soup accompanied by a deep pewter flagon of milk.

Her stomach twisted hungrily at the sight of food. She wondered when she had last eaten. Not recently if her growling stomach was correct. The man set the tray down on the nightstand next to the bed.

"How do you feel?" the man asked as he settled into the empty chair.

"Hungry…and confused. How did I get here?"

"I was out hunting on the mountainside when I heard goblin cries. I decided to investigate. Goblins are a constant source of fear to people in the mountains. They prey on travelers. Those of us who are able, kill them. When I reached the goblins, I saw they had something trapped in a net. It struggled against them. I realized that it was you they had captured."

"It was me? I don't remember any of that."

"Yes, it was you. There were only five of them. I had my bow with me and I was able to dispatch two of the creatures before they discovered my location. The goblins dropped you, the struggling prisoner, to attack me. You clawed your way out of the net as the goblins fought me. You took up a blade from one of the dead goblins and fought them. You killed a goblin, but a second clouted you from behind. You must have been weakened from your ordeal because the blow knocked you out. I was able to dispatch the last goblin. Then, when I couldn't rouse you, I brought you back here to splint and bandage your arm. You've been out for two days since then."

The man finished speaking, leaned back in his chair, and watched her as she stiffly ate the soup he had brought her. She stared back at him over the bowl.

"What's your name? Where am I?"

She continued to stare at him hoping to find out something about her identity. The man was tall, with legs covered in stained brown leggings and knee-high scuffed boots stretching out before him. Clad in an indigo shirt and black leather overtunic, his outfit clung to him bespeaking of the muscles beneath. The only truly distinguishing thing he wore was a finely wrought bright silver clip keeping his shoulder length raven hair back. His face was impassive.

"My name is Aodhan. You are in the home of the former Ranger Andrew. I live here with him so he can teach me the ways of the Rangers. What's your name?"

"I don't know…"

He frowned at her from under dark brows. "What do you mean you don't know?"

"I mean what I said. I don't know. I can't remember. I can't remember anything except a vague feeling of being surrounded by fire and feeling a net cast over me. That's all. I was hoping you would know my identity."

Aodhan sat silent in his own thoughts. After a few strained heartbeats he seemed to settle on a reply.

"I think I believe you. You suffered a hit sufficient to knock you out. Head trauma sometimes robs a man of his memory. It may return or it may not." He saw her face blanch fleetingly at his words, so he continued, "I must call you something in the meantime. How do you like Dara?"

"Dara would be fine, thank you."

"Then Dara it will be," Aohdan said.

"Thank you also for what you have done. I think I would be dead otherwise. Goblins are cruel creatures."

"Yes, they are most vile." He paused. "I would introduce you to Andrew, the master of the house, but he is gone at the moment. He'll be back tomorrow."

Dara took a long draft from the flagon. The creamy milk cooled her throat after the heat of the soup. The warm food had satisfied her hunger and now the need for sleep crept over her, though she feared another nightmare. Visions of green-skinned goblins with sharp teeth and leering faces danced in her head muddling her thoughts. She had a few more questions she wanted answered before she slept, so Dara pushed aside the heaviness assaulting her.

"Where are we? And was there a weapon that the goblins carried that possibly belonged to me? I sense that I am used to having a blade."

The blue eyes hardened for a moment at her question. She could see Aohdan weighing what he should tell this stranger. She didn't feel that odd, but she sensed that her appearance was unusual. She went over her exterior trying to see herself as this stranger would. Her clothes were of light cotton in neutral hues, ragged and torn from her encounter with goblins. Her hair was a strange color of burnished silver blonde, combined with violet eyes that burned with a peculiar fire that might be disconcerting if she stared at you too long. After a few moments, Aohdan seemed to decide that there was no malice in her demeanor.

"We are in a house on the edge of the farthest eastern Cascade Mountain. Beyond lies the Blue Fire Mountain range, the tallest range in all of Arda. To answer the second part of your question, yes, the goblins had a sword with them that was not goblin made. It is a rather odd blade. I will show it to you when you are stronger, if you wish."

A rush went through Dara at the mention of the Blue Fire Mountains. Something stirred inside her. She grappled with it hoping to turn up a memory but found nothing. She was not surprised that Aohdan was reluctant to give her a weapon. They knew nothing of each other.

"I appreciate your candor. I will be glad to look at the sword. Perhaps it will spark my memory."

"Perhaps. For now I will leave you to rest. I hope you found the food reviving."

Aohdan stood, picking up the tray. Nodding to her, he left the room closing the door with an air of finality behind him. Dara lay back pondering the exchange. It was certainly an ambiguous introduction. Neither trusted the other. Dara hoped that would change. She would need to rely on Aohdan's friendship until she regained her memory. Sleep overwhelmed her thoughts, and she rested in its relief.

She awakened the next morning to a tray of steaming porridge and a thick slab of bacon. Whatever Aohdan thought of her, he was at least keeping her well-fed. Dara finished the breakfast quickly. She was pleased to see a set of clean clothes for her on the chair. She felt strength returning to her body, enough to encourage her to get up. She pulled herself upright and walked slowly to the window.

The view looked out into a large, well-tended garden full of rows of sweet smelling flowers. Rainbow bursts sprayed across the tops of the plants in a lovely array of colors. A small plot of bright vegetables mixed with a variety of herbs sat close to the house. Billowing gracefully, a willow and some fruit trees made an incongruous picture in comparison to the mountain pines that ringed the house. A marble bench under the willow completed the garden. Rust colored bricks formed a path through it all, running to the bench. This was indeed an unusual house. Rangers, even retired, were not known for having such fine abodes.

Standing at the window Dara felt herself tiring. She hesitantly walked back to the bed, not wishing to leave the sunlight. She slept again for a few hours before awakening to voices outside her room. Both were distinctly masculine. Dara guessed that Andrew had returned. She caught the end of the conversation.

"…doesn't remember anything," came Aohdan's voice as the men walked into her room.

Aohdan entered first, followed by a tall, thin man, well-tanned by years in the sun. His hair was dark chocolate brown and streaked with gray. His intelligent brown eyes searched Dara's with keen interest. Aohdan went straight into introductions.

"Dara, this is Andrew. He is master of this house, and also guardian of this part of the mountains."

The puzzle of the fine house was now settled for Dara. This retired Ranger must act as magistrate for the area she surmised. *How did she know that? She wondered in frustration. How could parts of her mind work and others not?*

Andrew broke into her thoughts. "Welcome, Dara, to my home. I'm sorry to hear about your memory loss. You seem young and strong though. I think it will return in time and I am interested to hear your story when it does. Until then, you are welcome to stay here. Rest, heal, in body and mind. This house is a haven for travelers, though we get very few of them. Queen Avana herself commissioned me here so we are under royal protection."

"Thank you for your hospitality. I do not wish to impose on you, but without my memory I am grateful for a safe house until I am well."

"And you truly can remember nothing?" queried the old Ranger. "Tell us what you do know. Perhaps we can begin to trace who you are."

Dara combed through her mind. "It is true that I have no memory about myself. I feel that it is there, but I can't unlock it. I remember fire. I remember pain from my arm; I think that was when it was broken. I remember thrashing about in a net. I am familiar with Rangers, the Queen, and the Blue Fire Mountains sparked something inside me. I wonder if I am from there. I also know that I have carried a sword before. That is all."

When Dara spoke of the Blue Fire Mountains the men exchanged a quick glance with one another. She suspected that there was much more to them than what they had told her.

"Your story lines up with how Aohdan found you. I apologize for being suspicious, but it's my job to be wary. I wonder about your connection to the Blue Fire Mountains. As far as we know there are no settlements there. This house is the last taste of civil life before you cross the mountain range."

"I wish I could remember why those mountains call to me," Dara admitted wryly. "I simply know that the name burns inside of me when it is spoken. Perhaps I had been on a trek to cross them when the goblins attacked?"

Andrew nodded in agreement. "That is a possibility. Whatever the case you are here now. We shall do our best to help you recover. Are you feeling up for a tour of the house?"

"I think I would enjoy that. I have already had a walk to the window. The view is quite pleasing."

"Good. Aodhan will walk with you since you are still weak."

With that the men rose while Dara carefully shifted out of the bed. Aohdan courteously offered Dara his arm which she gingerly took. Standing beside him, she realized he was a good bit broader than Andrew.

They exited out of the room into a large kitchen and dining area. A heavy, well carved oak dining room table sat in the center of the kitchen. Chestnut grained cabinets lined the wall, matching the table. A wide range with a cherry glow in its belly occupied a corner. It was a space designed to hold about twenty people. It was homey but seemed too large for the current occupants.

"Our kitchen is a bit extravagant for us, I'm afraid. It does the job though."

Aodhan's voice echoed in the large room. Dara smiled up at him in reply. "It's very nice. I'm sure you can host a large number of people when the need arises."

"Those times are few and far between, I'm afraid. Visitors are uncommon."

"That makes me doubly unusual. I just can't be normal, can I?"

Andrew shook his head with a twinkle in his eye. "A bit of oddity in life improves it. You're giving us some needed variety."

"At least I'm good for something then." Dara laughed at his spin on her predicament. "Shall we continue on?"

They went into an arched hallway that had several rooms opening off of it, all similar to Dara's. Each was simply furnished with a bed, nightstand, and a chair on the side. Further in, the house widened into a sitting room that branched off to a full bathhouse. The sitting room boasted a deep cherrywood fireplace. Elegant, navy cushioned sofas and chairs lined the walls. Dust motes danced in the light pouring in through gabled windows, outlined by the same green damask drapes as in Dara's room.

Attached was a full porch with a finely wrought front door. After this, Dara was delighted to find a library with floor to ceiling books. It was comfortably furnished with chairs and a satin covered window bench. The corner of the library held a doorway that led to a staircase going to the upper portion of the house. The smell of vellum and dust pervaded the room. Dara inhaled the scent with a small thrill. She loved books. How did she know she loved books?

"Those are our quarters," Andrew said regaining her attention, pointing to the stairs. "Our rooms are comparable to yours. The upstairs is mostly storage. We keep our food stocks there."

"And I suppose it keeps you out of the way of highborn visitors on the odd occasion that you host them," Dara hedged.

"You catch on quickly. Now that you have seen it, you are welcome to wander the house, and eventually the grounds as you have the strength. We only ask that you respect the privacy of our rooms as we from now on will respect yours."

"I will do as you say, Andrew. I look forward to going about more than just my room. The library especially is promising. Could I perchance take a book back with me?"

"Of course. I must attend to the horses now. We keep a few for long distance travel. We also keep a cow and chickens for fresh milk and eggs. They are a necessity of living in a secluded area. Aohdan will help you with anything else that you need. As for meals we generally eat light during the day and save our big meal for the evening after our work is done. If you are up to joining us we will eat around six in the kitchen." With a bow to Dara, Andrew left the library and headed outdoors.

An empty silence fell as Dara surveyed the library. She left Aohdan's side and walked up to a shelf containing history volumes. She chose a book concerning the most recent events in hopes that something would jog her memory. As she stood poring over the book she felt a ringing stir inside her. Puzzled she looked over at Aohdan to see if he too could feel the vibrations. He stood engaged by a large book, looking not the least concerned. Dara wondered if it was a side effect of her injury. She paced toward the stairs and window hoping to shake off the strange feeling. Instead the ringing intensified, an insistent clarion. It felt familiar, like a calling or yearning for something that she couldn't identify.

Dara shook her head slightly, shrugging off the sound. She approached Aohdan, clutching the book tightly to her chest. Surely, she was just tired. A good nap would cure this strange feeling.

"I would like to retire now, Aohdan. Thank you for the tour. I hope I will wake for dinner."

Aohdan gently replaced the book he had been reading saying, "Sleep is most important now. Don't worry about skipping meals. You will make up for them in time."

Taking her book for her, he again offered his arm, and for the first time a real smile spread across his face. In his coldness he had been handsome, but warmth made him striking. Dara's pulse couldn't help quickening as he carefully escorted her back to her room. There she fell instantly asleep, worn by her adventure.

Chapter 2

OVER THE NEXT WEEK DARA CONTINUED to improve. She roamed the house, often spending time in the library. She eagerly read through the books hoping to find something to trigger her memory. Soon she took her strolling out to the garden. Often Dara would pick a book and take it out to the bench under the willow. There she would sit and read for hours caught up in the story. Her appetite for knowledge was unquenchable, eating up volume after volume.

She felt more alive in the outdoors, reveling in the fresh mountain air. Its bite accompanied by the fragrance of pine opened up a wild side of her that tugged at the block in her mind. The voluminous garden also garnered her attention. The orderly rows of flowers, swollen with vibrant colors, giving off their pleasant aromas drew her to them with sweetness. She was fascinated by the variety, spending time studying each plant. Dara even began to do small amounts of pruning as her strength allowed.

After his initial standoffishness, Aohdan quickly warmed to Dara. When he wasn't hunting or training with Andrew, he spent time with her. She discovered that he was musically talented. An old pianoforte in the sitting room became a meeting place for the two. Aohdan had a strong baritone that Dara matched with her alto. Aohdan's fingers would dance over the keys as they sang together.

Andrew enjoyed their music. He was friendly but maintained a separateness from Dara. He was still cautious of her. He sensed that she was more than what she seemed. On the other hand, Aohdan proved to be a suitable companion. He was often stern yet allowed the curiosity of youth to still shine through. Dara's presence softened his solemnity.

One warm afternoon Dara sat reading under the willow enjoying the cool of the shade. Aohdan was on the garden lawn, practicing with his sword. A long quavering howl broke their concentration. Aohdan broke into an enormous grin, while Dara looked alarmed.

"A friend has returned," Aohdan spoke happily. As he did so, a huge white creature ran through the pines toward them. A gigantic wolf the size of a draft horse burst into the garden. It flew at Dara snarling madly. It stood growling over her, fur on end and teeth exposed. She shrank back into the bench, curling into a ball.

"Fallon, stop!" Aohdan cried out in alarm. He dropped his sword and rushed up to the wolf. "She's a friend. Leave her!"

"What is this creature, Aohdan? It is not fully human. Its scent is strange." Fallon growled, every hair bristling with suspicion.

"We don't know. She's lost her memory. I rescued her from some goblins. I call her Dara."

Fallon's growls receded, his ruff relaxing, but he continued to tower over Dara. "Speak female. I wish to hear truth from your own mouth."

Dara peeked up at the wolf as she trembled. There was no longer anger in his eyes, only cold suspicion. Her voice faltered as she began.

"I truly don't know who I am, great wolf. I remember nothing of my past, but foggy memories of my capture. That is all. Please, you say I am not human. What am I then? I am anxious for an answer to my past."

Fallon bowed his head to level with Dara, eyeing her judgmentally. He nudged her gently with his wet black nose inhaling her scent. Dara stiffened at his touch. Aohdan was impressed that she held her ground as she faced off with Fallon, though he could see the muscles in her neck tense.

Fallon backed up a step from Dara. She slumped onto the bench. Fallon closed his eyes appearing to think hard.

"I have never encountered your scent before. It is similar to several other species yet matches none. You smell of human….and something I can't identify. I sense no malice or evil in you. Instead, I feel the stirring of powerful good magic. You are extremely unusual. I apologize for my reaction. It is not my intention to be rude. I simply was concerned over the welfare of my friend, Prince Aohdan."

"Prince…?" Dara's violet eyes widened, staring at Aohdan in shock.

Aohdan visibly reddened. He shifted from foot to foot, running his fingers through his hair, staring at the ground.

"Fallon, you and your overprotectiveness," he mumbled at long last casting the wolf a sidelong glance. "Yes, I am Prince Aohdan. My parents are Queen Avana and King Killian. I'm sorry for keeping you in the dark. Andrew and I don't make my heritage known for my safety, but also so that I can remain anonymous in my training and work."

"Of course, my Prince. I only wish that I had not been so ignorant," Dara replied bowing her head respectfully to Aohdan. She felt uncomfortable now thinking of how careless she had been in her manners with him.

"None of that 'Prince' nonsense, Dara," Aohdan lectured sharply, sensing her thoughts. "I am nothing more than any other man. My parents do not hold with grand titles and neither do I. I wish for us to continue as friends. Not as prince and subject."

Smiling hesitantly, Dara nodded. She stood up warily as Fallon approached Aohdan and nuzzled him affectionately, crooning a soft growl. Aohdan threw his arms around Fallon, fiercely embracing the wolf in a long awaited reunion.

After his welcome by Aohdan, Fallon turned back to Dara. "I have known Aohdan since he was a cub. I have watched over him as a token of friendship to his mother Avana, my adopted sister. We have journeyed far together. Recently, circumstances have kept us apart. His path led him to come to the mountains to assist Andrew and train with him. I was detained with pack matters among the Wild Wolves of the North. You took me by surprise. I don't like surprises."

"I understand, wolf. Would you permit me to call you by your name?"

"Yes. You may address me as Fallon. Draw near to me so we may have a more pleasant greeting."

Dara tentatively stepped toward Fallon who lay down in the grass as a sign of friendship. Mustering her courage, she reached out a hand to touch the shaggy white fur. The wolf leaned into her touch placing his head over her shoulder, pulling her into him. Pressed against Fallon she could feel his powerful heart rhythmically thumping against his ribs. Forgetting herself she returned the embrace the best she could while protecting her injured arm.

Abruptly remembering that she was hugging a wolf, Dara pulled away. Fallon laughed heartily at her swift departure.

"Wild Northern wolves have a way of charming people when they choose to befriend them," Aohdan said, laughing at Dara's discomfort. He gave her a roguish wink that was so uncharacteristic of him that she stared for a moment longer than was polite, causing him to laugh harder.

Finally, allowing herself to be infected by their mirth, Dara too smiled. "I will consider it the highest honor to call you my friend, Fallon. I trust that our friendship will be a long one. But, Aohdan, something bothers me. What is this work of Andrew's that you and Fallon allude to?"

"I suppose if my personal secret is out then I can tell you about what Andrew and I have been working on. Over the last few years there has been a drastic shortage of bright silver. The elves create the metal and then store it in carefully concealed caches. These caches have been raided. Almost every store is gone. Andrew has been following up on the evidence. He thinks it's the work of an evil black dragon named Killkari. The trail has led him here to the edge of the mountain range. That's where I joined him. We've been scouting far and wide. We are now sure that Killkari is not in the Cascades, but rather up somewhere in the Blue Fire Mountains.

"And there's another twist to the story. Killkari is responsible for the death of Andrew's wife. Fifteen years ago, Killkari burned down the small village where Andrew lived while he was gone on a Ranger mission. The entire town was destroyed. No one survived. Andrew was heartbroken. He quit the Rangers and began to search for Killkari. He sought revenge against the dragon for the death of his wife. Andrew devoted his life to finding the black beast. Killkari went on a spree of destruction for a few months after razing Andrew's hometown and then he disappeared.

"Andrew searched relentlessly for the black dragon but found nothing. It was only in the last two years that signs of the dragon resurfaced. Killkari is the thief. We intend to find his lair and destroy him. We must retrieve the bright silver at all costs. If the goblins got a hold of it, we'd all be in trouble."

Aohdan finished his long speech with a sigh. "Andrew drives himself too hard. He hates dragons. Even the good ones. All he can think of is revenge on Killkari."

"What an awful thing to happen! And what a desolate life to live. So he's spent the last fifteen years bent on revenge?" Dara asked quietly.

"Yes. And it's changed him. He's not who he was. I remember him from my youth as an outgoing, fiery man intensely interested in all aspects of life. I used to look up to him as much as my father. I still do, but he's changed. Now there's only a shell left of that personality."

Dara saw the pain in Aohdan's eyes as he spoke of his friend and mentor. *Loss drives each person differently*, she thought to herself. *Add grief, and it can drive you mad.*

"I am sorry, for both of you, Aohdan. I hope that you are successful in defeating Killkari. I don't suppose I could be of any help at the moment with my arm; however, if there was something I could do I would gladly volunteer."

"Thank you for your kindness, Dara," Aohdan's voice rang softly with gratefulness, "There isn't much we can do at the moment. We simply are tracking the beast down. That takes time. The good news is that since Killkari now has a horde, he is less likely to leave it, and that makes our job easier."

Fallon rumbled next to them. "And now you have my assistance again. You will be able to search farther afield. I do not tire as easily as your horses."

Aohdan laid a hand on the wolf's shoulder. "Andrew will be pleased that you are here, Fallon. He has been anxious to explore the upper parts of the Blue Fire Mountains."

"Something else still bothers me. Every time you speak of the Blue Fire Mountains I feel a connection to them, though I don't know why. It's excruciating to have this niggling sense and remember nothing!" Dara huffed.

"That will have to remain a mystery. My hope is that Andrew and I will discover something that pertains to you. Perhaps there is an unknown settlement there. The range is quite substantial and forbidding, so it stands to reason there could be people there we have never encountered." Aohdan also wished to solve the mystery of Dara's past. He had an overwhelming curiosity to understand her.

Dara allowed a flicker of lightness to stir in her heart. "I will hang onto that hope then. I must admit now that I am tired from all this excitement. I am so pleased to have made your acquaintance,

Fallon. My mind wishes to stay, but my body is resisting. I feel the need to retire for a nap. I hope to see you both at supper."

With that she withdrew from their company. She went to her room and soon fell fast asleep.

When she awoke, Dara realized it was morning again. She had missed supper, but she figured she needed the sleep more. Dara stood and stretched, mindful of her arm. As she did so, she again sensed the ringing inside of her that she had originally felt during her tour of the house.

Something was calling her. Dara decided to investigate. First, she peeked out the window in hopes of seeing Fallon. The garden was empty. Then she opened the door and walked slowly down the hallway. The ringing grew stronger. In the kitchen she stopped for a moment. There was evidence of breakfast from Aohdan and Andrew. A plate of muffins with fruit was set off to the side. Dara surmised this was meant for her. The food made her stomach rumble loudly, but the draw of the ringing was stronger.

She followed the ringing into the library, through the doorway, and up the staircase. At the landing she stopped. Here the ringing felt so loud inside her that she could barely think. Dara looked at the rooms along the hallway. Most of them were open. Whatever was calling to her was up here. She closed her eyes, allowing the ringing to engulf her. With her eyes still closed she slowly walked forward keeping one hand on the wall. One room, two, then three passed under her hand. At the fourth she stopped. She opened her eyes. This door was closed.

It had to be either Andrew's or Aohdan's room. A ripple of nervousness coursed through her. This was a private room. She had no wish to disturb or irritate either man. But the ringing was driving her crazy. Curiosity overcame her fears. She quickly knocked on the door before her courage completely left her. The floor creaked from the other side and the handle turned. Aohdan pulled the door open.

"What is it, Dara?" Aohdan appeared very perplexed and also very handsome in his confusion.

"Something is calling me. I can't properly explain, but it's in here. I felt it the first time you showed me around the house. Today I awoke and it was so compelling, I had to follow it." Dara looked imploringly at Aohdan as the ringing tugged insistently at her gut.

"I suppose you can look around. I haven't heard anything though."

Dara stepped into the room. Like hers it held a nightstand and bed, but there the similarities ended. A bulky rucksack sat on the floor. Two well-worn bed rolls occupied the space next to it. A deep closet held Aohdan's clothes, while the walls were lined with many pegs. These held a large variety of weapons, camping utensils, and a painting of the city of Amaroth.

Dara was drawn to the weapons. Aohdan watched her carefully. She gravitated toward an odd looking sword. The blade was a strange hue of purple that seemed to have a faint glow to it. A large white stone was set in the pommel. It was a hand-and-a-half sword, smaller than a long sword.

Dara felt herself pulled to the purple blade. The sword rang incessantly. It seemed to pulse in her gaze. She reached out for it, grasping the handle. At her touch the sword blazed a heatless, fiery violet flame jolting both Dara and Aohdan. Keeping her grip on the blade Dara turned to Aohdan. He stepped back in alarm. Dara's eyes burned with the same violet fire as the sword. Something in her had changed. There was a depth in her gaze that had been hidden before.

Lowering the sword, she spoke to Aohdan, feeling her eyes alight with excitement. "I know who I am. I remember! There is so much to tell you."

She took a step forward and collapsed unconscious to the floor. The sword clattered loudly next to her, losing its glow instantaneously.

Aodhan was stunned. What had just happened? Cautiously, he reached out a hand to feel for a pulse. It was there, but weak. He shook Dara in an attempt to wake her. She lay as if dead. He tried again. Still nothing. Alarm spread through Aohdan. Gingerly, he scooped Dara into his arms and carried her back to her room. He left her sword, fearing to touch it. Over and over he tried to revive her. She did not respond.

Andrew was out scouting with Fallon and wouldn't be back till luncheon. What was he going to do? He tried smelling salts and cold water. Dara didn't even stir. Aohdan paced the house, frantically waiting for Andrew. When the former Ranger returned, Aohdan immediately took him to Dara. He explained what had happened.

"I've never seen anything like it, Andrew. I thought for a moment that she was dead. All of my attempts to awaken her have failed."

Andrew stared at the still form lying in the bed.

"There is some magic in her Aohdan. That's why the sword called to her and behaved as it did. I think that the return of her memories came as a shock. That's what knocked her out. I've heard of cases like that before, but never had anything to verify them as truth. That's the best guess I have, I'm afraid. There's no knowing when she'll awake."

The two men sat in silence contemplating the enigmatic young woman who had fallen into their care. The only magic creature Aohdan knew was the dragon Zellnar. Part of him wished that Zellnar was with them. Perhaps his magic could heal Dara.

"There's not much we can do for her but wait and keep her comfortable. If she came round once already, she's likely to do it again," Andrew said with finality.

With that they left Dara to her peculiar slumber. Aohdan went out and found Fallon in the woods. He spoke to him over the strange occurrence. The wolf was also puzzled and concerned for Dara. Aohdan checked on her every few hours trying to awaken her but was still unsuccessful. That night both men fell into troubled slumbers over Dara's predicament.

Morning arrived in a cool flurry of breeze. Aohdan went straight to Dara's room. To his dismay he found her broken arm greatly swollen and her body burning with fever.

"Andrew! Andrew, come quickly. Dara's burning up!" Aohdan yelled.

Andrew hurried to Dara's room. He placed his hand on her forehead. Sweat beaded her brow. She moved restlessly in bed. Her eyes flickered under closed lids. Andrew attempted to wake her, but Dara stiffened under his hand and remained stubbornly asleep. He was even more disturbed by the swelling in her broken arm. Aohdan had loosened the splint so that it would not cut off circulation in her hand. Dara flinched when either of them touched it.

The two men were perplexed. What had caused this? They could only assume it was a strange side effect of her blackout. They decided to have Fallon check her for poison. Opening up the window to the room, Aohdan called for the wolf.

Fallon stuck his broad head through the window, a sight that would have been humorous at any other time. Whining softly, he gave Dara a vigorous sniff.

"No poison I can smell taints her blood. However, there is something very wrong with her. It's almost as if her body has turned on itself. I can't make it out. The sickness is coming from her, not from an outside influence. She suffers from some internal pain. You said you can't wake her?" Fallon opined carefully.

Aohdan shook his head. "Nothing works. We have tried everything we can think of."

Fallon said thoughtfully, "You told me that before she passed out yesterday, she recovered her memories. I fear it is those memories that are poisoning her. I'm not sure, but it seems to me she has remembered something better left forgotten. I think she is not wakening because she doesn't want to. I have seen it before in the pack, where a wolf loses their mate and is driven mad by it. Eventually they give up their will to live. They wither away. I think whatever Dara remembered is killing her. She's letting go. I'm sorry."

Andrew and Aohdan were appalled by Fallon's pronouncement. Andrew recovered first with a grim look on his face. "I hope you are wrong, Fallon. Nonetheless, I understand what you are saying. We will do all we can for her. Perhaps she will change."

With that, Andrew stalked out of the room before his own old wounds of grief overcame him. Aohdan sadly watched him go before he settled into the chair next to Dara.

Taking her good hand between his, he spoke to her, "Dara, if you can hear me, don't do this. Hang onto life. Live because life itself is worth living. You can't change what happened, but letting yourself die won't fix it. You have friends that care for you here. Are not Andrew, Fallon, and I worth something?"

Dara stirred again. Aohdan wasn't sure, but he thought he perceived the slightest pressure of her hand against his.

Aohdan stayed by Dara's side for the next two days. Andrew kept him supplied with the cool cloths that remained a constant on Dara's forehead. Her skin took on a sallow pallor, while her silver hair hung in damp strands on her shoulders. He force-fed her water, as much as he could get in her. Her fever lingered, burning fiercely at times, an ever present reminder of her internal struggle. Aohdan kept up his encouraging words to her, begging her to hang on.

On the third day he took a short break from his ministrations. Aohdan was beginning to feel despair creep over him. Dara's pulse had been almost nonexistent this morning. Her fever blazed as steadily as ever. He sat down under the willow tree rubbing his eyes, spent from the stress. As he rested he thought he heard Dara's voice quietly calling out his name.

Looking up he studied Fallon who sat at the window watching

Dara. He shook his head. In his exhaustion he was imagining things. If Dara was really asking for him Fallon would let him know.

"Aohdan."

There was her voice again. It was louder this time. He looked hard at Fallon. Surely the wolf had heard it, but Fallon gave no sign. Aohdan jumped up from the bench, walking briskly to the house.

"Aohdan, come to me."

The voice was more urgent now. Aohdan flung the front door open and sprinted to Dara's room. Fallon stared at him in bewilderment from the window.

"Take my hand, Aohdan. Hurry. I am fading."

In that moment Aohdan realized in shock she was not speaking out loud to him. She was communicating through his mind. It could only be with her magic. Pulling the chair closer to the bed he grasped her hand.

He was then pulled into another world. He was surrounded by a field of heatless fire filling him with panic. Orange flames licked at his legs but did not burn him. In the middle of the inferno stood Dara in a flowing lavender gown. She smiled and beckoned to him. Aohdan cautiously came toward her. The fire parted around him as he walked.

She spoke with a lilt to her voice. "You came. I am so pleased that you could hear me. It took almost all my energy to call you. I wanted to speak with you. I've heard your pleas for me to hang onto life. That's why I've called you, but really it's Andrew that I need to speak to. I wanted to tell you first though. I am indebted to you for your friendship."

"Dara, what is this place? Please explain what you mean by all of this," Aohdan said in bewilderment.

"To start my name is actually Saoirse. I am fond of the name Dara now, though. It was a good choice for me. As for the rest, I suppose giving it to you bluntly is best. Fallon said that I am not fully human and that I contained magic. He was quite correct."

Aohdan was completely on edge. "What are you then?"

"I am *Elestari,* a shape changer. I am two creatures in one. I am dragon and human. Equal, yet separate. The *Elestari* are more refined than normal dragons, even the good Zellnar from Lonrach Lake near your home. We are steeped in deeper magic. We can communicate to all species with our minds. We crave knowledge instead of hordes of valuables. Our people are often wizards when in human form. We also grow to greater size and live longer. We are close-knit, holding great banquets to spend time together."

"Where have you been hiding an entire people then? Surely someone would have found you out."

"Let me explain, and you will understand. My people are not numerous. There are fewer than five hundred of us. We live in the Blue Fire Mountains. The very tallest peaks are my home, wonderfully giant caverns decorated much like the dwarf city of your father. Thousands of books line the walls of my home. We have knowledge that spans thousands of years. From the time we hatch we are trained in all types of learning. We study everything from weapons to healing. The most trained healers in Arda over the years have been *Elestari* in their human form," Saoirse said.

"Are there *Elestari* in Amaroth right now?"

"I honestly don't know. Very few of my people ever leave. But to continue on, we also specialize in weapons. Our weapons are unique in that we encourage them to take on the characteristics of the wielder, hence the purple hue of my blade that matches my eyes. We rarely show ourselves as dragons because of the fear that surrounds that shape. We do not wish to be blamed for the tragedies caused by despicable creatures like Killkari."

Aohdan frowned and nodded in agreement. "I can understand wanting to avoid the stigma."

"Due to our seclusion and strength, we put very little value on security. We are only vulnerable in our human form. Even then we considered ourselves safe in our unapproachable eyrie. That was our downfall."

"Complacency is deadly, as Andrew would say."

"Andrew is correct, but there is little I can do now. We were attacked by goblins one night as we feasted at a banquet. All the *Elestari* were there in our great hall. No one was on watch. They started by setting one of our many libraries on fire. This threw us into a panic to put it out. Many of us, like myself, were in human form already for the banquet and simply stayed human to better take care of the flames. That's when the goblins struck. They were armed with swords of bright silver and slaughtered us left and right.

"So that's where much of the bright silver has gone."

"It would seem so. It is a powerful weapon. A few *Elestari* were able to shift to their dragon form. They were dismayed when the bright silver blades cut through their armor. No other metal is able to do so. It was a massacre. The dragons dared not use their fire for fear of doing further damage to the books. This left them vulnerable. And though our caverns are enormous, they were not meant for dozens of dragons in flight," Saoirse grimaced.

"How is it you came to be captured? And why didn't you use your magic?"

"Somehow the goblins managed to block our main entrance. We were trapped. Using magic depletes us. There was no way we could have successfully fought off that many goblins with just spells. Instead we took to personal combat, allowing as many as we could to flee down side passages into the mountain. It was chaos. Nonetheless, we fought bravely in the face of danger. Our losses began to grow. The space was just too small. I fought alongside my promised life mate, Colm. He in dragon form protected me from the brunt of the attacks."

"I take it the fight did not end well for you."

"It did not. We, and thirty or so others, were backed up against a wall. The goblins pressed their advantage and overwhelmed us. A handful of goblins were able to skirt around Colm. They captured me in a net, pinning me to the ground. I fought back desperately, attempting to shift to a dragon. The goblins were wise to our tricks though, and one managed to break my arm. Then I was stuck. Shifting would have caused greater damage to my arm as the bones move to accommodate the other form," Saoirse said.

"And rendering you nearly useless as a fighter."

"Yes, though I am equally comfortable with holding a sword in either hand, a broken bone is quite distracting. Colm heard my cries and saw my plight. He raged at the goblins. For a moment he turned them back."

"Then the unthinkable happened. Colm let his guard down as he checked on me. A goblin took the opportunity and plunged a sword deep into his chest. I could feel his pain, the way the sword twisted, and then the blood pumping out onto the ground. It was horrific. His dying cries rang in my ears as the goblins hauled me away."

Aohdan was silent for a moment before responding. "And that is why you were letting go of yourself, isn't it?"

"I snapped, Aohdan. I remember very little after that, only pain and fear. You see, *Elestari* are linked to their life mate from the time they hatch. Large clutches of eggs are kept together. A pair will hatch at the same time. They are linked from then on. They grow up doing everything together. When they are adults, they leave their parents and begin their own lives as a bonded pair. Mentally they are linked to each other. They are the complement to the other's strengths or weaknesses.

Elestari can live to be over two thousand years old. Pairs are inseparable their whole lives. When one dies unexpectedly it is like losing a part of yourself. Often the one left does not survive. It is too painful to live."

"If you are so heartbroken, then why did you call to me?" Aohdan asked.

'When I touched my sword, it brought everything back. It was too much for me. I wanted to die. But then you spoke to me. I heard you calling me to hang onto life. It encouraged me to not give up. I realized that I could do more good alive, than dead. However, there is one problem that I am afraid to address, Andrew. His hatred of dragons is deep seated. I don't know what he will do when he finds out my true identity. I feel that I have been unintentionally deceitful. He will undoubtedly want recompense for that. I expect him to kill me."

Saoirse ended her explanation to Aohdan with a serene look and folded her hands in front of her.

Aohdan stared at her speechless for a minute. At last he found his tongue. "How do I know that your story is true, Dara…or Saoirse…whatever your name is?"

Saoirse said gently, "I will shift for you. Protected in the confines of our minds I am free to show whatever form I wish without injuring myself."

With that Aohdan watched in astonishment as Saoirse's body began to blur at the edges. When it reformed, in the place of the woman, stood a silver colored dragon a bit bigger than Fallon, with violet eyes.

"Do you believe me now?" the dragon asked in the same lilting voice.

"Yes," Aohdan said huskily, "but there is one last thing that I don't understand. You said we are in our minds? Please explain that."

Saoirse nodded. "In calling you I linked my mind to yours. This link was solidified when you touched me. Outwardly no one would be able to tell anything different about us. We are speaking mind to mind. Unfortunately, the flames are a side effect of the fever that keeps plaguing me. It manifests as fire because of my dragon."

"I wondered about the fire. But how is it possible that there seems to be no record of the *Elestari*? I do not recall ever hearing of your people before," Aohdan questioned.

The dragon gave him a smile that could only be described as sly. "We have taken great pains to keep ourselves unknown. Over the years our wizards have hunted down any texts with reference to our people, changing them to omit anything pertaining to the *Elestari*. Our mountain has a spell so there is continuous heavy cloud cover. Only other dragons, perhaps the Northern wolves, and a few other magical beings know we exist."

"You wish to be a free people, don't you? Just like the dwarves, elves, and humans?"

"Yes, but because of our powers there is great temptation to enslave us. Three thousand years ago most all the *Elestari* were enslaved to an evil wizard king. He used the *Elestari* to wage war on the other races. They were forced to do despicable things against their will. Eventually the king was overcome by the elves, but it was too late. The *Elestari* no longer trusted anyone outside of their own people. This is why they decided to erase all evidence of themselves. Then they went into hiding. They discovered the tall peaks of the Blue Fire Mountains and made a home there. It has only been in the last thousand years that we have again mingled with the other races."

Saoirse shifted back to her human form. She stepped closer to Aohdan and took his hand.

"You are the first to see an *Elestari* in dragon form in centuries. I have come to trust you, Aohdan. I value your friendship. Please talk to Andrew. Bring him to me and let me tell him my story. I hope to win him over. If not, I am content to join Colm in death."

"I won't let him kill you. I will protect you from him," Aohdan vowed. "I will go to him now."

"Don't let me come between you and your mentor, Aohdan. I am releasing our connection now," Saoirse answered quietly.

With a jolt Aohdan came back to reality. Everything was the same. He was still holding Saoirse's hand, Fallon was still at the window, and Saoirse continued to lay unconscious in bed. Not truly unconscious he realized with an incredulous shake of his head. He had to get Andrew. But what to tell him? How would Andrew react?

He could guess Andrew's reaction, and his stomach knotted at the thought. Resolutely he hurried to the library where he knew Andrew would be relaxing. Sure enough, Andrew sat with a book on his lap looking tired from the last few days.

Aohdan took a gulping breath." Andrew, come quickly. I've spoken with Dara. She's not awake per se, but she managed to link her mind to mine. Her real name is Saoirse. She has much to tell and wishes to speak to you. She is very weak though. She is running out of time. She is not what she seems, but please hear her out. I promise you she is not evil. I know I sound crazy, so come see for yourself."

Andrew gave Aohdan a puzzled frown. Setting down his book, he rose from the chair.

"You're not making a whole lot of sense right now, but I've seen all kinds of strange things. You'd better not be making a fool out of me though," Andrew threatened in disgruntlement.

Aohdan countered Andrew as they reached the bedroom. "Everything is as I say. Saoirse will tell you her story. Please don't draw judgment on her until she is finished. She craves your approval. Take her hand and she will speak to you."

Andrew looked hard at Aohdan and then at Saoirse. With a heavy sigh he settled into the chair next to the bed. He took Saoirse's good hand and then suddenly went rigid. Hoping to be part of the conversation Aohdan laid his own hand on Saoirse's shoulder. He found himself pulled back into the world of fire.

This time he was farther away from Saoirse. He saw that Andrew stood facing her and he could hear their conversation. He stepped forward to move closer, but the flames roared up around him. He tried again with the same result. In frustration he tried rushing through them. He was repulsed by an invisible force. Clearly Saoirse was letting him see what was happening but would not allow him to interfere. He vibrated in irritation at this boundary, but he knew there was nothing he could do about it.

"Where are we?" Andrew asked, his voice laced with ire.

"We are in the confines of our minds. We are linked together, warded so that only those that I wish are allowed to enter," Saoirse replied calmly.

"That sounds awfully convenient for you. What about me? Am I safe from your prying? And anyway, what are you? Surely you are an enchantress of some sort."

Andrew crossed his arms glaring at Saoirse.

With a deep breath Saoirse answered, "I am *Elestari*, a shape changer. My tale as Dara is true. I remembered nothing of my nature until I touched my sword. I am not what you think though. I am two in one. I am both human….and dragon."

"DRAGON!" Andrew snarled, "You vile, deceitful creature! Worm! You came into my home under false pretense. I never fully trusted you. I see I was right. I should have killed you right off…"

Aohdan shouted, "Andrew! Hear her out. Please, for my sake listen to her. She is not the bloodthirsty monster you think she is."

"You would side with the beast? How could you, Aohdan?"

"Yes, I side with her. Just listen to her. Then you can decide what she is," Aohdan pleaded.

Saoirse interjected. "Listen to my story. Then decide my fate, Andrew. But first, please hear me out."

Andrew did not reply, only glowered at Saoirse with hatred. Taking this as a sign of his assent Saoirse launched into her story. She spoke of the events succinctly. Only at the mention of the loss of Colm did she lose her composure. Aohdan thought he saw something flicker across Andrew's face when she spoke of losing her mate. Andrew, better than anyone, could understand her pain. Finally, she brought her story back to the present.

"I do not know if any of my kin survived. It eats away at me to be unsure of their fate. It also galls me to think that your wife was murdered by the contemptible Killkari. I am ashamed to even be able to take the same form as him. He, and other evil dragons like him, bring dishonor to the *Elestari*. Though we are a separate species, it brings my people a shame that we would rather not have. I cannot express enough how sorry I am for your loss.

"I realize my words are little consolation, but I want you to know I will do everything in my power to destroy Killkari if you so wish it. I believe he is also behind the attack on the *Elestari*. I believe he provided the goblins with the bright silver. It is the explanation that best fits."

Saoirse finished, and a brooding silence fell between her and Andrew. When Andrew finally spoke, his voice was choked with a multitude of emotions.

"How do I know you're not lying to me? Show me your dragon. Then I will believe you."

Saoirse flickered and changed to the silver dragon. She stood determinedly before Andrew.

"I should kill you," Andrew whispered. As he spoke the words, a sword appeared in his hands. He held it threateningly. Aohdan struggled to reach them, but Saoirse's magic kept him stuck in place. Andrew stepped toward Saoirse. The dragon made no move from Andrew's advance. She stayed perfectly still when he placed the blade against her long, shimmering neck.

"You hold my life, Andrew. I will not resist if you choose to take it." With that she bowed her head.

Andrew's face twisted as he wrestled with his unspoken decision. With an angry roar that caused Aohdan to jump, he turned and flung the sword as hard as he could. He hurried away from Saoirse, Aohdan, and the field of fire, breaking his connection to Saoirse.

Aohdan staggered forward as he felt his invisible bonds release. He hastened to Saoirse who was still in dragon form.

"What were you thinking? He could have killed you!" he thundered in frustration.

Saoirse looked at him, violet eyes pulsing with energy. "I did it because he needed a chance to see that Killkari hasn't completely stolen his humanity. Revenge eats away at you, Aohdan. It leaves you empty and lifeless. The only way to fill the void is to give instead of take. Andrew has driven himself almost to the point of no return. I gave him the opportunity to show that there is more than hatred inside him, that he still has compassion and mercy."

"But he almost killed you. It was too risky. You shouldn't have chanced your life like that."

"I don't fear death. Yes, I gambled with my life, but in the end I won. Andrew is full of anger, yet I could see in him a spark of life when he spared me. That spark is worth my life. I have nothing. But if I can give him something then I would gladly do whatever it takes to restore him, regardless of the consequences."

"Are all *Elestari* as stubborn and audacious as you, Saoirse?"

"Most of them are more so. I am nothing special. I wish only to help, even if my methods seem a bit unorthodox."

"Will you choose to come out of your illness and help us hunt down Killkari?"

At his question, Saoirse flared her wings, arched her neck, and hissed with bared fangs. "I will kill him myself if that's what you want. He will not be easy to find. I can't hunt until I am healed though. But when I am well, I will track him to the ends of Arda and destroy him."

Aohdan nodded. "Then I will help you any way that I can. Andrew will spurn your aid, but he won't hinder you. I know it will not be easy to work with him. You are our best chance of finding Killkari yet. Fallon will also help us. He doesn't have the same prejudice as Andrew. For now, rest and recover."

"As you say, Aohdan. I will sleep now. The sooner my arm heals, the sooner I can fly again."

With that Saoirse broke the connection with Aohdan. He again found himself in her room with his hand on her shoulder. Fallon's cold nose was rooting in his back as the wolf vied for his attention. Andrew was gone already, not that Aohdan was surprised. He knew the old Ranger would be out alone for the next few days to control his grief and anger.

"It's all right, Fallon. Everything is fine."

"Fine?" the wolf exploded. "Both you and Andrew sat like dead men next to Dara's bed and I couldn't wake either of you. Then Andrew jumps to life, goes storming out of the house, and gallops off on his horse. What nonsense is going on here?"

Aohdan sighed. "It's a long story… perhaps I should come outside to explain everything."

"Please do," growled Fallon impatiently, silver fur bristling.

Aohdan looked at Saoirse one last time. He touched her forehead. It was cool for the first time in days. The fever was gone. Her arm already looked less swollen. She lay limp in bed, but he thought a touch of color had come back to her cheeks. *Saoirse would recover*, he thought smiling to himself.

Chapter 3

SAOIRSE AWOKE THE NEXT MORNING. SHE was weak but entirely herself. This time she knew her identity. There was no questioning of her past. A part of her ached to go back to sleep and never wake again. Aohdan had won out though. His words stirred her to action. She was going to live.

Slowly she pulled herself out of the bed. She stood still for a moment allowing her body to adjust. She took a deep breath; the lingering scent of pine laced the room while a hint of something cooking for breakfast wafted from the doorway. Saoirse tottered to the kitchen where she found Aohdan. He leaped up in shock when he saw her leaning in the doorway.

"You're up and walking. I did not expect this so soon." Delighted, Aohdan pulled out a chair for her at the table.

She carefully sat down into the proffered seat. "I am resilient if nothing else. At the moment I could use some food," she confessed.

"I'll fix something right away," Aohdan said as he hurried to the stove. "How do hotcakes sound? I've had some already so there is a pan out for them."

"They sound wonderful," Saoirse answered, full of gratitude. After a few moments she asked tentatively, "Where is Andrew?"

A frown creased Aohdan's face, and he paused. "Gone. He will be back in a few days. When he gets in a bad mood he goes off by himself to work through it. He won't have forgiven you, but he will at least be civil."

"I'm sorry that I have upset him. Part of me wishes that you had not rescued me. Then you would not be caught between us. However, I am glad for an opportunity to help. The thought of Killkari makes my blood boil."

"You and Andrew can at least agree on that. If you can show him that a dragon can do good, he may come around in his attitude."

"I will do my best. I don't want to push it though. I could end up doing more harm than good. Enough about Andrew. Tell me more about yourself, Prince Aohdan. Since my secrets are out, you should share some of yours. Give me more details about the city of Amaroth," Saoirse said as she eyed the hotcakes Aohdan was making.

"I'm afraid my life is not very exciting. My mother and father both have much more fascinating stories than me. It's hard to live up to their reputations I suppose. I grew up splitting my time between Amaroth and our house on the Tiered Mountain with the dwarves."

"I did not realize you had lived on the Tiered Mountain. I understand it is beautiful," Saoirse commented.

"It is. That's why I love this place. Mountains are where I am most at home. My father, Killian, is extremely busy. As an advisor to the dwarf king Halfor and his responsibilities with Mother in Amaroth, he was always on the go when I was young. Yet he made it a point to make time for me when he was home. He taught me both archery and smithy work. My mother, Avana, showed me how to use a sword, taught me how to track, and gave me a great love of reading. She had little access to books in her youth, which she regrets. She loves to read so she made sure that I had the opportunity."

Saoirse let an enormous smile cross her face at the mention of books. "I am glad to hear that Avana taught you to love books. They are knowledge, and knowledge is power. Besides, they teach you curiosity and how to grow. But I have interrupted, please continue."

"When we weren't in the mountains or at Amaroth, my family would spend time with the Northern wolves. Some of my favorite memories are of the three of us out hunting with High Chieftain Finris's pack, sleeping out under the stars deep in the Wilds. That's when I became friends with Fallon. He watched over me as if I was his own. He has been my closest friend." Aohdan gave her a smile of his own as he continued to prepare the hotcakes.

"You two do seem to have a special relationship. You are in a very unique position, Aohdan. You have a human mother and a dwarf father. They have given you opportunities very few others could even dream of," Saoirse stated.

A small frown flitted across Aohdan's features. "Sometimes it's been difficult to have parents of different races. I have both human and dwarf blood in my veins. I don't always fit in, though dwarves and humans are on excellent terms right now. Being prince doesn't help. That's one of the reasons I chose to come out to train under Andrew. Besides, I want to make a name for myself. I don't always want to live in the shadow of my parents' legacy. I love them, but I wish to be my own person apart from them."

Saoirse gave a snort. "Of course you're different from them. Don't let their actions intimidate you."

"Precisely, but I can't do that living in Amaroth. Even if I joined the Guard it wouldn't be the same for me as for everyone else. Therefore I chose to come here. I want to be useful."

Saoirse let out a soft hum in response. "I think I understand you better now. Thank you for sharing. But you still have not spoken of Amaroth. I am curious to learn about the city."

Aohdan laughed. "You are tenacious, Saoirse. I will tell you more of Amaroth. As for the city itself, it's old and beautiful. If histories are correct then it is thousands of years old. It is an excellent stronghold. Only once have the walls been breached."

"Truly? It must have a very strong defense then," Saoirse said in surprise.

"Yes. But it draws strength from its people. It is a conglomerate of cultures. Dwarves, humans, and elves all live together. There were always a few elves in Amaroth, but more began to filter in after the most recent war. Amaroth has become such a large trading city that it draws many merchants. You can find almost anything you want there for the right price. The markets are enormous. You should see the colorful stalls. The sound of trade and bartering is almost musical. Aside from that, there is the Guard and the districts which I have already spoken to you about. That's all there is to tell without you visiting yourself."

Aohdan set a tall stack of hotcakes on a plate in front of Saoirse as he sat down next to her, his chair squeaking noisily over the wooden floor.

"What about you? Tell me more about the *Elestari*. I confess I know little about dragons. I have been around Zellnar only a handful of times."

Saoirse smiled over the mound of hotcakes.

"I suppose it's only fair. My people love knowledge as I have already told you. I began studying histories and magic when I was just a hatchling. *Elestari* are all born with magic. However, it takes a great deal of training to become skilled with it. Not everyone chooses the path of wizardry. We are all taught basic skills that allow us to control our magic. Then we can decide what our focus for training will be."

"And what did you choose?" Aohdan asked with a curious expression.

"My interests were both in wizardry and weaponry. It was a bit unusual for an *Elestari* to take up two studies, but not unheard of. I thrived on it. I'm afraid I have not finished mastering either one yet. My training was to be considered complete after my 600th birthday. I am currently 587. Now I'm not sure if I will ever be a proper wizard and weapons master… Aohdan, is there something wrong? You're looking at me strangely," She bit into a hotcake, sighing inwardly in contentment at the warm, buttery flavor.

Meanwhile, Aohdan stared at Saoirse with a flummoxed expression. "You can't possibly be that old," he finally muttered shaking his head. "You don't look a day over twenty-five."

Saoirse burst out laughing, spraying hotcake crumbs all over the table. Once she got control of herself again she said, "I'm sorry for my poor manners. Yes, I am that old. I will most likely live to be around two thousand. I know of certain *Elestari* wizards living longer, but that's the average lifespan."

"That's incredible…I can scarcely believe it. Although elves also live long lives, so I suppose it stands to reason that there are other long-lived races," Aohdan marveled, seeing her in a new light.

Saoirse looked contemplative. "I do remember one story from our history where an *Elestari* fell in love with a human and chose to live a human's span of years. That was quite a long time ago though. I am not technically considered a true adult until I am 600. However, once you have reached the age of 500 you are treated as an adult, just without the privileges and responsibilities."

A hint of red colored Aohdan's cheeks. "And I thought I was the older, responsible one trying to take care of you. I myself am twenty-five. I must seem like a child in your eyes."

"On the contrary, Aohdan. You are an adult among humans and almost there in dwarven reckoning. I am still seen as a youth. You are still the elder, though perhaps not in years." Saoirse dabbed at her mouth with a linen napkin before taking another large bite of hotcake.

"Andrew is going to have quite a shock when he hears this." Aohdan chuckled regaining his composure.

"I don't know about that. I get the feeling that not much surprises him. He knew something was off about me before we knew my identity. Even retired, his Ranger training gives him an edge. May I go out and talk to Fallon after I finish eating?"

"Of course." Aohdan gestured to the door. "Fallon is very interested in speaking with you. He is curious about your background."

"Then I will hurry up and finish my breakfast." Saoirse wolfed down the end of the hotcakes. She thanked Aohdan for the food and went out to the garden. She sat down heavily on the bench, tired by her walk.

Reaching out with her mind Saoirse called for Fallon. She felt his presence in the woods nearby. She felt him jolt in surprise when she touched his mind. At first he instinctively withdrew, but once she made herself known he accepted the connection. His mind was not like a human's. His instincts guided his thoughts and actions: protect, hunt, care for the pack. The dragon in Saoirse related to Fallon in these.

She appeared to him in her dragon form in his mind. He regarded her curiously.

"So you are a dragon, but you're more, something much greater. Now the mystery of your scent is solved for me. We have tales of the *Elestari*. I did not think them true. I see I was wrong."

"You are a legend yourself, Fallon. Your brethren are held in high esteem among my people. Their actions have been noble."

The wolf's laughter rumbled through Saoirse. "I see you are not above flattery, but I mind it not. The old tales say that *Elestari* weave words as well as spells. You are like, yet unlike the elves. Your dragon separates you distinctly. I feel your dragon as one hunter to another. I know you wish for my friendship after your accidental deception. I will ease your mind by giving it. When you are healed we shall hunt and destroy Killkari together."

"I am pleased that we are of one mind, Fallon. I apologize for my ignorance during our first meeting. Would you be willing to overlook it, to aid in the search for Killkari? I suspect that he is behind the attack on my people. I burn with the thought of him."

"You are forgiven, shape changer. I wish to stop Killkari for the sake of my friends. I do not do so out of duty, only out of love for them. Take care to not become jaded and bitter like Andrew. I sense that though you fight the feelings now, you are in danger of giving in to them. The old tales among my people speak of an *Elestari* who let anger and power take control of him. He caused great destruction because of it," Fallon intoned.

Saoirse allowed herself a quiet growl. "I will heed your warning as best I can. It weighs on me. I will try to keep hope in my heart instead of revenge."

With that, Fallon broke the connection and Saoirse found herself back in the garden. The encounter had tired her so she closed her eyes, leaning back against the bench. When she next awoke she was in her room.

Aohdan, she thought to herself. Always the responsible prince. She sat up quickly. There was much to do even without being able to scout the mountains herself for Killkari. Maps to look at, accounts to be read, and strategies to be created. Killkari would be brought to justice.

Chapter 4

SEVERAL WEEKS OF RELAXATION AND HEALING had passed. When Saoirse stretched her left arm, it felt ready to be out of the splint. Not strong enough to shift though. It was sore, but usable within reason. The muscles were still weak from lack of use and would need some building up.

She was too soft in general. Recovery had made her lax. It was time to develop her skills again. Saoirse decided to ask Aohdan to help her train. Andrew had more experience, but he still shunned her. She hoped she would eventually earn his trust.

Aohdan was out searching the mountains with Fallon. She reached out with her mind for him. He was closer than she had thought. They were returning.

"Aohdan."

She tugged gently at the edge of his mind. She felt him respond to her touch.

"Saoirse, what is it? Is everything all right?"

"All is well. I tested my arm. It is healed enough to go without the splint. Not ready for me to shift though. I need to strengthen it first. Would you help me train to get back in shape? I feel that I am ready for light spar work." She made a fist reflexively. "I would like to begin working with my right arm in the meantime since it is whole."

"I will help you. And yes, we can spar, though perhaps you should work on grip strength with your left hand before you hold a sword."

"Good idea. It will take me a while to properly hold a blade. How did scouting go? Were you able to find the lower storage caves?"

"Scouting was uneventful. We found the caves. They have been ransacked. The goblins had been through them. Nothing is left there. The *Elestari* were not guarding it, so they must have moved on."

Saoirse's heart burned at this news. She had hoped that some of her people were using the storage caves as a temporary camp. It hurt to have her hopes dashed. She tried to ignore her disappointment.

"I'm glad you found the caves. I'm sorry you were not more successful than that. I was hoping that you would find some trace of my people or some proof that Killkari is working with the goblins. My patience is wearing thin staying here doing nothing," she said in resignation.

"You are helping more than you realize, Saoirse. Even if you are not yet able to search, you have given the rest of us very useful leads to check. It beats searching blindly. We will return within the next few hours. I will see about finding something to help you to develop a strong grip again."

Saoirse smiled to herself. "Thank you, Aohdan. I await your return."

Several hours later Aohdan rode Fallon into the clearing where the house sat. He was unsurprised to see Saoirse in the garden performing a series of complicated stretches. His limbs were tired. Five days of hard going had worn him down. He swung slowly off Fallon. He had been thinking about how to help Saoirse regain her muscle strength. He had an idea that he wanted to try before he forgot it.

Walking stiffly into the house, he took a small dish rag from the cupboard. This he took out to the stream that flowed close by. The banks were soft and sandy. Scooping up a large handful of sand from the river edge, he placed it in the center of the rag. With his knife, Aohdan cut off a short piece of cloth from the edge of his tunic. He used it to tie the sand-filled rag tightly shut.

He squeezed the bundle experimentally. It had just the right amount of resistance with give. Whistling, he tossed the ball of sand from hand to hand as he walked to the garden.

"I've got just the thing for your grip, Saoirse. Try it!" He gently threw the odd bundle to her and she deftly caught it. She gave the sand bag a trial grasp in her weak hand. A smile dawned across her face.

"This is excellent. It's small so I can play with it constantly. And so simple. Just sand, right?"

Aohdan nodded, feeling pleased with himself.

"Good idea. I think it will make a difference if I faithfully use it."

"It should. Is Andrew back yet?"

Saoirse flinched inadvertently. "Not yet. I don't expect him until dark."

"Andrew doesn't hate you. He just doesn't do well with reminders of his past. Don't take it personally," Aohdan said.

"I hate being associated with Killkari. It makes me feel like a monster."

Aohdan shook his head giving her a pointed look. "You're a far cry from Killkari. Come now, let's spar before I fall asleep on my feet."

They went into the house to each retrieve their respective weapons. Saoirse carefully buckled her sword around her waist. Aohdan noticed that her sword had a faint violet glow to it. He guessed that it had something to do with her excitement at finally feeling up to using it.

Saoirse and Aohdan hurried back out to the garden. Drawing her sword with her good right hand Saoirse stood in a ready stance.

"Go easy on me. I'm woefully out of practice."

Aohdan copied her with a saucy smirk. "I thought you were learning to be a weapons master. I highly doubt you're that rusty. I will watch your arm though. I've no wish to have to continue bandaging it."

Then he lunged for her. It was a lightning-quick thrust meant to catch her off guard. His sword clanged loudly against hers and purple sparks flew. He pushed her back a step. Saoirse countered with a thrust of her own, causing Aohdan to leap nimbly to the side. Aohdan flew at her with a series of hammering blows using his height as an advantage to push her another step back. He felt her mind reaching for his, probing his own weakness. He let her into his head, suddenly seeing things from her view. He sensed that she was weakening.

Saoirse could feel her muscles begin to ache from the heavy attack after a month of disuse. She could also feel the years of training coming back to her. She purposefully slowed down the fight so she could study Aohdan better. He had a very aggressive style of swordplay and he preferred to push forward with every swing than to conserve energy and fight within his own space. She would use this to her advantage. Aohdan was surprised to learn this detail about himself. He filed it away to work on later.

Saoirse began a complicated set of parries that grew faster and faster. These she turned into thrusts and jabs that forced Aohdan to stop his attack. Though he could see what she was thinking, she was still too fast. He knew her muscles were on fire, clamoring for her to stop. Still she lunged forward causing him to retreat. Feinting as if to push him back farther she instead called on her magic and engulfed her sword in purple flames. Surprise filled Aohdan at this move, causing him to step back. This was just what she wanted. Using his fraction of hesitancy, she gave a ringing blow to his sword near the hilt, sending it flying across the lawn.

Panting from her exertions, Saoirse collapsed to her knees on the lawn using her sword as a crutch. She withdrew her mind. Aohdan looked at her and laughed. He had been bested by her even with the advantage of mentally previewing her movements.

"Out of practice indeed. I knew that was nonsense. I've trained with only the best since childhood, and you made me look like a novice. Although I'm not sure that calling up fire was really a fair move."

"That's not true. You're an excellent swordsman. I'm so out of shape that had we fought any longer you would have overpowered me. The fire was a last ditch effort."

Aohdan snorted in response as he went to pick up his sword. "I don't know that my pride can take getting beaten by you all the time."

Now it was Saorse's turn to laugh. "You'll beat me easily on my left side. That arm won't be able to stand up to your pounding for a while."

"About your arm—I've been thinking about it and meaning to ask you something. If *Elestari* are healers, then why don't you heal yourself?"

Saoirse pulled herself upright. "Because it doesn't work that way. Magic takes energy. The energy it would take to heal my arm would deplete me. I would be worse off than before. You see every creature has energy in it. The *Elestari* use our magic to direct the energy of the wounded creature to heal itself. For instance, if you had a sword cut, I would use the energy that your body is already putting toward healing to speed up the process. Our bodies want to be whole. Magic is simply the catalyst for quick healing. Using my magic on my energy would sort of cancel each one out. It would work, but I would probably sleep for days afterwards, or if it was a severe enough injury it could kill me."

Aohdan mulled over this information. "So how can you heal someone with a mortal injury?"

"It is certainly harder. But no matter what, the body wants to be whole. It requires more magic and energy from the healer, though generally the side effect on the victim is a full day of sleep. You can only carry so much energy in you at one time. At my best I could heal one hundred men at death's door. After that I would be spent. And that's only if I was fully rested. If I had been flying or fighting beforehand I would be much more limited."

"I see." Aohdan paused. "But if you were training to become a wizard surely you would have a way to make yourself stronger."

Saoirse grinned broadly. "Excellent deduction! The *Elestari* store part of their energy in a stone. Jewels can hold a large amount of energy, enough to last for days. My stone is in my sword pommel because I was training in weapons. Many *Elestari* chose to wear their stone as a necklace or set in the head of a staff. There are many ways that we carry our stones. We are always careful to keep them near. My stone calling me is what caused me to go to your room that day, though I didn't realize that's what it was at the time. When I touched it the energy unlocked my memory."

"So essentially a part of you is stored in the stone?" Aohdan asked.

"Yes. That's the short version." She nodded.

"That is rather remarkable, Saoirse. Does your sword have a name? Many of our blades do."

Saoirse fingered the etching down the center of her blade. "Indeed it does. It is called *Elasair*, meaning dragon fire or dragon bite. I forged it from bright silver myself."

"It suits you well. It's a hand-and-a-half sword, correct?" Aohdan asked.

"Indeed. I needed something shorter to fit my frame. I am not particularly tall. A long sword is a bit large for me."

Aohdan chuckled. "My mother carries a long sword, but she also has great skill with a bow and saxe knives. Avana is unusual in many ways."

Looking up at him Saoirse returned his laughter. "Don't all children think their parents are odd?"

"I suppose that is true. I simply feel that I have the far end of the spectrum for strange parents."

"Shall I start calling you Prince Peculiar then?" Saoirse teased with a mocking bow.

Aohdan groaned, rolling his eyes. "Don't let Andrew hear you saying that. He'll call me that permanently. That's certainly one of the nicer names I've been called. Being a half breed garners some unpleasant names, even if you are the prince. Sometimes I think being prince makes it worse."

"People tend to be afraid of things that are out of their spectrum of normalcy. It didn't used to be that way. The great kings of old that you are descended from welcomed everyone. Magic was rampant and races freely intermingled without fear. Your parents are doing much to bring that back to rights." Saoirse suddenly went rigid. A strange look covered her face, and her eyes glowed slightly.

With a sigh she closed her eyes momentarily, then opened them again staring hard at Aohdan. "I've just had a brief glimpse at your future, Aohdan. The opportunity to finish what your parents have started. Under your reign Arda could fully regain its former glory. However, I also saw a darkness. Unrestricted power that would make all fear you. It will overtake you if you are not wary. Nothing was clear I'm afraid. I can only see pieces. I don't have true sight like some *Elestari*."

Aohdan looked shaken by her pronouncement.

"I don't think I'm ready to rule. I often wish I could live without that responsibility looming in my future. Your words are comforting but also add to my burden. I hope you don't think me a coward."

"Not at all. Few in your position ever feel ready. Don't let fear cripple you. Self-doubt will be your nemesis."

Aohdan stood silent, his face a mask. After a long moment he spoke. "I will have to think on your words. I'd like to be alone for a while if you don't mind."

Without waiting for an answer he sheathed his sword, turned on his heel, and strode into the house. Saoirse watched him go with regret. She had forgotten that humans did not always wish to hear about their futures the way the *Elestari* did. Sheathing her own sword, she began the slow process of stretching her muscles from the sparring match.

That evening after Saoirse had retired for the night, Andrew and Aohdan sat together in the sitting room in front of a roaring fire. Andrew was in a dark, brooding temper. He had been intensely morose at dinner, snapping at any perceived offense. The anniversary of his wife's death was drawing near.

"What do we really know about Saoirse?" he asked Aohdan in a sour tone. "She could be in league with Killkari for all we really know. Seems convenient that she shows up here as we are looking for him."

Aohdan's heart plummeted at Andrew's words. He had no wish to argue with his mentor. "She hasn't given us any reason to disbelieve her."

"She could be magicking us and we wouldn't even know it," Andrew countered petulantly.

"If she is, then it has not harmed us yet. I don't believe she means us ill."

"Aohdan, she's not human. Even if she didn't intend to harm us she could do so without even realizing it. I've been around my fair share of magic, and she's like nothing I've ever encountered."

Aohdan nodded. "I agree with you that she is powerful. Yet she has not hurt us. Spend some time with her. Saoirse craves your approval, you know."

Andrew scoffed, staring stormy-eyed into the fire. "She's a dragon. She will never win my approval."

"Saoirse is not Killkari. She's not a bloodthirsty killer. Can't you see that?" Aohdan asked earnestly.

Andrew glowered darkly at him then leapt up from his chair and marched angrily from the room. Aohdan heaved a sigh of frustration. He wondered if Andrew would ever give up his vendetta.

Chapter 5

A WEEK PASSED BY WHERE NEITHER Andrew nor Aohdan brought up their awkward conversation. Aohdan knew that it was only their deep-seated friendship that kept the old Ranger from dismissing Saoirse completely. But he was pleased when Andrew, after much wheedling on his part, agreed to spar with Saoirse.

Andrew spent every bout with the *Elestari* woman hurling insults as well as jabs, but he was an excellent teacher and a true sword master. Andrew had been the last pupil of the greatest swordsman in all of Arda, Aohdan's great, great grandfather, Mordecai. Years of real battle experience also gave him an edge over Saoirse. Their matches were close. They were almost even for the most part, but Andrew won more often.

Saoirse wanted to learn from him and gain his respect. This was not what his prejudice had expected, and it took him by surprise. Though he would not say so, he was starting to warm to the silver-haired woman. Aohdan could tell that Saoirse felt the ice between her and Andrew thaw over their mutual love of swordsmanship, giving him some hope.

Saoirse also started riding Fallon out into the wilderness. Just for a few hours at a time. After a full week she felt ready for a longer outing. Aohdan was going on a half day trek of the mountainside in search of deer for their larder. She asked if she could join him. It would be spot and stalk style hunting. Aohdan agreed to her request.

Early in the morning, long before light, they got up and began their trek over the mountainside. They hiked rapidly in the wee hours. Soon they came to a grassy clearing in the woods that Aohdan knew was a common place for deer to graze. Aohdan and Saoirse sat quietly hidden in the brush. Light began to filter through the trees as dawn's first rays came over the mountain. The scent of pine and dew combined to create a fragrant morning.

Three does appeared across from them in ghostly fashion. The deer nibbled daintily at the lush green grass. A buck joined them after the sun began to golden the tops of the trees. They stayed out of bow range, meandering in the field. Saoirse observed the creatures with pleasure. The peaceful grazing and relaxed demeanor told the hunters that their presence was undiscovered.

A shrill whistle from farther up the mountain broke the morning tranquility. Four heads shot up, four pairs of eyes and ears strained for the source of the sound. The deer stirred in agitation. Nostrils fluttered to catch the wind. Coming to a decision, they bolted as one back into the forest.

Aohdan sat back in disappointment, "Wonder what made that sound?" he murmured to Saoirse.

She shook her head. "Whatever it was, I don't think it was that far away."

"I agree. The deer won't be coming back for a while. Why don't you stay here while I go take a look around? I'll come back for you in a half hour or so."

Saoirse exhaled a dissatisfied huff. "I'd rather not stay here. However, you will certainly move faster without me. I'll wait."

"I'll be as quick as I can. Soon you'll be able to keep up with me. Alright then. I'm off."

Aohdan stood up, and with soft tread, shifted into the shadows. His strides were swift. He had done his best to pinpoint the sound that had frightened the deer. Taking note of the sun to help keep him going in the right direction, Aohdan searched the woods for any signs of disturbance. He saw no tracks out of the ordinary or broken limbs that would signal some large animal passing through.

Aohdan proceeded up the mountain, ranging back and forth. Still nothing. Pumas roamed the mountains, but they were few and far between. A big cat was the best explanation, though it nagged at Aohdan that he had seen no indicators of one in the area. Something felt off.

His time was beginning to grow short. Aohdan turned to go back down to Saoirse. As he did so a dull glimmer on the ground caught his eye. He reached for the object. It was a short, crude dagger with a roughly carved handle. A goblin blade. Not far from it he found tracks of at least four of the creatures. *This is what frightened the deer*, he thought to himself in disgust. He needed to get back to Saoirse.

As this last thought crossed his mind, he heard the sound of goblin war cries echoing up from below him. They had found Saoirse. Aohdan sprinted down the mountain, skidding over rocks, weaving through the trees. Drawing his sword, he held it at the ready as he dashed to the aid of his friend.

Aohdan berated himself as he ran. Of course it had been goblins that had scared the deer. He should have trusted his instincts that the intruder was not a puma. As he drew nearer the yells grew louder, then suddenly stopped. Aohdan hastened his steps. The silence was worse than the war cries.

He could see the light of the clearing just ahead. Gathering himself he leapt into the field with a cry of righteous anger only to be cut short by the scene that met him. An enormous silver dragon stood across the field from him over the bodies of six green-skinned goblins. Blood dripped from its jaws as it looked up sharply from the goblin it had been consuming. The dragon's eyes narrowed into wild purple slits, while the spines along its back stood on end. At the same time it flared one wing and hissed menacingly at Aohdan.

"Saoirse. Saoirse, it's me, Aohdan," he said in a wary voice, gulping down his surprise.

Recognition flashed through the violet eyes, and the wildness left them. Instead a look of utter shame crossed the dragon's face. She seemed to shrink in on herself, flattening her head to her neck and pulling in her wings. With one last humiliated glance at Aohdan, the dragon turned tail and dashed into the woods leaving him stunned.

Regaining his composure Aohdan called after her, "Saoirse, wait!"

He chased after the fleeing dragon. She easily outdistanced him but left a wide trail in her wake. Aohdan pursued her doggedly. He eventually caught up to her on a mountain ledge.

Saoirse was curled into a tight ball with her spiny, horse-like head facing away from him. Again, he called out, "Saoirse!"

"Leave me alone, Aohdan," she rumbled miserably.

"No, I won't. Why did you run from me?" Aohdan asked in helpless frustration.

"I'm a monster. Just like Andrew said. I don't deserve your friendship. Leave me." The dragon kept her eyes averted and head turned from Aohdan as she spoke.

"You're not a monster," he said sharply in exasperation. "Don't speak such nonsense."

Saoirse snuffled in response. "But I killed the goblins…and ate them. I enjoyed it. I'm a monster."

Compassion kindled inside of Aohdan consuming his previous frustration. "Oh, Saoirse, you're a dragon. You were doing what dragons naturally do."

Saoirse finally turned to him, violet eyes full of mortification, "But I hated them too. I wanted to destroy them for what they did to my people. I let rage take over. I didn't even try to restrain myself."

Aohdan considered her words. Then he walked up to her and

cautiously placed his hand on her silver scales. She radiated warmth. He felt her great body trembling with emotion. Stroking her side he finally answered.

"Goblins are evil creatures. I would not have spared them had I come upon them. I do not think ill of you for what you did. I think you have learned a valuable lesson from your encounter. Please don't be too hard on yourself. Everyone makes mistakes. You're not a monster. You're my friend."

"Do you really mean that?"

"Yes," Aohdan answered with equanimity.

A shudder ran through Saoirse and she brought her head round to look directly at Aohdan.

"Thank you. Your kindness is more than I deserve."

"I want to help you. Will you trust me?" He stared intently into her glowing eyes.

"I will trust you. I do trust you," she amended.

A deep thrumming like a cat's purr emanated from her. Aohdan felt it vibrate through his body. He could physically feel her happiness. Her consciousness linked to his, and she spoke to him without words. A wave of emotions swelled over him from the silver dragon. Gratitude, relief, and a sense that her trust in him was not given lightly. She put a high value in trusting him. He hoped he could live up to it.

All too soon she severed the connection, withdrawing to herself. Aohdan felt himself reaching out to her for a fleeting moment. Then he remembered himself and stepped away from the dragon.

"How were you able to shift? I did not think you were well enough to do so," he asked, pushing aside his feelings.

Saoirse winced at his words. "I am not. Do you not see how I cannot properly unfold my wing? I won't have use of it until I am fully healed. Shifting was excruciatingly painful. I did not see any other option though when I was attacked. I may be skilled, but six to one with a half-mended arm was not a good match-up."

"So you shifted instead."

"They did not carry bright silver. They were easy to dispatch once I was in dragon form and posed no real threat to me. Now I must face the painful decision of whether or not to shift back."

"I don't think Andrew should see you as a dragon. I realize that shifting will be painful, but I fear his goodwill toward you will dissipate if you return in this form," Aohdan said with a frown. "You have made significant progress in your relationship with him. It would be wise to keep it that way."

Saoirse closed her eyes in apparent resignation. "You speak truth. I will shift."

A strange violet glimmer surrounded the dragon. The huge form contracted into a murky human shape. It solidified into the familiar woman Aohdan had grown used to seeing. She gasped and pitched forward, crumpling to the ground. Distressed, Aohdan dropped to his knees, gently helping her to sit up. Saoirse was nearly as pale as her hair from the pain.

He could feel her heart hammering an erratic rhythm against her ribs as she leaned against him for support. Her breathing was ragged, her eyes closed as she regained her composure. At long last she let out a quivering sigh. Slowly, using Aohdan to pull herself up, she stood with a soft moan.

Aohdan too stood up. "Are you all right?"

"I will recover. I still feel a bit lightheaded. I'm sorry to say that I doubt I will be able to continue hunting. I am spent from the pain of shifting." Saoirse gave him a wan smile.

"Can you make it back to the house?"

"Yes. The walk will clear my head. I'm weak, but sleep will put me to rights."

Aohdan studied her carefully. Already he could see Saoirse becoming steadier as the pain receded.

"Then we shall return so you may rest."

Chapter 6

Saoirse recovered quickly from the failed hunting venture. Neither she nor Aohdan told Andrew the details of what happened. Saoirse knew that Andrew was not fooled by their story, but she was relieved when he didn't press them on it. Her shift had been a setback in her healing. She chafed at it. She had missed her dragon.

Time could not go by fast enough for her. Saoirse pushed herself in training until she was exhausted. She went on daily rides with Fallon. She prowled around the house driving Andrew and Aohdan mad with her pacing. Both men could sense the electricity of her magic building in her as she grew stronger. Yet Saoirse was unwilling to practice her wizardry fearing that it would eat up energy that she required for healing.

Andrew soon banished her from the house except for sleeping and meals. Saoirse didn't mind. She was past the time of map reading and researching. Now was the time for honing her skills again. Then the day came that she had been longing for.

Saoirse got up early, eating a quick breakfast. She went out to the garden and began her stretching routine before she started weapons practice. Andrew and Aohdan were awake inside preparing their own food. As Saoirse stretched her muscles, she used a small bit of magic to probe the injured site. She wanted to know how the healing process was going.

She could tell the bone had fully knit. It was sound through and through. The muscles that had been weak and injured were now strong. A thrill of excitement ran through her. She checked once more to be sure. It was well.

A pulse of pure joy emanated from her. It vibrated off the mountainside sending the birds into song. Fallon leapt up in surprise, while Andrew and Aohdan both felt an absurd need to shout with happiness.

For a moment the two men glanced at each other, perplexed over the strange feeling that had come over them. Then Aohdan broke into an enormous grin. "Saoirse."

They both left their breakfast and ran out into the garden looking for her. Saoirse was not on the lawn where she normally exercised. She was nowhere to be found. The men were puzzled.

"She can't have disappeared into thin air." Andrew huffed in annoyance.

"I don't know about that. She's got a good bit of wizard in her," Aohdan answered.

Andrew shook his head. "That may be, but we've been around her enough we would still be able to sense her presence. Saoirse gives off a huge amount of magic. I've an idea she doesn't have the experience yet to fully hide herself. She's just not here."

"Then where is she?" Aohdan voiced the question they both were asking themselves.

As he spoke, a strong wind picked up in the pines on the mountain far above them. It moved downwards, buffeting them with the strength of the gust. The unusually keen wind drew their attention to the sky.

High in the clouds, circling the mountain, was a small shape that looked like a bird of prey. It flew with extraordinary speed. As it came lower from the heights, they soon realized it had only appeared small because of the great distance it had been from them. It rocketed from the sky growing steadily in size till they could make out the shape. It was a dragon.

Scales burning like molten silver in the morning sunlight gave the dragon an ethereal glow. The wings were nearly translucent as light poured through the delicate membrane. The dragon let out a roar that shook the mountain, sending Andrew and Aohdan reeling from the concussion. As it roared it spouted a long stream of purple flames.

The dragon continued to hurtle toward them. Aohdan guessed that it had to be nearly three times as big as the house. With its size and the rate it was going the dragon would surely obliterate everything in its path if it landed. A flicker of fear passed through him. He realized that Andrew must have had the same thought as a worried expression crossed his face.

The wind grew stronger until neither was sure they could continue to stand in the gale. Then, unexpectedly, it began to lessen. The dragon continued to bear down on them, but something had changed about it. At first Aohdan didn't understand what it was. Then it clicked. The dragon was shrinking. As it got closer there was no doubt it was losing size. It went from double the size of a house, to a single house, then down to about Fallon's proportions. As it shrank it slowed its flight, lessening the wild wind created by its wingbeats.

The silver dragon banked above them. It wheeled in the sky, emanating another pulse of happiness that swept away their previous fear. Slowly, the dragon began to spiral down to them. When it drew near, it gracefully flared its wings and landed gently on the grass in front of them.

"I am well," Saoirse's voice echoed in their minds as her eyes blazed with a pleased violet fire.

"So you have recovered, dragon," Andrew spoke with a note of bitterness in his voice. "Will you be leaving us now?"

Aohdan felt himself flinch in surprise at Andrew's question. He realized, however, that Saoirse might have changed her mind about helping them.

The silver dragon seemed to contemplate his query. "I will only leave if you so wish it, Andrew. But with your permission, I would like to stay and help you find Killkari."

Andrew glared at her in contempt for a moment before answering. "Know this, dragon, I do not need your help to take down Killkari. Nonetheless, it would be foolish of me not to accept your offer. You are free to stay as long as you like."

"I appreciate your generosity. I will not take it lightly," Saoirse answered his sharp words graciously. Then her attention turned to Aohdan.

"Aohdan," she rang in his mind, "will you fly with me? It would please me to share the skies with you as a token of my gratitude for all you have done."

Aohdan felt a thrill of excitement at her words. He cast a glance at Andrew who simply shrugged. What would it feel like in the open sky?

"I will take you up on your offer."

"I suggest you put on your cloak then. It's much colder where we are going."

Aohdan hastened back to the house pulling out his hat, gloves, and cloak from his pack. Striding purposefully back outside he approached Saoirse. As he did so a wave of nerves overcame him. What right did he have to ride a dragon? His steps slowed as he neared her.

Saoirse looked at him in expectancy and crouched low to the ground so he could pull himself onto her back.

Gulping down his anxiety, Aohdan stepped tentatively onto the large silver leg that Saoirse offered him. Reaching for a spine he cautiously swung up onto Soairse's back settling himself down in the hollow between her shoulders. He could feel the excitement rippling through her. Her heartbeat was elevated but steady.

Aohdan felt Saoirse bunch her muscles, and for a split second she crouched even lower. Then with a mighty leap she was in the air, wings pumping strongly. Aohdan clutched the spine in front of him in a moment of terror as Saoirse flew steadily upward.

Saoirse leveled out above the trees. Aohdan found that he could relax his grip a bit. He risked a peek over the side of the dragon. The forest below was a thick green carpet. Small, gleaming creeks undulated through it creating a patchwork quilt. He was starting to feel more comfortable. Ahead he could see the Blue Fire Mountains capped with snow rising up out of the mists like silent sentinels.

"Beautiful, isn't it?"

Saoirse's voice shook Aohdan out of his reverie. He again realized the height at which they were flying and clutched at her spine. Saoirse's laughter rumbled through him shaking him to the core.

Feeling his face redden at her laughter, Aohdan answered, "Indeed. I never knew it could be anything like this."

"It gets better."

Aohdan wondered what she meant as Saoirse started to climb higher into the sky. He could sense her exhilaration as they flew. The temperature of the air around them dropped as they rose. Aohdan risked moving a hand to pull his cloak tighter around him. The clouds soon surrounded them so thickly that he could barely see the outline of Saoirse's head in front of him. Moisture beaded his cloak and steamed off her scales.

Suddenly, they broke through the clouds. Sunlight bathed them with a warm, refreshing glow. The clouds shimmered in ethereal beauty beneath them. The brightest whites accented in hues of gold, blue, and pink glittered in an ever-changing rainbow that played over the tops of the clouds. Cotton soft mists, swirling and rippling in a kaleidoscope of shapes, made towering columns that Saoirse flew between with grace belying her great size. Above them the sun glowed a cheery yellow, set against the clearest sapphire sky Aohdan had ever seen.

Aohdan was astonished at the loveliness of the world Saoirse was sharing with him. It was breathtaking. Saoirse thrummed in contentment beneath him. All fear left Aohdan as he took in the surrounding brilliance. He allowed Saoirse's happiness to wash over him.

"I missed this. More than I can say. What do you think of it?"

"I don't have words to describe it. I understand why you missed it. I wish Andrew could see it."

Saoirse snorted a stream of violet fire. "He would never ride a dragon. His hatred runs too deep. You're right though. He would like it. It would do him good."

"Yes, he needs more light, and to not constantly be bent on revenge."

"Poor Andrew." Saoirse sighed with such feeling that it brought tears to Aohdan's eyes. Blinking quickly, he pushed aside his sadness for his mentor.

"Would you like to see a bit of magic?"

"Magic?"

"Watch," Saoirse thrummed.

Ahead of them a column of clouds congealed into the form of a dragon identical to Saoirse. It hung frozen in the sky. Saoirse flew over the cloud dragon bathing it in a stream of fire. The cloud dragon shook itself, then flapped its wings coming abreast of them. Saoirse banked, and the cloud banked with them. She dove, and it dove. Every move she made the cloud dragon mimicked perfectly.

Aohdan gaped openly at the marvel Saoirse had created. At an unspoken command the cloud dragon split into two dragons and split again to create four. They flew away from Saoirse and Aohdan in an intricate dance weaving around the clouds, wings leaving a sparkling trail of light. Higher and higher they flew gaining speed. When they were directly above Saoirse and Aohdan the cloud dragons careened madly into each other in a glittering explosion of rain. Tiny droplets sprayed over them from the cloud dragons.

Aohdan laughed out loud for the joy of what he had seen.

"If more people could see such sights, the world would be a much brighter place, Saoirse. Your people could make an enormous contribution if they were willing to share their magic like this instead of living in hiding."

"Perhaps we will after this. Apparently, we are not as invincible as we thought. The time may be coming when we will mingle as our true selves within Arda."

"There have been few times in my life that I have felt that my title as prince could be useful. But in the case of the *Elestari*, my friendship would be beneficial if you wished to live openly in Amaroth or the surrounding country. You would be welcomed if you were known to be friends of the crown. The Northern wolves are an excellent example. Once a feared fairy tale, they are now considered one of our greatest allies."

"That is a pleasant hope. If there are any of my people left, I'm sure they will seriously consider your offer. I thank you for your generous proposition," Saoirse radiated a sense of appreciation that quickly turned to sadness. "But what if I am the last of my kind? This question haunts me. I'm afraid of the answer, but I'm desperate to know the truth."

Aohdan laid a comforting hand on her neck, "You are strong, Saoirse. I believe we will find your people. No matter what we discover, having answers will give you peace of mind. It is better to deal with grief than eternal worry."

"You speak wisdom. There is solace in hearing it. I miss Colm. Nothing will bring him back. But hope for my people takes the sting out of the pain. Now that I am back to full health, we can search for them and Killkari. We should return to the house or Andrew will think that I have eaten you!"

Aohdan grinned broadly. "He's going to be put out with me for flying with you. It's worth it though. You have shown me wonders that I will never forget. I am keen to meet your people."

Pleased, deep thrumming emanated from Saoirse as she descended back to the clearing of the house.

Chapter 7

"YOU'LL HAVE TO LET ME FLY you, Andrew." Saoirse glared icily at the retired Ranger. "It's enormously difficult to reach the caverns without a guide. Not to mention the climb itself is tortuous. Flying you, Aohdan, and Fallon up is much more practical."

Saoirse and Andrew had been arguing about how to reach the *Elestari* home in the Blue Fire Mountains for the last twenty minutes.

"Besides, there's no way Fallon could get up that way. He's agreed to let me carry him at least," she accused, eyes flashing.

Andrew glared back, "I refuse to ride a dragon. I'm not budging on this either."

Weary of their quarreling Aohdan broke in. "Andrew, we have no idea if the place is crawling with goblins or if Killkari is there. It wouldn't be wise for you to go alone on a path you've never traveled."

"You'd do well to remember I've been in dozens of unknown, treacherous places and come out just fine," Andrew snapped at Aohdan.

"But this is Saoirse's home. No one knows it better than her. Surely you can admit that's a huge advantage."

"Of course it is. That doesn't mean I need a ferry ride from a dragon."

Saoirse's eyes glittered. "I do not appreciate being compared to a rough barge, old man. I am not some cheap transportation. I am a dragon. If I was not trying to help you, I would never offer you a ride. You don't just ride a dragon."

"You puffed up, silver boot leather, I'm not accepting your offer. I'll keep my feet firmly on the ground."

"Boot leather!" Saoirse spat, her hands slapping the low reading table.

"ENOUGH!" roared Aohdan, fed up with the harsh words. "Andrew, you will ride Saoirse whether you like it or not. She's our best route to the mountain top. In the meantime, you will both keep a civil tongue with each other. Our enemy is Killkari. Act like it or don't go searching for him. Agreed?"

Saoirse flushed brightly and ducked her head for a moment, clearly feeling a stab of shame. "I agree."

Andrew huffed out a disgusted breath before finally relenting. Grimacing, he said, "All right. I'll do it." Turning on his heel he abruptly left, leaving Aohdan and Saoirse alone in the library.

Aohdan sighed in relief. Andrew and Saoirse could argue all day. They had been butting heads ever since Saoirse had fully recovered and started giving input on finding Killkari. Peace had been difficult to come by. Strong wills tempered by passionate opinions made the two formidable opponents.

The look of abject repentance in Saoirse's face softened Aohdan. He realized her intentions were meant for good. Andrew could irritate anyone with his obstinate ways.

"I'm sorry. I shouldn't let Andrew's prejudice upset me. I fear I am letting my anxiety get the better of me." Saoirse's violet eyes searched Aohdan's.

"It's all right. Nonetheless, you must learn to let his remarks go. Reacting won't improve things." Aohdan let a stern tone edge into his voice, though his heart wasn't in it.

Saoirse sagged into one of the chairs across from Aohdan. "You're correct as always. His mulishness galls me when I know I am in the right."

"Don't fret about it. We've got more important business to attend to. Are you prepared to return to the Blue Fire Mountains? It may be…challenging… for you," Aohdan articulated carefully.

Saoirse stiffened, inspecting the rug on the floor instead of meeting his eyes.

"I feel inadequate. Yet I am drawn home by an inexorable force. I am terrified, but hope lingers. I am also full of anger. It's a constant boil that's waiting to erupt. I am driven by it."

Her face blanched. Aohdan felt a sting of pain shoot from her as she collected herself. "There is also a duty for me to fulfill. I dread it. If there are no *Elestari* left on the mountain, it will be my job to care for the dead."

"Surely, the bodies are…no longer able to be buried?" Aohdan hazarded in an endeavor to be delicate.

"That's not an issue. When we die, we turn into the same kind of stone as our energy jewels. We stay that way until dragon fire is breathed over the statue and it shatters into millions of pieces. These can be gathered and kept by the family or spread like ashes as your traditions do. This will be my responsibility. I worry I will not have the fortitude to do so."

"We will support you. Comfort you if you wish or stand aside if that's what you prefer. Even Andrew will be sensitive in this. I think he will surprise you. He is more aware of your pain than you think. He too feels loss." Aohdan watched as she internalized his words.

Saoirse absorbed his reassurance, bringing confidence to her spirit. She felt a great sense of security having his strong solid form standing near her. It was a sensation she'd not felt since Colm's death. It settled over her in a warm cocoon.

"I am eased by your compassion. I again find myself indebted to you."

Reaching out with her mind to Aohdan, she linked with him conveying a silent thank you. A tendril of him seemed to attach himself to her. She felt him softly wind through her heart. A strange bond had formed, but she didn't know how to respond to her feelings. Quickly she severed the connection but still felt his presence.

His bright blue eyes brought forth a conflict within her. Saoirse muttered an excuse for leaving and fled from the library. Aohdan watched her go with lingering curiosity. Something had happened between them just then. It was inexplicable, but it had joined them. He wondered what it meant. He wanted to pursue Saoirse to ask her. Instead, he tested the new bond and reached across the house for her. Aohdan found her in her room. Her emotions rolled over him in waves nearly overwhelming him.

With a start, he realized he could hear her thoughts. She was torn over the connection that had just been made between them. Confusion abounded. Her mind was unguarded and open to him. After a moment it became clear that his presence was unknown. With a rush of discomfiture, and not wishing to intrude, Aohdan withdrew his probing. This mysterious connection would require some tact. It would also take some getting used to.

Aohdan kept his wonderings to himself over the next two days as they made final preparations to ascend the mountain. He could tell Saoirse was avoiding him, but he didn't let it bother him. Instead he focused on his work. He had created a leather harness for Saoirse to wear so he and Andrew could travel more comfortably on her back without fear of falling. They each were to clip a cord to their belt that attached to rings on her harness. In this way, even if one was unseated, they would not be lost. The harness also gave them something to tie their packs on.

The only shortcoming with the harness was it prevented Saoirse from growing in size or she would break it. Aohdan knew she hoped this would not be a hindrance in their flight to the mountain. She had decided to stick with a larger form in order to comfortably carry

Fallon. The leather crisscrossed her scales in stark contrast with her shimmering silver. From a distance the lines looked like exotic tattoos, adding to her mystique.

On the third day, in the chilly dark of early morning as the sun began to color the horizon, they readied to leave. Saoirse ate an enormous breakfast. Eggs, biscuits, and a side of ham all vanished before her. She was eating for a journeying dragon. Fallon had already left the day before to join them on a towering peak where Saoirse could easily pick him up. He too wore a broad leather harness, giving Saoirse's talons something to grasp instead of trying to hold the wolf without injuring him.

Fallon was agitated over the prospective flight. It went against every fiber of his being to leave the ground. Yet, he wished to aid his friends. He growled fearful epithets to himself from the house up to the summit but lay stoically at the top waiting for them.

Saoirse shifted to her dragon in the lawn. Steam rose in ripples from her armor as the crisp air kissed her fiery warmth. Aohdan carefully buckled the harness about her body, rechecking each strap a final time. Then he and Andrew took their packs and clambered onto her broad back. Andrew had been silently morose all morning. It was only when he clipped himself to Saoirse's harness did he speak.

"Alright, dragon. We are ready," his voice cracked, betraying his nerves.

Saoirse let out a bass thrum of acknowledgement. Aohdan recognized the meaning winding through the thrum. It wasn't words so much as word pictures she was giving off. Satisfaction that they were leaving, the thrill of flight, worry of what lay ahead, and a serenity in finally taking action. He looked over at Andrew, wondering if he had caught Saoirse's words. Andrew's face was impassive, though a shade paler than normal. Aohdan's wonderings were cut short as Saoirse pushed off the ground with a thunderclap of wingbeats.

The heady sensation of climbing into the sky washed over the two men. Saoirse leveled out, catching a draft beneath her wings. It would be a full day's flight to reach the hidden peaks of the Blue Fire Mountains that Saoirse called home. A green sea of forest flowed beneath them. The white caps of peaks thrust sharply out of the jade carpet.

The air was cold, drawing tears to their eyes. But heat radiated from Saoirse protecting the men from the wind's full bite. Ahead of them the Blue Fire Mountains were illuminated with fire from the rising sun in the east. Gold mist wreathed the zeniths till the range appeared to be a castle of liquid gold.

Aohdan drank in the sunrise with awe. "Look," he murmured to Andrew.

Andrew was indeed looking. The grandeur was not lost on him. His fear and anger trickled out of him as he allowed the beauty of the skies to cleanse him.

"I am glad you convinced me to go, Aohdan. Saoirse...." Here he laid a hand on her scales, "I admit this is worth it. Thank you for carrying us."

"You're welcome, Andrew." Saoirse vibrated beneath them. Again, she sent out a sonorous thrumming. This time Aohdan felt it was full of happiness. Happiness for Andrew, happiness for friendship, and perhaps something more.

Saoirse's thrumming song continued as the day wore on. They spoke no more as they flew. Aodhan ascertained that he could choose to hear Saoirse or block her out. Her thoughts were mostly contemplative memories that Aohdan did not wish to encroach on.

Midday drew upon them and they reached the apex where Fallon was waiting. His stark white fur lit up by the sun contrasted brightly against the dark stone of the mountain. Saoirse landed with lithe ease on the wide ledge. Stiffly the men slid off to stretch their legs. They took a small repast on the mountainside. Saoirse curled up with her head under her wing and slept while the men ate.

It was only a short nap. When she woke Saoirse informed them that she too needed food. With a snap of her wings, she flew down the mountain disappearing into the trees. A short time later she returned, talons stained red, her maw smeared with rust-colored flecks.

Andrew shuddered at her appearance. Aohdan, on the other hand, was reminded that while Saoirse might have a human side she was still as wild as Fallon. Fallon was the least disturbed by her exterior. He grinned a sharp smile in appreciation of a successful hunt. Saoirse primly washed her claws and muzzle in a leftover snow bank, then declared herself ready to continue their flight.

The men climbed onto Saoirse clipping themselves to her harness. Taking to the sky she circled back around in order to pick up Fallon. The wolf stood on the edge of the precipice. Banking steeply with fore legs outstretched, Saoirse lowered herself toward him. Fallon's ears flattened against the wind she created. With cautious dexterity, she slid her talons through the straps Aohdan made, wrapping her talons around them. Then with a mighty heave she lifted the wolf off the ground.

A yelp escaped Fallon that he could not suppress. It required every ounce of his will not to thrash wildly. This was not a natural place for him, dangling from the claws of another predator. His heart raced uncontrollably till he felt Saoirse reach out to him with her magic, soothing his terror. He clung to her peacefulness as his pulse slowed. Soon he began to enjoy the bizarre flight. His tongue lolled and the tenseness left him. He pondered over the spectacle they made. A dragon carrying two humans and a wolf. What a tale to tell the pack when he returned.

Chapter 8

THE LATE AFTERNOON RAYS DANCED THROUGH the mist. The adventurers threaded pockets of light and damp clouds nearing Saoirse's mountain. Saoirse had become utterly silent upon braving the cloud bank that protected her home. Tension sparked like lightning between the travelers as they drew near.

Finally, they burst through the blanket of thick fog. A towering island line of peaks stretched below them reaching the far horizon. The nearest monolith boasted a set of enormous stone doors carved with writhing dragons, running wolves, towering trees, and stern faced men. A gigantic tree trunk had been wedged across these doors, keeping them firmly shut. Two smaller, human sized entrances flanked the stone doors. One of the smaller entries' russet wooden doors lay twisted and broken off to the side. A goblin sentry wearing crude dark armor stood next to the ravaged wood.

Black fury descended over Saoirse. Fallon and the men felt her poorly concealed rage. Her potent emotions caused them to meet her ire with their own.

"We are undiscovered," she hissed in their minds. "There is a platform above the doors that we used for stargazing. I will drop you off there. A staircase leads down to the main gateway. If you can kill the sentry without raising the alarm, we can take them by surprise. I do not think Killkari is here. The doors would be open if he was. Be prepared for me to open the main gates. I do not know what we will find. If it goes ill return to the platform and I will come for you."

Stealthily, she allowed a draft to glide her to the platform where she alighted in elegant silence. She gently allowed Fallon to gain his footing first. Then she herself landed, the men scrambled from her retrieving their packs. Aohdan hurried to unbuckle the harness from Saoirse. Andrew was already peering over the edge at the goblin. He motioned for Aohdan to take up his bow.

Aohdan pulled his bow and quiver from his pack. He slung the quiver over his head where it rested next to Saoirse's blade on his back. Taking an arrow and nocking it, he inched his way to the edge. Below him, the goblin leaned lazily on a tall spear. Aohdan's vantage of almost directly above the creature created a challenging shot. If he didn't kill it instantly, the goblin would betray their presence.

He felt, rather than saw, Saoirse hovering above them ready to remove the tree from the stone doors. With a deep breath he drew the bow, calculated his mark, and released the arrow. The goblin stiffened, transfixed by the arrow that pierced his skull. Then the goblin toppled dead over his spear, muffling its clatter. The air rushed out of Aohdan before he realized he had been holding it. *Another bad habit*, he berated himself.

Andrew and Fallon were heading down the staircase as soon as the goblin fell. Saoirse's voice jangled their thoughts.

"Beware, for I will be using my fire. I do not wish for any of you to be caught in it. Are you ready?"

All three gave their assent. Aohdan raced down the stairs to catch up with the other two. Saoirse flew in close to the stone doors, grasped the tree blocking them, and with a mighty heave wrenched it free. She threw the trunk over the edge of the mountain, wings straining to keep her balance. Then, uttering a quiet word of magic, she flung open the stone doors.

A vast expanse of cavern stretched out before them. What should have been a bustling, glowing city entrance was now a lifeless hole. Statues of dead *Elestari* littered the entrance eternally frozen in death's embrace. Bile rose in Aohdan's throat, his lunch threatening to escape. The foursome tentatively walked through the doors.

Then the air was filled with the humming of arrows. The first round was incinerated by a quick blast of violet flame. Out of the dark recesses swarmed a horde of goblins. A rumbling growl emanated from Saoirse that grew to a tremendous roar. Launching herself into the air she flew low over the goblins enveloping them in fire. A few escaped her flames. These came shrieking at the other three on the ground. Fallon was on them in a trice before the goblins could reach Andrew and Aohdan.

Instead, arrows again sang around them as they dodged for protection behind a stone dragon.

"We must pick off these archers if we are to join the fight," Andrew said tersely.

Aohdan nodded, sheathing his sword and pulling out his bow. Andrew too had a bow with which he quickly fitted an arrow. The two men inspected the cavern before seeking to identify the goblin archers. Three groups of bowmen harried them, standing behind a long balustrade that wrapped part way around the cavern. Andrew and Aohdan alternated their shots moving closer and closer to the fray. Their arrows were well placed and soon the goblin ranks were severely diminished above them.

Meanwhile, Saoirse and Fallon continued to battle the goblins in the center of the room. They dogged the goblins mercilessly. Fallon would drive them back into a corner where Saoirse would blast them with flame. Andrew and Aohdan now joined them drawing their blades, standing on either side of Fallon. Swords clanging fiercely, they drove the goblins back against a wall, hemming them in.

Because of the close proximity of her friends, Saoirse could no longer utilize her fire. Instead, she used her claws and tail as weapons. With their escape cut off, the goblins grew desperate, and Saoirse's lack of fire emboldened them. They fought savagely now. Some were carrying bright silver blades that could pierce the hides of Fallon and Saoirse. With these they tried to hack at Saoirse with every sally she made. They were successful only in inflicting minor cuts. Fallon suffered more than Saoirse, his white coat ribboned with red from the glancing blows. Now the goblins were in a true state of panic. Their original number was slashed to a fourth of what it had been.

The goblins shrieked angrily at their predicament. In a last frantic attempt, they rallied.

"FALL BACK!" Saoirse's voice echoed in the three fighters' minds.

They each took a few quick steps backward leaving a space between themselves and the goblins. Instantly, Saoirse let loose a massive fireball over the trapped goblins turning them to ash. Now it was time for the men to finish the fight. They turned their attention to the few goblins left above still loosing arrows on them. Sprinting toward the stairs, they yelled out a challenge. Seeing the rapidly approaching men, the goblins fled.

Andrew and Aohdan pursued the creatures, following them into a twisting maze of rooms that were offshoots of the balcony. The rooms they ran through varied in size from human quarters to rooms large enough to house Saoirse's dragon form. Many had been ransacked by the goblins with belongings strewn carelessly across the floor. Putting on a fresh burst of speed they assailed the goblins that lagged behind.

A blow from Aohdan's sword brought the nearest goblin to a swift death sending the others into screeches of fear and fury. Andrew leapt ahead bringing down another goblin with a sweeping stroke. This redoubled the goblins efforts to flee. They stayed grouped together continuing on their track further into the mountain.

"They are headed somewhere," Andrew huffed out as he ran after the goblins.

Aohdan grunted an assent as he focused his breathing on the chase. There must be an escape of some sort or possibly another host of goblins that their quarry was trying to reach. Otherwise, the goblins would have split up by now to try to pick off him and Andrew. *Saoirse would know what's ahead*, he realized. He felt the tendril that connected him to her. Now was as good a time as any to test it. Reaching out across the expanse he found her mind. He plunged through her barriers, loudly calling out her name.

Saoirse jolted at his presence. He felt the shock echo through her, though she tried to quickly brush it aside.

"What do you need, Aohdan?"

"The goblins have purpose in their flight. They are headed somewhere. Is there another exit?"

"A few, small obscure ones. They only open from the inside. They could escape from those."

"Thank you."

Withdrawing he focused on the task at hand. Suddenly, a picture flashed into his head. It was a map of the rooms ahead of them, a short distance away was a door leading to the outside of the mountain. The goblins were heading on a direct track for it.

"Thanks again, Saoirse," he muttered softly to himself. He imagined he heard her rumble in response.

"Andrew, there's a way out. The goblins are trying to escape. Saoirse showed me a map."

His words were clipped from shortness of breath. The long run was beginning to tell on him.

"Can you head them off?" Andrew questioned.

"I think so."

"Good. I'll keep tailing them."

Pulling up the image of the mountain again Aohdan took a sharp deviation from the goblins. It would be close, but he had to chance it. The goblins must not escape. This knowledge imbued his legs with an extra fire. He sprinted recklessly forward. It was a race now. Left, right, long corridors, vaulted rooms, ornately tiled floors all passed beneath his feet.

He was almost there. According to the map, it should be at the end of the next hall. He turned a corner into a large chamber. Along the wall, opposite from him, a pair of windows slit into the rock allowed slim rays of sunlight onto the floor. A short, heavy door stood between them. The exit! He jogged the last few steps, stopping squarely in front of the door.

From his left, the clatter of feet and the sound of raspy breath intensified till the goblins came running doggedly into view. Shrill cries of surprise emanated from goblin lips at the sight of Aohdan. They came to a stumbling halt, gibbering fearfully. Heart clattering from his wild run, Aohdan waited in anticipation for them to make the first move. It was Andrew, coming in swiftly behind them that threw them into action.

Faced with a choice, the goblins decided to attack the foe blocking their exit. They swarmed Aohdan. Keeping his back to the door Aohdan made sweeping blocks with his sword. He was ringed by the foul creatures. Andrew reached them, battering away at the wall of enemies trying to overcome his friend. Goblins fell before him. Suddenly, the goblins turned from Aohdan to Andrew, who was dealing destruction. Now Andrew was surrounded. Aohdan agonized for a moment about whether to leave the door unguarded. A grunt of pain from Andrew made the decision for him.

Roaring furiously, Aohdan hacked at the goblins. Blades clanged and slithered off one another. An overhand stroke dispatched one goblin and continued on to wound another. Bodies began to litter the floor. Unexpectedly, a glare of sunlight broke over them. Taken aback, Aohdan faltered. A blade took him across the thigh bringing a hiss from his lips. Across the mountain he felt, rather than saw, Saoirse's head go up in response to his pain.

A goblin had escaped, he thought angrily. He couldn't afford to let anymore get away. Shaking off his daze he turned his full attention to the remaining goblins. Five were left. They fought as a trapped animal does, with claw and fang. Andrew and Aohdan were not unscathed by their fervency, but soon the bodies of the five joined their comrades.

Both men stood heavily panting. Weariness shackled them to the ground. Neither spoke, too winded to do so. Soon though, their hearts began to settle back to a normal rhythm.

"One got away," Aohdan broke the silence.

"It will mean trouble for us," came the grim reply. "He'll be back with friends. It will be a while though. They can't get up here easily. I doubt they will be back tonight at least. I think we will be safe to stay till morning," Andrew spoke with assurance.

"Let's take a look at where that door leads." Aohdan turned from Andrew to the door in the wall. Stepping over the goblin bodies he cautiously opened it, keeping himself behind the dark wood. No arrows came hissing through the gap, only late afternoon sunlight. Slowly he peeked around the edge. Andrew stood at the ready behind him, blade still drawn. The sun warmed his skin with a red glow.

Satisfied that there were no goblins, he swung the door completely back on its hinges. The doorway opened onto a narrow ledge. Dropping away from the ledge, steps zig-zagged nearly vertically down the mountain. The stairway was shallow, without a railing, and contained numerous gaps that one would have to leap over to cross.

"That looks pleasant to traverse," Andrew commented drily, his eyebrows raised in distaste at the steep descent.

Aohdan nodded, eyeing the stairs. "Saoirse did say that the path up here was difficult."

"I'm inclined to believe her now."

Aohdan gave his mentor an incredulous look. Andrew stared back at him gravely for a moment before bursting into laughter.

"You're becoming too gullible living with me, Aohdan. I'm going to have to send you back to Amaroth to spend some time with the money lenders. That will teach you not to believe everything I say."

Despite himself, Aohdan found that he was grinning broadly at Andrew. "I suppose I am. I prefer the truth, but I need to remember that certain people enjoy sarcasm."

A wolfish smile crossed Andrew's features. "I think that would be wise on your part." Still chuckling to himself, he asked, "Now how do we get back through this rabbit warren?"

Aohdan thought carefully. He pulled up the map in his head. In surprise he realized that it had grown to show the entire mountain colony.

"I can see the way. It will be a long walk," he said.

"Then we better get started," was Andrew's philosophical answer.

"Wait, I have a better idea. Why don't I have Saoirse send us Fallon? I'm sure he can follow our scent. In the meantime, we can start walking in that direction."

"That sounds like an excellent plan."

Opening his connection to Saoirse he relayed to her their request. She promptly dispatched Fallon to them. With a nod to Andrew the two began the journey back.

Chapter 9

THEY RETURNED TO THE GATES AND found the ground covered in the fine dust of billions of tiny gems. The statues were gone, Aohdan was relieved to see. The glittering carpet spread across the cavern was the only evidence they had ever existed. Saoirse was not in sight. Her sadness billowed from a nearby room telling Aohdan that she was not far from them. Andrew and Fallon had both become subdued.

"Bit eerie, isn't it?" Andrew broke the silence.

"Better than the statues. It's disconcerting to walk through this dust though. Rather depressing when you think about the origin," Aohdan replied tersely.

Andrew grimaced. "I'm glad we won't be staying long."

A low moan from one of the side rooms cut off any more conversation. Saoirse's link to Aohdan twisted painfully causing him to flinch. He followed the connection to the room she was in with Andrew and Fallon trailing behind.

At one time it had been a beautiful library. Now parts of it were charred, with shelves broken and books strewn across the floor torn apart by goblin hands. The remains of an elegant chandelier lay shattered over the blackened shell of a large writing desk. In a third of the room scorch marks ran from floor to ceiling. It was a large space meant to hold dozens of scholars. Instead there were dozens of statues in various forms. Some hunched protectively over a pile of scorched books. Others were locked in a deadly embrace with the moldering skeleton of a goblin.

The trio looked over the scene with heavy sadness. Saoirse was at the back wall hunched next to the large form of a jade stone dragon. Great sobs wracked her body. Her pain nearly brought Aohdan to his knees. For every shudder she gave, he felt the deepest ache in her heart as his own. But this was her grief. He knew she had come to terms with her mate's death; yet that did not make living with it any easier. Only time would ease the pain. For the moment it was still fresh, a sorrow that needed to be released for her to begin healing.

A tiny sniff came from Andrew. For the first time in his life Aohdan saw tears streaming down Andrew's face. Never before had he seen his mentor cry; even in all of his bitterness and loss. Now the tears flowed freely. Aohdan watched in astonishment as Andrew slowly walked to the side of the silver dragon. He laid a hand on the bowed neck. Aohdan immediately felt his presence through Saoirse.

Andrew too was grieving, lamenting the loss of his wife to Killkari. Yet in the midst of his heartbreak, Andrew offered sympathy and comfort to Saoirse for her tragedy. The two stood with heads bent shedding tears and time seemed to stand still. Aohdan and Fallon gazed solemnly at their companions.

At long last a flicker went through Saoirse. A sigh escaped her. She turned her proud head to Andrew butting up against him. He embraced her. A shared understanding came between the two. Each had lost someone dear to them. This brought dragon and man together breaking down the enmity that had separated them.

No words were spoken, and none were needed. Now looking to Aohdan and Fallon, Saoirse spoke, "Favor me and draw near as I give Colm the last rite of dragon fire."

Hesitantly, Aohdan and Fallon approached. Standing with Andrew they looked on as Saoirse blew out a stream of violet flame. This fire was different from what they had seen earlier. It gave off no heat as it covered the jade body of Colm, dancing over him till he appeared to glow. Then in an instant, the statue disintegrated into a shower of jade sparks.

Turning heavily, Saoirse proceeded to bathe each statue in flame. When she was finished the library was covered in tiny gems. Without a backward glance she trudged out of the library, tail dragging, weighed down by her sadness. The three friends followed her as she walked back to the gates of her city.

Once Saoirse was outside and on the wide balcony before the doors she stopped. With a deep moan she allowed her legs to buckle beneath her, head facing the expanse of darkening sky in front of her. Aohdan could sense she was emotionally spent.

In silent agreement the two men went and retrieved their packs from the observation deck above them. Fallon laid down next to Saoirse, head between his paws. Stars were beginning to pop out in the deepening sky.

Andrew started a small fire and Aohdan set to making dinner for them. Soon they were eating a savory stew that buoyed their spirits. The moon had risen and cast a dim glow over Fallon and Saoirse. From a distance scales and fur flickered in the moonlight.

Aohdan could feel Saoirse slowly gaining mastery over her pain. The fear of inadequacy that had plagued her was gone. A calm had settled over her. She had mastered her fear and said her final goodbye to Colm.

Sleep was tugging at each of the travelers.

Fallon gave an enormous toothy yawn. "I will sleep inside to keep watch for any goblins. Rest in peace, my friends."

With that he got up and padded softly into the black mouth of the mountain. Andrew set out his bedroll, promptly falling asleep. Aohdan made preparations to rest, yet as he lay looking up at the twinkling stars, sleep evaded him. He was too keyed up from the day's events to relax.

He was bothered by several details that would not let his mind rest. Why did the goblins attack the *Elestari* in the first place? They were foul creatures that destroyed wantonly, but to go against a formidable opponent was unusual for them. The *Elestari* held little that the goblins would be interested in. Armories yes, but most of their valuables were in books and magic. Someone or something must have wanted them to attack. Was Killkari behind the plot? What did he have against the *Elestari*?

It didn't make sense. Where were the rest of the *Elestari*? Were they carried off like Saoirse? Or did they escape to some unknown mountain eyrie? Aohdan felt frustration roll over him as the questions circled endlessly. They were missing a piece of this puzzle. And there was another mystery that he wasn't sure how to deal with—Saoirse.

He knew that his connection with her was highly unusual. What did it mean? Saoirse had alluded to the fact that a bond between *Elestari* was a powerful thing. Her link to Colm and subsequent loss of him had nearly killed her. Aohdan wasn't sure what his feelings for Saoirse were. She was a tangle to him. Drawing him in, then repelling him with their differences.

He rolled onto his side restlessly. The fire was burning low. Across from him Saoirse lay motionless like a silver statue reminding him uncomfortably of the dead *Elestari* they had encountered that day. Aohdan could feel that she too was awake. Should he ask her about their connection? He knew eventually they would have to broach the subject. Their bond was getting stronger.

He lay still, concentrating on the dragon. He could feel her heart pumping a steady beat. He felt the blood pulsing through her veins, warming her body. Strengthening the connection, he reached for her mind and found himself looking through her eyes. Saoirse's eyes saw the sky in a myriad of deeper colors than Aohdan had imagined were there. The stars were clearer with startlingly bright edges. The space beyond was a vast indigo expanse varying from a deep blue to obsidian.

Abruptly, Saoirse threw up her head breaking the connection. She glared at Aohdan over the fire.

"You were in my head."

It was a voiceless accusation that caused Aohdan to squirm. Rising, he walked over to Saoirse.

"Yes, I was. I'm sorry. I shouldn't have."

"How did you do it?"

"I don't know. I followed my connection to you. The more I opened myself up the more I felt of you. Then I was looking through your eyes. The way you see things. It's beautiful."

Saoirse did not answer. Instead, Aohdan could sense that she was troubled. He decided that this might be his opening to question her.

"Please," he said, "I don't understand this link between us. What is it? I can tell that it both gratifies and alarms you. I feel the same. I don't know what to make of it." Withdrawing himself from the connection, he waited for her response.

Saoirse closed her eyes tightly. This was the question she had been asking herself. She wasn't sure she was ready to answer it. She didn't even know if her suspicion was correct. Their connection defied everything that Saoirse was familiar with. With great hesitancy she finally answered.

"I'm not entirely sure if I am right. Nonetheless, I cannot ignore the signs. I believe that we have somehow bonded."

There. She had gotten it out. It seemed less fanciful now that she had said it. What did Aohdan think? She desperately wanted to peek into his mind, but that would be improper. Opening her eyes, she looked into the bright blue gaze of Aohdan. His look was akin to wonder with something more. Then his eyes filled with terror.

Saoirse's heart plummeted. Then she realized Aohdan's terror was not caused by her. Her instincts suddenly screamed of an oncoming enemy. She saw through Aohdan's eyes that a jet black dragon was attacking. An instant later a massive weight came plunging down on her pinning her to the ground. Sharp talons bit into her wings and back. Jaws clamped down on her neck shaking her savagely. Saoirse let out a bellow of fear and anger.

Bucking ferociously, Saoirse sought to unseat her attacker. Rearing up she threw her head back wildly attempting to seek release from the jaws that held her. The dragon held on tenaciously, its weight slamming her back to the ground. She knew this was no *Elestari*. It was Killkari. She sensed the malevolence of his thoughts bent on destroying her. Sending a shard of lightning toward his mind she tried to overpower him mentally. Her bolt slammed into a heavily fortified wall of blackness that billowed with evil.

Saoirse reeled in shock, causing Killkari to laugh at her in a deep granite rumble. She had not expected him to be prepared for her attack. She knew she could defeat Killkari in fair combat, but she had been caught unaware. How had he known she would attempt to breach his mind? This was all wrong. Saoirse's confusion was to Killkari's benefit. He pressed his advantage grinding his teeth deeper into the scales of her neck. Yanking viciously, he used this hold to try wrench her over onto her side. Without her feet beneath her it would be much more difficult for her to fight him.

Suddenly a bright sting of pain buried into his thigh. Killkari howled angrily, lashing out with his tail at the unseen enemy. This was the break that Saoirse needed. The moment Killkari released his hold on her neck she launched herself off the ledge in a mighty bound taking Killkari with her. For an instant the two dragons were free falling.

Saoirse knew that self-preservation would force Killkari to cease grappling with her in order to unfurl his wings and not plunge to his death in the depths below. Infuriated, Killkari let out a roar as he pulled away from Saoirse. She too spread her wings. As she did so she grew to her full size. She was larger than Killkari now, but not by much. Her onyx opponent was bigger than the average dragon with the strength to match.

Letting out an ear-splitting screech she banked and barreled toward him claws extended. Saoirse engulfed Killkari in flame sending up a crackling fireball as the two crashed together. Fangs slashed, while talons sought weaknesses in their opponent's armor. Saoirse ripped a long tear in Killkari's wing, and he in turn scratched a gash in her foreleg. They broke apart.

They circled. Again, Killkari laughed at her, eyes burning red against the dark sky. This time he taunted her in a gravelly voice.

"You call yourself a dragon! You travel with those weakling humans as if they are equal to you. They are nothing! You say you crave knowledge. Rubbish! You should crave power. You could own the world."

"You speak foolishness, Killkari," Saoirse spat.

"It is you who are the fool," Killkari hissed sibilantly. "I will reign over Arda. I will not bow to some stupid human. Men, dwarves, and elves should serve us. They will not be easy to bend to our will, but with the *Elestari* I will prevail. I have already turned the goblins to me. You are a fair dragoness. Join me, and you could rule by my side."

Saoirse glared at Killkari with overwhelming hate. "I will never join a cowardly worm like you. You destroyed my people. I would rather die than join your cause."

"I did not destroy your people," Killkari scoffed. "I simply subdued them. I have many of them kept safe to serve my purpose."

"WHAT? You dare imprison my people!" Saoirse flamed a violet streak, then attacked.

Her momentum threw Killkari back, tangling them together while his wings beat irregularly to adjust to her force, his unbalanced body giving her an opening. Thrusting a taloned forepaw into his throat she forced his head up and away from her. This left him exposed for a fraction of a second. Taking the opportunity, Saoirse bit down hard on his left foreleg. Her fangs sank deep into his flesh. Unhindered, she felt his bones crunch between her teeth.

Killkari let out a wail. He thrashed his way from her grasp, leg hanging limply. Now crippled, he fled before her. Saoirse was harrying him mercilessly when she heard Aohdan calling for her. Roaring angrily, she pulled away from the black dragon, watching him fly away with vexation.

Aohdan's voice was strident in her head. "Saoirse, come back. Andrew is badly hurt. He may be dying."

Fear for her friend flooded the silver dragon. She rocketed back to the mountain. Killkari would wait for another day. Dropping heavily to the outcrop she hurried over to the still form that lay propped against one of the doors. She was greeted by Aohdan and Fallon.

Aohdan spilled out the story. "When Killkari attacked you I was thrown aside by your thrashing. I had the wind knocked out of me. I was struggling to rise when I saw Andrew rush to your aid, seeking revenge, his sword drawn. Killkari was so focused on you that he did not see Andrew's approach.

"Andrew struck the beast in the leg causing him to release his hold on you. But then Killkari set to flailing his tail about. He caught Andrew with a spine of his tail and flung him against the door as you see him now. It's very bad, Saoirse. I hope we are not too late."

Saoirse turned her focus on Andrew. His body looked lifeless. Probing with her magic Saoirse found that Andrew was barely breathing. Blood pooled next to him from a large hole in his abdomen. The spine had pierced through him front to back. His ribs were crushed from the impact of hitting the stone door. His internal organs were torn or bruised. A tear slipped down Saoirse's snout. Andrew was on the brink of death. She hoped she could heal him in time.

Breathing out a heatless purple flame she covered Andrew head to toe in fire. Holding the flame steady, she proceeded to knit him together from the inside out. She focused on the most severe injuries first, knitting sinew and repairing blood vessels. Concentrating, she allowed her spare energy to ebb into Andrew. Finally, she was finished. She stepped back wearily.

Now it was up to Andrew. Would he cling to life or was it too late? Andrew's pulse slowly grew stronger. He stirred, eyes fluttering. Aohdan allowed a gasp of relief to escape. Andrew would live. Clutching his mentor's hand he gently shook him awake. Fallon too nudged at Andrew, grateful to see him alive.

"What happened?" Andrew rasped out. "Did you kill that filthy monster, Saoirse? Last thing I remember, I was flying through the air."

Aohdan was too choked up to answer properly. Saoirse replied sadly instead, "I failed you, Andrew. I let Killkari get away. I'm sorry. When you wounded Killkari he impaled you with his tail spine and threw you across the landing. You were mortally injured so I came back for you. I healed you."

Andrew spoke tiredly, a wan smile crossing his face. "I owe you my life. You didn't fail me. You did an honorable thing coming back for me. Thank you. I doubt Killkari got away easily."

"It was a close contest. I broke his leg, and he fled from me. Killkari will need some time to recover," Saoirse elaborated.

"Coward," Andrew growled with a trace of his old humor.

Fallon interjected. "He won't be bothering us tonight at least. I'm glad for that. And to see you alive, Andrew. I doubt we will have anything else to worry about for what's left of the night. Let's try to get some sleep."

"Fallon is right. Andrew, you will need much rest before you are truly recovered. I may have healed your wounds, but your body is still exhausted from the trauma. We should all try to rest," Saoirse pronounced.

Aohdan helped Andrew over to his bedroll where the retired Ranger sank down gratefully. Sleep overcame him, allowing him to rest peacefully. Fallon retired to his previous post inside the mountain.

Lastly, Aohdan brought over his medical kit to Saoirse. She shrank down to the size of a large horse. She gratefully permitted Aohdan to tend to her injuries, daubing a healing salve over her deep but not life-threatening, wounds. The worst were the bites ringing her neck. They bled freely with every move Saoirse made. Her blood appeared as a dark stain against her moonlight-colored scales.

"I ought to bind your neck," Aohdan said as he lightly probed the fang marks. "We need to staunch this blood flow. It will only weaken you if I don't."

Saoirse groaned wearily. "It will make it difficult for me to grow, but I suppose a few hours this size won't hurt anything. Do as you wish."

Grimacing she extended her neck for him. Aohdan packed each deep fang mark with herbs making Saoirse wince. Once every gash was filled, he bandaged her neck making sure to keep it from becoming too tight and choking her. When he was finished Saoirse looked like she had a strange scarf wrapped round her. Aohdan smiled tiredly at the sight.

"All done. I expect you will be stiff and sore for a while."

Saoirse snorted. "I'm stiff and sore now. But thank you. I'm not a very good patient, I'm afraid. It seems I'm destined to always be patched up by you."

Aohdan allowed his smile to grow. "Would that really be such a bad thing?" he teased her gently.

"No." She ducked her head slightly avoiding Aohdan's gaze.

He felt a tinge of shyness emanating from her. He decided to not press the subject. He was tired. The day had held too much excitement. They both needed rest.

"Good night, Saoirse," he said fixing her with a steady look.

For a moment she held his eyes, losing herself in the bright blue. Her heart betrayed her, racing wildly. She looked away. "Good night, Aohdan. Sleep well."

Chapter 10

THE SUN AWAKENED SAOIRSE MUCH SOONER than she would have liked. Her body ached from snout to tail. Her neck twinged with every movement, but it no longer bled. What she wouldn't give for a hot bath. She yawned, then stretched catlike in the sun. She was hungry. She looked over at the two men who were also waking up. Ambling over to the now dead fire she shot a tiny spurt of flame reigniting it.

Andrew looked decidedly pale. Saoirse hoped that he had the strength he would need to fly today. She needed to eat. Her energy was zapped.

"I need to hunt. I will be back soon." Snapping her wings open, she left before they could reply.

Fallon padded out in time to see her leave. "Gone hunting, I assume? I dined on rats this morning. Not my favorite repast."

Aohdan nodded. "Yes, she is hunting. She will need all the food she can get."

"At least we don't have to feed her. She would eat our supplies up in a trice," Andrew quipped.

Chuckling, Aohdan answered, "She saves your life, and you begrudge her a meal, Andrew?"

"I would if it means I have to go hungry," Andrew groused.

Fallon and Aohdan laughed heartily at the grumpy old Ranger who glowered back at them.

Aohdan set about making a pot of coffee to take the edge off his sleepiness. Quick rising bread with jerky strips soon warmed their bellies, bringing contentment to even prickly Andrew. They basked in the warmth of the morning sun as they waited for Saoirse. The bright rays were a welcome diversion after the terrors of the night. Once again Aohdan was struck by the beauty of the mountain view. The clouds surrounding them gave the illusion that you could step off into them, walking in a boundless field of pink and gold cotton. The sky above was changing to a crystalline blue, fading white against the fiery eastern sun.

Soon Saoirse returned. Her posture was relaxed for the first time in days. Judging by her pleased humming Aohdan guessed that she had been successful in her hunt. He made no attempt to pry into her mind. Eventually, questions would be answered, but now was not the time.

Saoirse went straight to the point. "Killkari has taken the *Elestari* captive. Not only that he holds the goblins under his sway."

The three blanched at her pronouncement.

Andrew's already drawn face grayed. "I had suspected as much from the evidence we have seen. This poses a grave problem. Arda is in danger."

"Yes. Killkari said as much to me," Saoirse intoned. "He wants to rule. He spoke to me of not just overtaking your throne, Aohdan, but he wishes to reign over all races - elves, dwarves, and men alike."

Fallon growled in a low voice. "That would be very difficult to achieve."

"Not so difficult as you think, my friend." Aohdan's brow darkened resignedly. "We have to assume that Killkari has supplied the goblins with our stores of bright silver and that they have used it to make weapons. Armed with bright silver alone makes them more formidable. Let's also not forget that if he holds the *Elestari* then it is certainly not for their good that he does so. They are powerful. He will try to harness that power for his purposes."

Andrew nodded vigorously. "Precisely. However, there is hope. It was only the last few years that the bright silver caches were raided. He wouldn't have had enough to supply an army until recently. Also, the *Elestari* were a free people until a few months ago. Killkari cannot possibly be ready to make his bid for domination. It takes time to create weapons and amass an army. Our coming to this mountain was a fluke in his planning. But now we have a chance. We have to force his hand and destroy him before he is ready."

"But we don't know where his lair is," Fallon rumbled impatiently. "The infernal dragon could be hidden under any number of mountains. He could even be in the Cascades for all we know."

"Excellent point, Fallon," Aohdan agreed fingering his sword. "I think we have overlooked a very important piece of evidence…Saoirse."

Saoirse gave a puzzled snort, cocking her silvery head. "How am I evidence?"

A dark smile crossed Andrew's face and he chuckled mirthlessly. "Of course! How could we have been so blind? You are the clue, Saoirse, because we rescued you. The goblins were taking you somewhere, probably to Killkari's lair. We were incorrect in thinking that Killkari was hiding in the Blue Fire Mountains. He must have been scouting out the *Elestari,* not making a lair there.

It makes perfect sense. All the time Aohdan and I were searching for signs of Killkari we would have had little thought for goblins. They plague the mountainside already so proof of their passing through would not have brought us undue alarm. They could have transported many prisoners without our knowledge as much as it pains me to say. We were so focused on Killkari we missed the most important evidence of all."

"So now what do we do? Where do we go from here?" Aohdan mused.

"I think we should go to Amaroth," Saoirse replied. "There may be *Elestari* living there in human form. I also would like to see the archives of the city. I might be able to find important information from the past that could help us locate Killkari's hideout."

Andrew considered her words. "I think that would be a good idea. We can find out if there have been any other attacks or if any news of goblins has come to light. Also, we need to alert the Queen of the approaching danger."

"My mother has an excellent spy network that is constantly gathering intelligence. We will benefit from their information," Aohdan added.

"Well, what are we waiting for?" Fallon's impatience grew more apparent as he paced back and forth. "Let's be off."

"Indeed, we should take advantage of our limited time," Saoirse agreed snapping her wings wide. "Aohdan, please remove the bandages from my neck so I can grow unencumbered. Then let us leave as soon as possible."

Aohdan did as Saoirse asked while Andrew set about repacking their things. He was pleased to see that the bite marks on her neck were now well scabbed over. He gently probed the ugly marks marring her perfect shimmering scales feeling a deep seated anger at Killkari for inflicting them. He also inspected her other cuts, particularly the one on her foreleg. He worried that it would reopen from the strain of carrying Fallon, but he kept his reservations to himself. Saoirse would want to fly regardless of injury, so worrying about her would do him little good.

It took all of Saoirse's composure to keep from quivering under Aohdan's practiced touch. A shadow of stubble graced his normally clean-cut appearance making him all the more appealing. His dark hair was wild around his shoulders having mostly escaped its bright silver keeper. His hands again reached for the wounds on her neck, checking them one last time. Saoirse could feel his distaste for Killkari rolling off of him in waves. An almost imperceptible tremor defied her stubborn self-possession in response to his anger on her behalf.

Aohdan's hands stilled at the tiny vibration. He caught her violet eye, transfixing her. How could he make her feel such confusion? Losing her nerve, she ducked her head to avoid his blue eyes. She felt his disappointment keenly, a stab in her heart, but despite their connection would not reach out to him. A ball of misery curled in her stomach. The gap was too large between their worlds. Free from the bandages, Saoirse grew in size to fit her harness. She continued to evade Aohdan's keen looks while he placed it on her.

His sadness at her withdrawal made her anxious to get on with the flight. Saoirse longed for someone to confide in, someone to advise her. Forcing her emotions down she mentally rehearsed the path she wished to take back to the mountain house. Andrew was efficient and quickly had everything prepared for the return journey. Aohdan had outfitted Fallon in his harness so all was ready.

Fallon bounded up the steps to the observatory while Andrew and Aohdan pulled themselves onto Saoirse. With a glimmer of good humor at being in the sky again, Saoirse leapt off the mountain circling around for Fallon. She again repeated the tricky maneuver of grasping his harness. Then with a few powerful wingbeats she rose toward the heavens.

Saoirse found a strong updraft and coasted along on its warm lift. She thrummed a steady rhythm that was full of pleasant memories tinged with sadness. Aohdan, meanwhile, felt lost. He was sure that Saoirse cared for him, that much was clear. Yet why did she rebuff him? He knew that she did not dislike him in any way. The dragon woman was as much a mystery to him now as she had been when she didn't remember who she was.

Aohdan sighed inwardly. Patience was the best course of action. He couldn't force her to love him. With a start he realized what he had unconsciously thought. He was falling in love with Saoirse. A pleasant thrill came from this surprising thought. Acknowledging it helped to make up for Saoirse's recalcitrant attitude. He remembered the times when his father Killian had joked about taming the heart of the headstrong Queen Avana. If his father could do so, perhaps Aohdan himself had a chance with Saoirse.

A wide grin crossed his face, erasing his previous gloom. Saoirse had blocked him from her thoughts, but he knew that she sensed his abrupt change of mood. He guessed that curiosity was eating her, desperately wondering what had caused the switch. He also knew she would be too stubborn to ask him. Her discomfort only made him smile all the more. Two could play this game. A little teasing might draw her out.

Aohdan was grateful that Andrew couldn't see his smile otherwise he would surely question him. He wasn't ready to face Andrew's thoughts yet. The flight back to the mountain house went without incident. There was relief in reaching their destination as each had harbored a fear of attack after their encounters with Killkari and the goblins.

On reaching the house, the serene setting felt out of place with their previous adventure. Saoirse landed with a heavy thump on the lawn. She had dropped off Fallon where she had originally picked him up. He would come back in his own time. Now she was ready to be rid of her riders. She wished for nothing more than to sleep.

Saoirse politely lowered herself as much as she could for the two men on her back. They slid off stiffly, first Aohdan then Andrew. Andrew went straight to the kitchen to start a fire in the stove in order to prepare a meal for them. Aohdan on the other hand began the process of unbuckling Saoirse's harness. He took the packs from her, setting them on the ground. When he finished removing the harness, she gave a violent shake, then stretched like a cat.

A moment later she changed back to her human form. "Thank you, Aohdan."

Violet eyes smiled up from a weary face at Aohdan. Then reaching for a pack, she picked one up and slung it over her shoulder.

Turning on her heel she headed for the house. Shrugging in resignation at the silver-blonde figure walking away from him, he shouldered the other pack following in Saoirse's footsteps.

The threesome ate hungrily that night. The blazing fire in the range made the kitchen feel cozy. It was a welcome feeling. They soon retired to the living room where they sprawled out on the couches and chairs in front of a crackling fire. Silence still reigned supreme, but none of them felt the need to break it. It was enough to be together safe at home.

Home. Saoirse felt a bittersweet twinge at the word. Her home was gone. It was a strange thought that it was no longer there for her. She realized that this mountain house she was staying in was more a home to her now than her birthplace. A sting of sadness bit her heart, yet she was also grateful. She was safe and dry with good friends to watch her back.

She looked over at Andrew and Aohdan. Andrew was spread out over the sofa snoring softly. His lean face took on a peaceful appearance in sleep. It took some of the age from him. Aodhan leaned back in a deeply cushioned chair. His head lolled against the side of the chair with chin resting on his chest. His breath came in a deep even rhythm. Saoirse watched the two fondly for a minute. They were her family now. Rising stealthily Saoirse padded to her room, crawled into bed and fell soundly asleep.

Chapter 11

AFTER A DAY OF REST AND waiting for Fallon's return, they began preparations to visit Amaroth. It was a four day ride to the Tiered Mountain and three after that to reach Amaroth. They all agreed it would not be wise for Saoirse to fly into the city. She wished to keep her true identity as secret as possible. Instead, she petitioned that while they rode she would fly most of the way then finish the journey on Fallon.

"Fallon can guide me from the ground. Besides, I would benefit from solitude as I require some time of reflection," she argued pensively.

"You could ride Fallon with us just as easily," Aohdan countered not wishing to be separated from her.

Andrew, now softened in attitude, stuck up for Saoirse. "Let her be, Aohdan. A little contemplation never hurt anyone. It takes time to process events. She's lost her family and her home."

In displeasure Aohdan gave in to their wishes. He knew they were right even if he didn't like it.

Soon they were outfitted for their journey. The first day would be slow as Andrew and Aohdan's cow had to be taken to the nearest village. The young shepherd boy who normally looked after her while they were gone on short trips could care for her more easily there.

They started off on a fair morning with a warm breeze blowing at their backs. It would be midsummer soon. The air was pleasant in the mountains, but Aohdan knew they would feel the heat of summer when they began to descend. However, the stiff wind from Lonrach Lake would cool them in the city. It had been nearly a year since he had last seen his parents. He was pleased to have an opportunity to reunite with them. He missed their presence. Aohdan even missed the bustle of Amaroth. The city held a vibrant, ever changing kaleidoscope of curiosities.

Mostly he missed the peaceful times living in the mountain house his father Killian had built. Of all the places he had lived, that to him felt the most like home. It was the one place that both of his parents truly relaxed and allowed themselves to be carefree.

Killian built his mountain home with the utmost comfort in mind. Everything in it was elegant, with each section house more comforting than the last. It was secluded away from the dwarven city with a lovely terrace garden. Green marble steps led down to a cedar-ringed lawn. Aohdan's memories of the place were so peaceful. Life was not as full of trouble when he had lived in that house. Their home in Amaroth was a different story.

Aohdan dearly loved the city of Amaroth. The people were strong, overflowing with talent, inquisitive, intelligent, and kind-hearted toward the other races that now lived among them. But keeping the people safe came at a price. In Amaroth his family lived in a keep that had been built as an extension to the Guard barracks. It was plain, in keeping with the military forces surrounding them. Inside, Aohdan remembered the furnishings had been improved to show the state of the royal family, but it was not a particularly welcoming place. Its value lay in its position in the city. Having ready access to the Guard of Amaroth along with all of the other districts and their respective Elders, allowed the Queen a powerful vantage point. Any complaints of difficulty in accessing her would not stand up.

The intricacies of power and ruling were the one thing that Aohdan truly wished he did not have to understand. The petty quarrels and grabs for influence between the Elders disgusted him. He was grateful that most of the Elders who remembered a time before Avana was Queen would be replaced by younger, less contentious successors when he ascended the throne. There would always be those vying for more control, but most of the denizens of Amaroth loved Avana and her family. Aohdan knew that this loyal following would be much more willing to follow his lead than the current, crabby old Elders.

How he wished some days that he could simply disappear into the Wilds. But that was not his course. He cared too much for Amaroth and for Arda to abdicate. Aohdan had always had a sense of duty. It ran through the very core of his heart. Protect, care, watch over. These were the values that spoke deeply to him. Ingrained not just from his parents, but also in his heritage of the Rangers and kings of old.

He also had a longing for adventure. This drive felt at odds with his upbringing as Prince of Amaroth. Yet he knew that this too was part of his birthright. He came from a line of fierce warriors not content to simply sit by, watching, while others performed great deeds. This was why he had come under Andrew's tutelage. The search for Killkari was freeing to him. Aohdan knew he would have to face many challenges in his life. This one though, might possibly prove to be the greatest. There was nothing holding him back from meeting it head on. Killkari was a terrifying opponent made more so with the goblin hordes under his control. Nonetheless, Aohdan was filled with a fire to bring the evil dragon to justice.

He wished to bring recompense to the lives of Andrew and Saoirse. Ah, Saoirse! She was an incomparable mystery to him. He knew now without a doubt that he loved the *Elestari* woman. However, he was also afraid. Saoirse was powerful beyond anything he had ever seen. And he was a prince. He remembered the history she had told him of the *Elestari's* enslavement by a wicked king. His link with Saoirse was strong. He had already once seen through her eyes for a time without her knowledge. He guessed that he could do so again.

Deep down a part of him knew that he could control her for a short period if he so wished and that Saoirse could also do the same to him. It was a frightening ability. He had no desire to force Saoirse into anything against her will, but what if she could save Amaroth from a great danger? Would he be able to stand by knowing that he could protect the city through Saoirse?

But it was also a two-way street. What would the people of Amaroth think of a king whose will could be overtaken by another? These thoughts troubled him profoundly. They kept Aohdan nearly silent during their first three days of riding. Andrew did not disturb him, sensing that the young prince was grappling with something. Andrew knew that there was a special bond between Aohdan and Saoirse. He guessed that whatever troubled Aohdan had to do with that.

When they camped the third night Andrew decided to question Aohdan about his brooding. He hoped that he could set aside any lingering prejudice over Saoirse in order to help Aohdan. Their horses were hobbled and nibbling peacefully on the short grass in the glade they were camping in. The warm fire sent strange shadows flickering onto the firs that surrounded clearing. A pot of hot coffee now hung over the blaze to finish off their meal.

Andrew, who sat across the fire from Aodhan, cared little for niceties. He preferred straightforward answers and so went right to the point.

"Care to enlighten me on the problem that you have been puzzling over the last few days, Aohdan? I might be able to help you solve it."

Aohdan, who had been sitting and gazing into the leaping flames of the fire, looked up at Andrew. A dozen thoughts raced through his head. What should he tell Andrew? Should he tell him everything? What would Andrew think if he did? With a fervent sigh he decided to trust his mentor and tell him everything.

Andrew watched in interest as the cascade of thoughts crossed Aohdan's face. This served to pique his curiosity so he was less surprised with Aohdan's eventual answer.

"I'm in love with Saoirse," Aohdan finally hurried out.

Andrew's eyes widened. He had suspected that this was the root of Aohdan's anxiety, but he hadn't been able to quite convince himself. Now that his suspicion was correct, he did the last thing that Aohdan would have ever expected. He threw his head back and laughed.

It was a deep, barrel-chested laugh that rang out over the mountainside. Aohdan looked on in shocked surprise as Andrew persisted with his gut-wrenching mirth. After a moment, Andrew regained control of himself wiping tears from his eyes as his laughter died down to quiet guffaws.

"Aohdan, you fool, what a predicament you have gotten yourself into." He chortled sympathetically. "No wonder you are troubled. The Prince of Amaroth in love with a dragon. They say the apple doesn't fall far from the tree. How true! Your mother married a dwarf and here you are pining away for an ancient creature of legend. You indeed have a struggle ahead of you."

Aohdan glowered at Andrew for a moment before giving in with a groan. "You don't know the half of it."

He then proceeded to fill in Andrew with everything that had gone on between him and Saoirse. He made careful note to explain the strange bond that linked them as best as he could. As he did so he saw an inscrutable look cross Andrew's face. When he finally explained his current worries about the bond, he watched Andrew sag under the weight of his words. When he finished his account Aohdan felt a sense of relief. A yawning silence stretched between the two men as he waited for Andrew to speak.

"You're right to be apprehensive about this bond," Andrew said at long last sounding weary. "I think that it could be beneficial or extremely dangerous. I am now convinced that Saoirse means us no harm. I also believe that her people are peaceful. However, this matter of the *Elestari* being captured by Killkari is disturbing. If he wishes to take over Arda then he must have a way that he thinks he can bend them to his will. If he could somehow take over Saoirse then through her he could also possibly access you."

Aohdan was aghast. Andrew's assessment was a horrifying possibility. He shuddered over the thought of Killkari taking control of his mind. His thoughts ran immediately to Saoirse's safety. He knew that for the time being there was little chance of an attack from Killkari due to his injury, yet he couldn't help fearing for her.

"What do you think I should do then?" he asked feeling queasy.

Andrew sighed deeply. He stood up and paced around the fire. "It doesn't sound like you can sever this connection if it's the same kind that Saoirse had with Colm, not without catastrophic side effects to both parties. I don't think that either of you should try to distance yourselves from the other. For now, use the bond as positively as you can. On the flip side of all the evil that could come of your connection, there is also the potential of it becoming a nearly unstoppable force.

"When we reach Amaroth I think we should visit the Noble Library. There are tomes of Arda's ancient history buried deep in their vaults that could prove to be beneficial to us. I wish that there was another *Elestari* that we could speak to, particularly an older one. If they really are guardians of knowledge as Saoirse says, then he or she could possibly shed some light on this situation.

"And there's one more thing. Something Saoirse told us that has been bothering me, especially after learning about Killkari's plans. Problem was I couldn't remember exactly why it worried me until now. It's finally come to me, and it may be vitally important.

"You recall how Saoirse told us that the *Elestari* went into hiding after being enslaved by an evil wizard king?"

Aohdan nodded thoughtfully remembering Saoirse's distaste over the matter.

"I didn't think much of it until we discovered that Killkari had taken the *Elestari* captive. Then the story came back to me and gnawed at me, but I couldn't figure out why. How well do you know the history of the Rangers?"

Aohdan shrugged in confusion. "That they are the descendants of the old kings of Arda?" he hazarded.

"Yes, and what about the old kings?" Andrew pressed.

"They kept order over the Wilds and ruled Amaroth?" Aohdan guessed. Then smiled sheepishly. "I don't really know a whole lot more than that."

Andrew smiled. "Exactly. Because of the span of time that Amaroth was without a monarch, much of the history has been lost. But what if it wasn't just the loss of a leader that erased some important information? What if this information was removed by the *Elestari* in an attempt to protect themselves?"

Aodhan was floundering to understand Andrew's words. There was clearly something to them, but he hadn't grasped it yet.

"So how does this all fit together?" he asked feeling exasperated. "You haven't yet told me what you remembered."

Andrew's grin widened. "Because I think I found a history book that the *Elestari* missed. I read it years and years ago in the Noble Library. I happened upon it when I was searching for details on the abilities of Rangers to communicate with animals. It was forgotten and buried in the oldest lore vaults. I hadn't remembered what it said till now. The book told of a powerful wizard king that could not only speak to animals but could also shape shift. Guess what form he could shift to?"

The thought crystalized before Aohdan. "A dragon." He breathed out feeling that the puzzle was finally becoming clear to him.

"A dragon," Andrew agreed with him. "And not just any dragon.

Though the book didn't say so I believe the king may have actually been an *Elestari*."

"Of course! It all fits together. But how did he become king in the first place? And why would he want to enslave his own people? And why wouldn't Saoirse have known that he was *Elestari*? Aohdan exclaimed excitedly. He jumped to his feet joining Andrew in his pacing around the fire.

Andrew contemplated for a moment before answering. "I have no idea how he became king, and I can only guess as to what desire would drive him to do such a cruel thing to his people. But I can speculate over Saoirse's lack of knowledge. Her people went to great lengths to disappear. If one of their own really did turn on them, I doubt it is something they wish to repeat. It would make perfect sense to erase that piece of information from history, especially if it involved some forbidden spell or other such thing."

"You're right. I can only imagine their fear if it was bad enough to make them want to completely isolate themselves. Saoirse did mention that it wasn't until many years had gone by that the *Elestari* had made contact with the outside world. They must have thought that enough time had passed for whatever terrible thing the king had used against them to be forgotten or destroyed."

"Agreed. I think it's safe to say though, that Killkari has discovered the secret to controlling the *Elestari*. Their magic would be extremely useful to him. But here, I just thought of another mystery. What happened to the king's offspring? Did they inherit the ability to shift? And if so, why is there no mention of it? Is this also the *Elestari* at work?" Andrew threw up his hands in sudden frustration.

Aohdan picked up several branches and laid them on the crackling fire as he mulled over Andrew's questions.

"Are we not forgetting an important part of the story?" he said quietly. "Saoirse told us that it was the elves that defeated the king in the end. Perhaps they will have the answer. They too are secluded and long-lived. Their memories are extensive. I think we should find out if they can help us."

"Hmmmm…I had forgotten that," Andrew admitted ruefully. "Going to the elf kingdom might not be a bad idea. It will require a long journey across the Wilds though. And we would need a guide to find it. I have never been there myself. I fear that it will take up precious time even if it does yield solid answers."

"I have a feeling Saoirse could help with that. If we flew our journey would be significantly shorter," Aohdan countered.

Andrew objected. "But we still would need a guide. We want as few people as possible to know about Saoirse's identity. I'm not sure that I even trust an elf with that information. Only Valanter and his councilors should be privy to her secret until we have answers."

"There's always my grandfather Caleb. We can trust him…or there's also Mother," Aohdan spoke with a slight hesitation.

Andrew let out an incomprehensible grumble. "Your mother is always looking for excuses to run off on an adventure. She's the Queen now! She can't just go off on a lark the way she used too. Caleb would be a better choice."

Aohdan chuckled at Andrew's ire. "You know when she hears about all of this she's going to want to join us."

"That's what I'm afraid of," Andrew said with an exaggerated eye roll. "I've been debating on how to keep her in Amaroth since we left. You know for being a distant cousin of mine she sometimes feels like an annoying sister."

Smiling gleefully Aohdan teased, "I hope you don't see me as a burdensome child of the annoying sister that you have been saddled with to get me out of my parents' way."

Andrew tossed a pinecone in Aohdan's direction.

"I would NEVER allow myself to be burdened with someone I didn't think was worth it to train. You have as much potential as your parents, probably more. Anyway, if you had been a spoiled brat,

I would have sent you back without a second thought, regardless of whether or not you were prince."

A deep laugh boomed from Aohdan. "You're certainly keeping me humble if nothing else, Andrew. I must say it's refreshing to hear candid truths. Your honesty and wisdom has taught me much in my time with you. Thank you. I wish that everyone could think like you."

Suddenly feeling uncomfortable by Aohdan's thanks, Andrew muttered something about needing to rest, then made a great show of setting out his bedroll.

Now laughing softly to himself, Aohdan settled against a tree to take first watch, his mind full from his conversation with Andrew.

Chapter 12

NOT MUCH FARTHER AHEAD OF WHERE Andrew and Aohdan were camped, Fallon and Saoirse were bedding down for the night. Both could have traveled much faster than their friends, but they felt little need to hurry. They had kept up a steady pace with Saoirse flying low over the trees as she followed Fallon.

While Aohdan was wrestling over their bond and the events that had transpired, Saoirse too was troubled. She felt lost. Always there had been an older and wiser *Elestari* that she could turn to for advice. It was disconcerting to no longer have that support, especially with all of the confusing and frightening things that had happened. Her mind buzzed with unanswered questions.

Fallon, at least, was a comfort. He listened to her ramblings without judgment. He understood her need to find her people. Wolves were extremely clannish. He could relate to her acute desire for family.

Dragon and wolf curled up next to each other in the moonlight, scales and fur blending together to create a strange silver silhouette. They spoke mind to mind, not breaking the gentle song of the pleasant breeze sighing through the pines around them.

"How do you think Killkari plans to control the *Elestari*?" Saoirse mused to Fallon. "They won't work for him willfully."

"Magic? A promise of freedom after they serve him? I don't really have an idea. Hopefully Amaroth will hold some answers for us," Fallon grunted in reply.

Saoirse shivered from nose to tail. "Amaroth. I've heard so much about it. Studied its' history. I've often longed to walk the streets, to take in the entire city. Now I journey to see it. I have spent my entire life researching and reading about the world around me, yet I have never truly ventured out into it. The Blue Fire Mountains have been my home, and this is the first time I have left them to seek the world outside. For all of my great learning I feel very small indeed, now that I am faced with the prospect of seeing places I have only read about."

Fallon nudged her gently with his nose. "You have been sheltered, my friend. Enjoy this experience, but don't fear it. I think you will find Amaroth surprising. It will be like and unlike what your books have told you."

"But what will people think of me when they find out what I am? I know that my identity won't be hidden forever," Saoirse fretted.

"They will accept you. Some will resent your power, but Amaroth is an old city. It has seen a great deal. Even if a host of *Elestari* showed up at the gates I doubt it would affect the citizens all that much. Do not worry about their feelings toward you," Fallon intoned mildly.

"I admit that I am mostly worried about meeting the Queen. You know her so well, Fallon. What will she make of me? What is she like? Aohdan speaks so little of his parents."

Fallon let out a growling laugh. "She should be the least of your concerns. Avana will love you. She will find you fascinating and probably pester you with questions. What is she like? She's wild and fearless, but she has a tender heart that cares for her people. Avana can disappear out in the Wilds in an instant or use her words to placate Amaroth's leaders. She is fiercely loyal. She protects those she loves without a thought to herself. She also has a deep hatred for goblins. She will relate to you profoundly through your similar experiences."

Saoirse cocked her head in confusion. "Similar experiences? What do you mean by that?"

"Didn't you know that Avana's family was killed by goblins? Surely you knew that her father was held captive by them for years?" Fallon said in obvious surprise.

"I had known that her father was a goblin captive, but I didn't know anything about the rest of her family. Oh, how I feel for her!" Saoirse breathed out, feeling the tight pain in her chest from the loss of her own loved ones.

Fallon growled in agreement. "I'm guessing you also didn't know that Killian lost his only brother during the Great War. Avana and Killian each have a reason to harbor bitterness, but they have chosen to overcome it."

"You're right. I had no idea that Killian too had lost someone dear to him," Saoirse whispered. A sensation of belonging was beginning to close over her, listening to Fallon.

"Avana and Killian will welcome you, Saoirse. They will want to help you. I think you will find solace in them. My adopted sister will care for you to the best of her ability." Fallon pressed his body even closer against Saoirse in a comforting manner.

Saoirse hummed a quiet song of thanks to him, her apprehensions receding. She was almost asleep when Fallon spoke again, this time in a still small voice that she had never heard him use. So soft she could barely hear him.

"My mother, Rista, was killed by an Ice Troll. It nearly drove my father mad. He went for days barely eating or drinking. He recovered, but it changed him. Watching him was the hardest thing I have ever gone through, worse than losing my mother because I thought I was also going to lose Finris too. I suppose I should have told you before. You knew of Andrew's history. I was afraid to dredge up the pain though. You are not alone, Saoirse. You are surrounded by those who understand loss. We will ease your pain any way we can."

Tears filled Saoirse's violet eyes and flowed down her muzzle. They dripped to the ground in fat sizzling drops. Unfurling a wing she placed it protectively over the wolf lying beside her.

"I'm so sorry, Fallon. You humble me with your words. Thank you."

Saoirse's humming resumed, taking on a poignant tone that echoed the sadness both she and Fallon felt. Her song wove a story of loss and pain, but eventually the notes turned to gratefulness for friends and hope for the future. With this tune echoing in their heads, dragon and wolf fell into a deep, dreamless sleep.

They awoke the next morning with the cool mist of dawn wreathed over them. They were to travel to the crossroads that sat before the Tiered Mountain and there meet their companions. At the crossroads Saoirse was to change to her human form and ride Fallon over the roads through the dwarf kingdom. Then she would resume her dragon until they were near Amaroth.

Dragon and wolf both stretched, then shook, flinging the wet dew from their bodies. They would hunt for their breakfast as they went along. Wriggling her wings in a thrill of happiness Saoirse snapped them out and leapt into the golden sky above. The sun rose behind her, casting a rosy glow over the mists that rolled up from the trees. Saoirse loved this time of day. Everything seemed bright and new. The colors of the sun promised life as the rays ran from the palest shades of pink and blue ending in the brilliant white light of full daylight.

Her contented thoughts were broken by Aohdan's voice in her head. A ripple of pleasure spread through her unbidden. Hoping he hadn't sensed her feelings she hurried to answer him.

"What is it, Aohdan? Is everything all right?"

"All is well, my friend. However, last night Andrew and I think we have stumbled on a vital piece of information." From here he filled Saoirse in on everything that he and Andrew had spoken of, minus his feelings for her. When he broached their suspicions of the old king being *Elestari* he felt Saoirse radiate with shock. He gave her a moment to mull over his words.

"It makes perfect sense," she admitted after recovering herself.

"Which is why Andrew believes we need to visit the elves. After all, they were the ones who deposed this evil wizard if your history is correct," Aohdan finished.

Saoirse jumped onto the idea. "Of course! I should have thought of that sooner. I am glad that I have your help in this matter."

"One thing that we are not sure of is, if this king was an *Elestari,* how could he have enslaved others of his kind since you are a magical race? We can only guess, but we wondered if it was some spell or perhaps a magical object. We were also guessing that whatever it was, Killkari has found it and is using it for his own purposes."

Saoirse strongly agreed. "Fallon and I were talking a bit of that as well. We were wondering how Killkari was going to control the *Elestari*. If he has found an old secret, then that would certainly explain things."

"Indeed," Aohdan replied shortly. A pause stretched between them for an awkward moment that Aohdan broke by abruptly changing the subject.

"I wish you could see my home on the Tiered Mountain if we had more time. It's beautiful. My father built the house specifically for my mother. It has always been my family's haven of peace."

Saoirse was taken aback by this statement. "I didn't know that your father built your house. That must give it special meaning to you."

"It does. It's the only place growing up that I truly felt at home," Aohdan said with a note of wistfulness in his thoughts.

"I would be honored to visit there one day if the chance arises," Saoirse declared with mixed emotions. Part of her longed to unlock the secrets of Aohdan's past, while another side warned her to not become anymore entangled with this handsome prince than she already was.

Sensing her discomfort, Aohdan smiled to himself and decided to try a different question. "Are you looking forward to visiting Amaroth? I will enjoy showing you the city. It has much to share if you know the right places to look."

This was a subject that Saoirse was more at ease with so she hurried to answer. "Yes! It is a place that is almost as old as my people. Just the history surrounding it is intriguing, not to mention all of the people to meet. I have never met a dwarf or an elf. Amaroth is a place that I grew up longing to visit. I have been fascinated by it for years so it is a great treat to finally have the opportunity to see it with my own eyes."

"I hope that we won't be in too great a hurry, though I fear with the threat of Killkari hanging over us it won't be as much time as I would like. It takes days to truly get a feel of the place. We will be visiting some of the most important places, however. The Guard and the Noble Library are impressive. I have a feeling that you will enjoy the library."

Aohdan projected a picture of an enormous building full of books to Saoirse that gave her a sense of prestige and age. Her curiosity and excitement spiked over the image.

With a throaty laugh, she replied, "Now I really look forward to Amaroth. Don't show me anymore. I wish to be surprised."

"Alright. You should probably come down soon. The crossroads are not far off."

Sending Aohdan an image of the crux of two winding roads far ahead, Saoirse agreed. "I see it. We will meet presently."

Thus she broke their connection and reached out to Fallon instead. "I will be coming down now. I've spied the crossroads not far ahead. I wish to shift in the safety of the trees. Is there a clearing that I could land in?"

Fallon growled assent. "I just came into one. I'd guess that it's bigger than it looks from above. You should have no problem with it."

Careful perusal of the forest revealed the hole in the treetops that Fallon had spoken of. Saoirse angled for it spiraling down into the clearing with heavy wingbeats. She landed with a soft thump shuddering her wings and stretching herself. Fallon watched from the edge of the trees with interest as a warm violet glow surrounded her. She proceeded to shrink, changing to her human form.

For a moment she rested on her knees, silver hair falling around her face taking stock of the new body she was in. Tossing her hair back, she stood up stretching again. Her light linen clothes hung gracefully off her frame. Fallon stalked over to her and nosed her hard in the back causing her to jump.

"That's not nice, Fallon!" Saoirse scolded halfheartedly as she smiled at the large wolf.

Golden eyes glimmered mischief back at her. "Just keeping you in line, dragon girl."

Feigning indignity, she huffed and swung up onto his back. Saoirse buried a hand in his thick white ruff. It always amazed her how Fallon's fur could be so incredibly dense and yet silky soft at the same time. With Saoirse perched on his back, Fallon took off at a brisk trot. He knew from the scent of Andrew and Aohdan that they were now ahead of them.

Chapter 13

THE TRAVELERS MET AT THE CROSSROADS. From now on Saoirse knew that they would be in more civilized territories and that she would have to be very cautious about shifting. Traveling with Fallon would draw some attention, but not nearly as much as her dragon would. Saoirse couldn't suppress the enthusiasm bubbling up inside of her.

She knew that Aohdan could feel her elation. He cast a sidelong glance at her, hiding a grin from Andrew. Fallon also sensed her tension and walked with a stiff legged bouncy stride echoing Saoirse's eagerness. She didn't have to wait long.

Their steady pace quickly overtook four dwarves traveling to the Tiered Mountain. Saoirse was nearly overcome with curiosity. She stared hard at the dwarves trying to memorize every detail. They were all shorter than her, with curling beards of varying lengths. Most kept their thick hair back with intricate braids or clips, similar to the one Aohdan wore. Their clothes were sturdy in make and they seemed to prefer rich hues. The dwarves carried weapons of a heavier, harsher lined style than Saoirse was accustomed to, which seemed to perfectly match their appearance.

They looked upon the strangers with fierce eyes. Saoirse sensed surprise at the presence of a wolf in their company. Yet they called out courtesies to the riders with friendly voices. The four friends replied in kind, though Saoirse struggled to keep her greeting short.

How she longed to converse with these dwarves, learning all that they would offer about their lives.

She couldn't help turning round on Fallon and giving the dwarves a shy smile as they rode past. The lead dwarf gave a wide grin in return, winking at her. Saoirse blushed brightly, smile growing at his brazenness. *Were all dwarves like this?* she wondered. Soon they came round a corner of the mountainside and the dwarves were no longer in sight.

Instead, something else took up her attention. A huge mountain peak jutted out. It twisted and curved in a unique manner, appearing to have sections of rock stacked on top of each other. This was her first glimpse of the Tiered Mountain.

Saoirse turned to look at Aohdan and Andrew for confirmation. The two men smiled, "Yes, that's the Tiered Mountain," Andrew answered her unspoken question.

"It's not nearly as big as the Blue Fire ranges," Aohdan admitted ruefully.

Saoirse responded quickly. "No, but it is much more impressive. It is distinctive in a way that my home lacks. It's incredible, really. Pity we can't stop there."

Andrew replied thoughtfully, "Another time. We ought to pick up our pace. The roads are better now. Saoirse, I wonder if perhaps you should just ride Fallon. I'd like to push us now that we are near the end of our journey. I've got a sense that time is precious."

"Whatever you think is best," Saoirse said. Personally, she agreed with Andrew's words. As much as she enjoyed her dragon, she had felt a growing sense of urgency. Good sense told her that Killkari would need time to heal, but another part of her worried that this would do little to hinder him from continuing his plans.

Urging their horses into a lope that Fallon easily kept up with, they began to eat up the final miles between them and Amaroth. To Saoirse's delight they met more dwarves on the road as they traveled.

Though stopping wasn't an option, she could at least study them in passing. There were also a variety of human traders and travelers. She was captivated by the diversity.

Their speed soon brought them to the city. They crested the mountain ridge in the late afternoon sun and now before them spread Lonrach Lake and Amaroth. The tall stone ramparts of the city glowed a deep red gold from the light of the westward falling sun. Lonrach lay as a flat obsidian mirror next to Amaroth. The Thraicin River flowed out of Lonrach to the distant horizon, a black ribbon disappearing into the rolling plains that made up the Wilds. All the ground was in crimson and gold hues. Far away the sun blazed scarlet against the deepening blue sky.

To Saoirse it was magnificent. Below her spread the living, breathing city that was now hers to visit. A small sigh escaped her, turning the heads of the two men. Her awe did not escape them. Neither could help but smile at her pleasure. Saoirse let out a mental thrum that resonated through them all echoing to the very core. It was a sound full of eagerness.

"Not much farther," Andrew stated matter-of-factly, despite feeling Saoirse's anticipation.

They followed the winding track of road to the city gates. People of all races flowed in and out of the entrance. Guards stood on either side of the road, shining in red and silver armor. The stone arches that formed the gateway rose majestically in front of them. Saoirse's mouth fell open in shock at the carving of the twined dragons in the arches.

"Those dragons! Look at them. The lines of the wings, the scales are different, and the eyes. They are *Elestari*. I'm sure of it," she said breathlessly. "Who made them?"

Aohdan gave his head a shake with a wide grin. "Those walls have been here since Amaroth was built. The arch is a gift from the dwarves. The carving is theirs."

"Then they must have known *Elestari*. I didn't realize that we were represented in Amaroth." Saoirse smiled back at Aohdan.

Andrew studied the arches. "This city is ancient. There's probably hundreds of subtle details that we don't know about. It's an interesting choice by the dwarves to use dragons. I've wondered about that myself. Right now we have a great deal to go over with the Queen so let's keep moving."

With that statement he spurred his horse and rode into the city leaving Aohdan and Saoirse behind him.

"He's right. We'd best be getting on." Aohdan smiled apologetically.

They followed after Andrew, earning curt nods from the guards who recognized Aohdan and Fallon. Saoirse noticed that Aohdan sat up straighter as he entered, his gaze becoming more watchful. He gave respectful nods to those who saluted him as they rode past. *This was a prince coming home*, she mused. His regal bearing and welcome was a strong reminder to Saoirse that there was more to her friend then she was used to seeing.

Riding down the cobbled streets over twisting roads they eventually found themselves in front of the walled off barracks that were the Guard. They were quickly ushered inside with many greetings for the two men. The horses were taken to the stables to be attended to by the cavalry attendants. Saoirse dismounted from Fallon to walk alongside the men inside a large open courtyard clearly used for training.

Wooden posts battered by dozens of swords stood anchored deeply into the ground along one side of the yard. A ropes course hung from a wall, while a raised platform near the center could serve as a match ring and for making important announcements.

Soldiers and trainees hurried efficiently to and fro through the courtyard casting sidelong glances at the newcomers. Recognition and curiosity glimmered in the eyes that perused them. Saoirse felt alternately intrigued and uncomfortable as they walked across the wide space. Her discomfort was short lived. A running figure drew her attention.

"Aohdan! Andrew! Welcome home!"

A lithe, red-haired woman ran with cat-like grace toward them from a doorway, arms outstretched. A thin, twisted gold circlet graced her brow. Her steel blue eyes shone bright with intelligence and she wore a gown in utilitarian greens and browns. A large long sword was slung across her back.

"Mother!" Aohdan called back.

The beautiful woman flung her arms around her son. He lifted her up, swinging her around. She laughed, a rich warm sound that spoke of her joy. Coming up behind the two strode a tall dashing dwarf, who was nearly the height of Aohdan and the Queen.

Saoirse couldn't help the sharp intake of breath at the sight of him. Andrew raised an eyebrow at her reaction, which Saoirse studiously ignored. Aohdan was nearly an exact image of the dwarf. Black wild hair and an air of complete confidence made the two exceedingly handsome. As Saoirse looked closer, she noted though, that the variances were in the eyes and build. The dwarf had dark eyes and had the broad stature of all dwarves. Aohdan's eyes were a bright shade of blue, and he took more to his mother's litheness than the breadth of the dwarf. Yet the resemblance was still remarkable.

Setting his mother down, Aohdan turned to his father whom he embraced with just as much enthusiasm. Saoirse was surprised when Fallon stepped forward to the woman, and she made as great a fuss over him as she had Aohdan.

Saoirse suddenly felt very lonely. Here was a close-knit family. In that moment her heart yearned for her people. As if sensing her isolation, the red-haired woman released Fallon and took Saoirse's hands in her own with a warm smile.

"Welcome. You must be Saoirse. Aohdan has told me about you in his letters home. I am Avana. I'm so pleased to finally meet you!"

Saoirse bowed her head respectfully in return. "It is good to meet you, Queen Avana. I hope that Aohdan has spoken kindly of me. I have long wanted to visit your city. From the little I have seen so far, it is beautiful."

"Thank you. I hope you can explore it to your heart's content, but from Aohdan's words it doesn't sound as if that will be happening any time soon."

"I'm afraid not. I am looking forward to perusing the library though. If it's anything like what the men tell me, I could stay there for days."

"It's certainly impressive. I've made it a point to have it restored. Aside from the elves, Amaroth has the oldest library in Arda."

As Avana spoke the dwarf came up beside her. He offered Saoirse the same winning smile that Aohdan had, leaving her feeling a bit breathless.

"Greetings, Saoirse. I am Killian, Aohdan's father. He speaks highly of you. Welcome to our home."

He spoke with a rocky tone that was slightly deeper than Aohdan's. His eyes sparked with a jauntiness that spoke of confidence.

"Well met, Killian. I hope that I can live up to Aohdan's words." Saoirse blushed lightly.

"I've no doubt you will." Killian clapped her on the arm and leaned into her smirking, "You seem to have him rather bewitched. I don't blame him," he added quietly with a roguish wink.

Saoirse turned positively red. Avana gently swatted aside her husband, muttering rude things about him under her breath as she rolled her eyes. Killian grinned wickedly at his wife taking her hand in his. Avana sent him a sidelong glare that he impishly ignored, instead giving her an adoring look.

Something hitched in Saoirse's heart. These two were so obviously in love. It made her think of Colm, yet his loss was not as sharp as it had been. She realized that someone else was filling the void. Her gaze flicked to Aohdan who was watching his parents with a bemused smile. He caught her watching him, holding her captive. His eyes shone. Their connection sparked with unspoken words and feelings, sending a shiver through Saoirse. Her heart skipped again. She knew that Aohdan had felt it because he gave her a look that bordered on adoration.

Feeling herself coming undone, Saoirse tore herself from his gaze to focus on the words of Avana.

"Please come and join us for a meal. You must be hungry after your journey. Fallon, you are welcome to stay in the barracks, or if you would rather stay outside the city no one will hinder your passing."

Fallon growled an acknowledgement. "I shall stay outside of the city. I won't be far. Saoirse can find me when we are ready to move on. I know you love the city, sister, but it is too confining for my taste."

"I understand, Brother Wolf. It is good to see you. I miss your presence," Avana said as she caressed Fallon's thick fur.

The wolf nuzzled her gently, then turned and trotted back the way they had come. Saoirse watched him leave with a hint of sadness. It would be strange to not have his company after spending so much time with him. Andrew broke her reverie.

"How about this meal you were talking about, Avana? We could use some decent food after our camping rations."

Avana gave a clear ringing laugh. "We won't keep you waiting, Andrew. Although it might be wise for you to clean up first."

"Are you implying that I need a washing, my Queen?" Andrew replied tartly.

"That is exactly right, you grumpy old Ranger." Avana raised an eyebrow at him.

"Hmph," was the only audible response.

Ignoring Andrew, Avana motioned for the rest of them to follow her. They walked through a maze of halls ending up in front of a wide steel door. The golden dragon of Amaroth was etched into the metal to signify the crown residence and a matching gold door handle with keyhole finished off the picture. Saoirse noted the symbol with interest. She had noticed the dragon on the armor of the Guard and on the flags flying on the city walls. *It was an interesting choice*, she thought to herself. *Perhaps it held some connection to the ancient Elestari.*

Taking a silver key from a hidden pocket, Avana unlocked the steel door. It opened outward toward them. Killian took a step into the doorway, beckoning them to join. They walked inside, and to Saoirse's surprise the house looked similar to the mountain lodge. They were in a large, open living room with a deep fireplace made of the same cherrywood as the one on the mountain. A smattering of navy, cushioned sofas and chairs were scattered around in a comfortable fashion. These also were identical to the other house. The only thing missing was a pianoforte, though Saoirse suspected it might be elsewhere.

"There are three washrooms, Saoirse, so you needn't worry about sharing with the men," Avana said kindly. "The first is right here, adjacent to our sitting room. It's the left hand door there." She motioned to a door along the wall. "Aohdan and Andrew, you both know where the others are. I will bring fresh clothes for you, Saoirse, and Killian will attend to you men. I suspect you could all use a bath which will take a bit. That will give me time to request something for dinner."

The three nodded appreciatively as Killian and Avana smiled at them.

Chapter 14

SAOIRSE LOST NO TIME IN HURRYING to the washroom. She was gratified to find that it was a large stone room with the floor covered in soft fluffy mats to prevent one's toes from getting cold. An ornate pewter basin sat on a counter under a pump. A gilded oval mirror hung over it while a shelf full of towels and toiletry items stood next to it. A plain commode stood in the corner. In the back a large bathtub could be seen peeking from behind a heavy screen to preserve privacy.

Longing for a soak in hot water Saoirse moved back the screen in order to see how to fill the tub. Two pumps sat at either end. One had the letters HOT engraved on the handle and the other was labeled COLD. This was absolutely fascinating to Saoirse. She had grown up using magic to heat up a bath, while on the mountain they simply had boiled water. This mystery of the pumps would have to be explained. Curiously she tried the pump labeled HOT.

To her delight a stream of warm water came flowing out, getting hotter as it came. Then she tried the COLD pump. As the name implied, cold water came ricocheting out. Saoirse was enthralled. It didn't take her long to fill the bath full of steaming water. Pulling the screen back in place she hurriedly took off her dirty traveling clothes and eased into the hot water with a grateful sigh. A wicker basket on a stool held an array of soaps to choose from.

Picking one with a lavender scent, she scrubbed till her skin was pink from her efforts. A groan of pleasure escaped her. The lavender permeated the air, relaxing Saoirse even more. She hadn't known such comfort since before the attack on her people. It was a delicious feeling to be pampered if only for a short time. A soft knock on the door followed by Avana's voice broke her reverie.

"May I come in?" she asked.

"Please do!" Saoirse replied.

Avana opened the door to be greeted by the steam striving to escape the enclosed space. She quickly shut the door behind her to keep the warmth inside.

"I've brought you some dresses of mine. I am a bit taller than you so they may be a tad long, I'm afraid. Hopefully you will find one of them satisfactory. Enjoying the bath?"

Avana carefully laid the dresses over the shelving next to the basin as she listened to Saoirse's answer.

"It's lovely. And much needed. Wonderful for all the aches from traveling. Thank you for your hospitality, my Queen. It is greatly appreciated."

"Forget the queen bit, Saoirse. Please just call me Avana. I don't care for titles. I'm glad to hear that you are happy so far. We have been slowly improving the plumbing of the city, a task that had been much neglected in years past. We have only recently been able to reap the benefits of our labor, hence the running water for baths."

Saoirse gave a blissful sigh. "You have done a great service to the city then. I am impressed with your ingenuity."

Avana laughed. "I simply finished what others had started long ago. Let me know if you need anything else."

"I don't believe there is anything else at the moment. I have a meal to look forward to, so all my needs have been met," Saoirse said gratefully.

"Then I will see you at dinner. Keep on down the hallway and you will reach our dining room," Avana intoned with a smile. Then with a swirl of steam she left the washroom.

Saoirse soaked for a few minutes longer after Avana's departure, her aching muscles soothed by the warm water. It seemed like her bath ended all too soon, but she had no wish to keep everyone waiting. After toweling off, she sorted through the dresses Avana had brought her.

There were two blue dresses, a green, and a gray all made of sturdy, soft material. A white under chemise had also been provided. Saoirse settled on a dark blue dress. She pulled the chemise over her head before donning the dress. Then she put on the dress. The bodice was embroidered with silver stitching that created the effect of tiny stars. A plain black leather belt pulled the dress tight around her waist. The skirt was pleated with slits up the sides in the manner of a riding habit.

She stared at herself in the mirror over the basin. Though the dress was fairly plain, it made her look much more refined than she was used to seeing herself. With a quick word of magic, she dried her hair. Then taking one of the combs from the stand, she brushed out the tangles. She carefully pulled her hair back in a loose braid that hung over her shoulder. Satisfied that her appearance was presentable enough she opened the door and stepped back into the sitting room.

Remembering Avana's words, Saoirse followed the hallway away from the sitting room. She found herself in a comfortable dining room. Paintings of Amaroth hung along the wall and a long wooden table ran the length of the room with one end laden with a haunch of venison, a variety of vegetables, and two loaves of brown bread. Avana, Killian, and Aohdan were already seated at the table catching up on events.

Aohdan's eyes widened when he saw her enter. This was a different Saoirse than the one he was used to seeing. He sprang up from his chair, gesturing for Saoirse to come and join them. His parents shared a knowing look behind his back as he beckoned Saoirse over.

"Feeling refreshed?" Avana queried, trying to hide a smile.

Saoirse nodded emphatically. "I feel ever so much better. The food looks wonderful!"

"And it smells good too," Killian rumbled. "Andrew ought to hurry up or we will have everything eaten without him."

"What's this about not leaving me any food?" Andrew groused as he strode into the dining room.

Aohdan winked at him. "You were slow. We are hungry. We almost ate everything without you."

Andrew harrumphed. "When you get to be my age, you'll understand why I slow down a bit sometimes. These old joints aren't what they used to be."

Avana laughed. "Do you ever quit complaining, Andrew?"

"Not if I can help it." He grinned back at her.

The meal was not what Saoirse had expected. There was nothing fancy to it. Though she had to admit that the venison and bread were some of the best she had eaten. The venison was tender with a spicy tang, while the bread was soft and warm. The meal was accompanied by a sweet, honeyed mead that sent a delicious swirl of warmth through Saoirse with every draught.

Finally, when everyone was finished and plates had been cleared, the travelers began their tale. Avana and Killian listened intently, breaking in often to question details. Eventually the story was brought back to the present. A long moment of silence ensued as each were lost in their own thoughts.

Killian was the first to break the pause. "This is certainly a fine kettle of fish you've gotten yourselves into. I think you would do well to visit both our esteemed library, and our friends the elves. To sum everything up, we need to know how Killkari is able to control the *Elestari*. If we can break that power, Saoirse, do you think the *Elestari* would fight against him?"

"I believe they would. However, not all are trained to be warriors. Some are healers and lore masters. They have no interest in battles.

Even in their dragon forms they would be little help. Our people have always relied on the strength of the wizards and weapons masters to protect them," Saoirse replied earnestly.

"So perhaps half of them would choose to fight?" Avana said thoughtfully as she fidgeted with her glass.

Saoirse shrugged. "It would be hard to guess exactly. Many wizards are also lore masters. Not all have wished to study warfare in wizardry."

"Essentially what you are saying is that most *Elestari* are civilians, not soldiers. Correct?" Andrew clarified.

"Yes, that's correct." Saoirse nodded emphatically.

"If that's the case, then why would Killkari want them to fight for him? Assuming that's his plan." Aohdan frowned.

Andrew gave a short bark of laughter. "Because even an untrained dragon is still a dragon. They can do a good bit of damage with or without any knowledge in fighting."

Saoirse winced causing Aohdan to glare at Andrew. "I'm afraid you are right, Andrew. Besides if Killkari had some sort of mind control over the *Elestari* then he could dictate their movements without them even having to be trained warriors. I've been trying to figure out how Killkari could possibly bend my people to his will, and the explanation that makes the most sense would be some form of mental domination. As Aohdan and Andrew are familiar with, I use my mind to often communicate with them. All *Elestari* use mind communication. Threats and torture would not be enough for the *Elestari* to bow to his rule. However, if he could somehow overpower them mentally, I think they would be forced to do his bidding."

"That does make sense from everything else you have told us. Do you have any idea possibly how Killkari could do so?" Killian asked, looking serious.

"Unfortunately, no. I've never heard of any spells or objects with the power to subject multiple people to the user's will. I know that

Elestari can control the actions of another being for short periods, but it would be impossible to try to control more than one person at a time. It requires far too much concentration. Even the most skilled wizard could only keep up control for several days. Perhaps a week at most. It would be exhausting anyways. You could do it, but you would sleep for days afterward. Additionally, they would be unable to do anything else except focus on controlling the person or animal."

Saoirse's words made Aohdan's stomach churn. He was glad he hadn't made any more attempts to control her mind. There was more to be learned than he had realized. What if his foolishness had caused him to pass out when Killkari had attacked? He would have to be more careful in the future.

Andrew gave a dark smile. "I doubt Killkari would care about the consequences. Winning and domination are his ultimate goal."

"Precisely. He's a rogue dragon with nothing to lose. We can hazard that he's been plotting this for years," Saoirse said quietly.

Silence reigned over the table as each person pondered the implications of her words.

Aohdan finally spoke up. "Do you think Grandfather would be willing to guide us to Mirava?"

Avana looked up, eyes blazing. "Grandfather? Of course he would guide you. But he won't be going. I will."

Killian cocked an eyebrow at his wife while Andrew groaned loudly.

"You can't just go gallivanting off on a whim, Avana," Andrew blustered.

Avana smiled with a dangerous glint in her eye. "Oh, I can't, eh? It won't be on a whim. It will simply be a diplomatic visit to the elves. I have only visited Valanter once so far as Queen. It's high time I paid him another visit."

"But this needs to be a secret visit. Besides, it will take far too long to cross the Wilds on horseback. We were planning to fly," Andrew argued.

"And there's no reason we still can't," Avana said smugly. "I plan to only bring a few trusted individuals. We will all ride until we are a day from the city. Then we shall fly and they will continue on horseback. Besides I can stay on in Mirava for a while after you have found out what you can from the elves. It's a perfectly reasonable plan."

Killian touched her arm. "Except for leaving me out of it. If this is a diplomatic mission, so to speak, I'm coming with you. Besides, I don't want to miss out on a bit of an adventure. As long as you can carry me, Saoirse."

"Four riders will be pushing it, but I should be able to manage. I will have to grow to my full size for me to do so. I won't fit my harness anymore." Saoirse gave a pointed look at Aohdan.

Aohdan's eyes darkened reflectively as he considered her words. "I think I could tie extensions onto the straps. It's only a system of buckles, after all."

"Good. Then I am willing to carry you all. I admit that I want to hurry though. Once we are off I wish to fly at top speed to the Greenwood. I warn you all that it won't be the most pleasant flying experience," Saoirse said seriously.

Killian nodded for all of them. "We will accept the discomfort. Time is not our friend. A small discomfiture now will most likely pay off in the long run."

"I will begin preparations at once," Avana added. "You three get to bed now. You still have a good deal of searching to do in the Noble Library. I will send a note tonight to the librarians to assist you in whatever fashion you require. They get strange requests often so I doubt your investigation will draw undue attention.

"One librarian in particular might be able to help you. Cynthia. She is a bit of a wizard and has lived in Amaroth since before my father was born. She may be old, but she is very sharp in mind and word. She organized the library for me. If anyone can find the information you want, it's her."

Aohdan exclaimed, "I'd forgotten all about her! She's certainly a spitfire. Cynthia gave me my first book after I had learned to read."

Avana smiled fondly. "She did indeed. She often asks about you, Aohdan. She will be pleased to see you tomorrow. Her good graces will aid your search. She can be a bit prickly."

"That's an understatement," Andrew muttered, causing the others at the table to give him a serendipitous look.

Flinching under their gaze he stammered out, "We ahhhh…may have not left on the best terms the last time I visited the library." He finished looking sheepish.

Laughter broke out across the table and Andrew reddened. "Cynthia will put you in your place if you disrespect her," Killian said still laughing, "I suggest you all put on your best manners. She'll forgive you, Andrew."

With that the discussion ended. A warm fire and a soft bed were on their minds and so the three retired gratefully for the night.

Chapter 15

MORNING FOUND THE THREE TRAVELERS BACK in the courtyard of the Guard. They claimed their horses again with an extra mount for Saoirse. They rode deeper into the city until they reached a positively ancient structure. It towered over them, walls glistening. The stone appeared to be the same as the outer walls. On further inspection, however, Saoirse realized that it was made up of a patchwork of new and old stonework. Aohdan sensed her unspoken curiosity.

"This was the original palace. There has been more than one attempt to destroy it. After the last attempt, where it was set on fire, the city simply left it and built around it instead of repairing it. Years ago, the Elders had the building evaluated to see if it was still usable. When the base was deemed sound, the Noble Library was moved here after the building was rebuilt. Mother has seen to it that even more improvements have been made."

"It's certainly impressive from the outside," Saoirse replied genially.

They dismounted and left their horses at a nearby livery. Then they walked up the steps to the doors of the library. The doors were of polished chocolate-colored wood with black iron handles. A shining gold dragon graced each of the doors.

With a forceful tug to open the heavy door, Andrew held it open for Saoirse and Aohdan. Stepping inside, Saoirse let out a small gasp of pleasure. The room they had entered was enormous with a high, vaulted ceiling covered in delicate paintings. They stood on a marble tiled floor in an open space facing a forbidding librarian's desk. Books lined the walls of the room in a shaggy carpet while rows of shelves marched imperiously from the entryway. To Saoirse it was heaven.

A tall, severe-looking woman approached them. Her raven hair was streaked with silver and pulled back into a thick braid that fell over her shoulder. Her deep blue eyes sparked with a sharp intelligence. Her long, elegant dress matched her eyes. She was an alarming figure.

Despite her fierce appearance the woman broke into a wide smile at the sight of them.

"Aohdan! My dear Prince! How delightful to see you again. It has been far too long. I have missed your presence haunting these halls. Welcome!" she reached for Aohdan taking his hands in hers. "And I see you have brought a friend. But tell me, why do you associate with this troublemaker?" she questioned, casting a withering glare at Andrew who seemed to shrink under her baleful gaze.

Aohdan answered with a laugh. "Cynthia, I am heartened to see you well. This is Saoirse. She is a mountain dweller here to learn about Amaroth and its history. And Andrew is also my friend. Whatever his past deeds, please forgive them. He is assisting us in our search for knowledge."

Cynthia's brows lowered fractionally and her mouth tightened. Then she sighed, "Whatever you wish, my Prince. But if that man so much as speaks out of line, I will have him thrown out."

"Whatever you wish, Cynthia. You're the head librarian, after all." Aohdan smiled disarmingly at her.

She inclined her head, but gave a disdainful sniff in Andrew's direction, pointedly ignoring him. Then she turned to Saoirse, taking the young woman's hands in her own as she had done to Aohdan.

At the touch, the two felt an instant internal jolt. Saoirse reeled as her mind was overwhelmed by a consciousness that was vastly older than her own. Cynthia's mind roared in response to the encounter of another like it. With a gasp the older woman yanked back her hands from Saoirse like she'd been scalded.

Panting heavily she said, "You're *Elestari*."

It was not a question but a statement. Too stunned to speak Saoirse simply nodded dumbly.

Hey eyes narrowed in suspicion, Cynthia asked, "What are you doing here? I have not seen another *Elestari* in over one hundred years."

Saoirse hesitated. It was an overwhelming question to answer. Cynthia's frown deepened at her pause.

"We are here for information about the relationship of the *Elestari* to Amaroth. But more than that we are in search for a rogue dragon named Killkari. He is responsible for the destruction of my home in the Blue Fire Mountains. With the help of the goblins, he killed our people and took them captive."

Cynthia stared at her in utter shock.

"WHAT? The *Elestari* have been subdued by that pompous idiot of a dragon! How on earth did this happen?"

"It's an unpleasant tale. Killkari must have given the goblins the location of our mountain home. He also provided them with bright silver. With surprise on their side and bright silver weapons we were overwhelmed. They came when we were ill prepared. We were foolish to trust in our anonymity and magic to protect us." Saoirse hung her head in shame.

Anger and sadness alternately flitted across Cynthia's face.

"This should not be," she said at long last, and then addressing everyone, "Come with me where we can talk in private. I have some things to tell you."

Without a backward glance she strode off into the depths of the library. With a shrug to one another, the threesome hurried after her. The librarian kept up a fierce pace leading them down a series of stair-cases to the basement of the library. There she opened a small door that led into a musty smelling room. It was filled with shelves of ancient books. Dust motes sparkled in the air in the light from the glow orb on the wall. A rickety desk and chair sat off to one side. The strangest part of the room was the floor. It was littered with cushions.

Cynthia answered their unspoken question by throwing herself unceremoniously down on the nearest pillow with a vitality that did not match her age.

Meeting their perplexed gazes she said, "The best study occurs in a relaxed setting."

Shrugging, the three settled themselves down much more slowly than Cynthia. It felt unnatural to be this informal, but the old librarian seemed to care little for appropriateness.

"It would seem that you have already guessed at some of the history between the *Elestari* and Amaroth. Otherwise you would not be here." Cynthia eyed each of them.

Andrew nodded. "Years ago, I came across an old tome that spoke of a king that could shift to dragon form. We suspicioned that he was *Elestari*. We came to find more evidence if that was true or not."

Cynthia sighed knowingly. "You managed to find one of the few volumes that I had not weeded out. Your suspicion is correct. Long have the *Elestari* remained hidden, but I think that in light of these events it is time for their presence to be made known once again. I will tell you what I know."

"Thank you, Cynthia, for your cooperation," Aohdan said gratefully.

The old woman gave a bark of laughter. "You may not thank me after you hear what I tell you." She crossed her legs and leaned against the wall, closing her eyes in a contemplative manner.

"My dear Prince, would it surprise you to learn that the ancient kings were *Elestari*? Our people and humans once lived together in harmony. Intermarriage was common, and the royal line had a strong dose of dragon in it. It was a glorious time. The city thrived, knowledge was sought after more than gold, and peace reigned over Arda.

"Then a new king ascended the throne. He was the most skilled wizard that had been seen in a millennia. Hopes were high for what his rule would bring. At first, he seemed to be everything that Amaroth could ask for in a king. But he suffered a great sorrow when his eldest child died. Then there began to be subtle changes in his behavior and interests. Amaroth has always had a strong army, but he wished to increase its power. He sought to enlist every able-bodied man and woman in Amaroth, putting particular emphasis on *Elestari*.

"Soon he began to show arrogance towards our allies, the elves and dwarves. He claimed that his people were the greatest, and therefore did not need to hold to the same standards as the other races. Next, he shut down trade, isolating Amaroth. Then he did a despicable thing. He used his powerful magic to bend his people to do his will. He turned humans and *Elestari* alike into automatons. Every movement was controlled by the king. His goal was to create an unstoppable army.

"This he did efficiently and ruthlessly. The people of Amaroth became the greatest army Arda has ever seen. The king wished to rule the whole of Arda, dwarf, elf, human, and *Elestari* alike. He cared little of the consequences. His was a quest for power. Nonetheless, a few individuals were able to escape the king's control, fleeing in horror to warn the dwarves and elves of the king's intentions. The warning was of little use, however. The king attacked the dwarves who fought back valiantly but found themselves being subdued by the superior might of the Amaroth army.

"Though the distance was great, the elves crossed the Wilds marching to the aid of the beleaguered dwarves. They found the dwarves hard pressed, the battle going ill for them. The *Elestari* were all in dragon form, making them fearful opponents. The elves joined the fray and found that it was a nearly impossible task to defeat the

Amaroth army. The soldiers fought to the death never giving quarter even when mortally wounded. They were held under the control of the evil king.

"According to history, the elves drew back after their first encounter to reevaluate their strategy. Their only chance of defeating the Amaroth army was to snare the king. They hoped that by capturing him they could break his hold over the army. With this desperate plan the greatest elven warriors wove their magic together and rejoined the battle. At great cost of life they managed to reach the king. Rallying the last of their magic, the elves pitted themselves against the king. The struggle was immense and a storm raged over the battlefield in response to the magic.

"Lightning struck the ground in jagged lines. Suddenly, a great tremor shook the earth as the elves gained mastery over the king, breaking his magic. How they did so is a mystery known only to them. Though the king relinquished his hold over the will of his army, he was not willing to give himself up. Instead he called down a bolt of lightning that killed him instantly.

"With the king dead, the army immediately laid down their arms and surrendered to the elves. The people of Amaroth found relief in their release from the king's spell. Yet, there was also a sense of remorse, particularly among the *Elestari*. They felt responsible for empowering the king in his knowledge of magic. All *Elestari* crave knowledge, and they had allowed their quest for wisdom to overcome good sense by delving too deeply into black magic.

"Their guilt led to two outcomes: first, they pronounced a curse over the rulers of Amaroth, and second, they went into hiding. The curse they put on Amaroth stated that there would be no contact from the *Elestari* for two thousand years. Also, that the royal line would be stripped of all *Elestari* magic until the two thousand years were over. Long life, the gift of language, and wisdom would still be theirs, but no longer would they be able to shift to dragon form or wield spells.

"The guilt of the *Elestari* was so great that not only did they separate themselves from the people of Amaroth, they fled to exile. They feared the past. They began a campaign to completely erase themselves from history. Once they built their eyrie in the Blue Fire Mountains, the *Elestari* completely withdrew from the outside world, only venturing out when completely necessary. There, as you know, Saoirse, they built a new life.

"Now we come to the present. When the two thousand years were over, *Elestari* like myself ventured into the world once again, but most opted to stay in the mountains. It cost me dearly to leave. Many did not think we should ever truly return to the real world. They are afraid to tempt fate into repeating itself. I now understand their fears, yet I have no wish to forever hide. It is time for us to reunite with the rest of the world."

Cynthia finished with this bold statement, looking directly at Saoirse. Speaking mind to mind with her she said, "You, Saoirse, will be the link."

Saoirse startled inwardly. "What do you mean? How am I the link?"

"Your bond with Aohdan. You are bound together. He feels for you and I know you are afraid of that. You fear loss because he is human and you are *Elestari*. You also fear your bond because it could be abused. My advice is to not fear it. If you also feel drawn to him then do not keep up this wall I sense between you. *Elestari* blood flows in his veins and his dragon could be woken. However, if you cannot love him at least keep your relationship strong. That is what will prevent any abuse by either party." Cynthia blinked wisely at Saoirse. "You have a brave heart, but don't let it lead you astray. Both heart and mind must be in agreement."

A heartbeat passed before Saoirse replied, "Thank you, Cynthia. You have eased my mind on this matter. I've been wrestling with my strange bond to Aohdan for quite some time. I'd appreciate it if you wouldn't say anything to anyone else about this for the moment."

"Of course, dear. You will make the right decision when the time comes," Cynthia said comfortingly.

The dragons' silent conversation only took the span of a few breaths in the eyes of everyone else present. Andrew was still mulling over Cynthia's words and had no inkling of the exchange. Aohdan sensed their connection, but he had been blocked from hearing by both Saoirse and Cynthia. Dragons, he supposed, were allowed to be secretive when they wanted to be.

"So you're sure that the elves hold the knowledge of how to defeat Killkari?" Andrew asked cautiously.

Cynthia looked cross. "No, I'm not sure, but they will have the most answers. My personal belief is that the ancient king found some sort of powerful stone and he took it as his power source. Through it he was able to magnify his own magic like all *Elestari* do with their gemstones. Only his magic was already imbued with its own power, making him stronger than anyone else before him."

Aodhan crossed his arms. "If that's true, then it stands to reason that the elves were able to separate him from the stone. That's what allowed them to win the battle."

"Correct. But it's all conjecture. The main point is that *something* gave the king powerful magic and whatever that was Killkari has gotten hold of it," Cynthia said with a deep sigh. "And it is imperative that we take it from him or all of Arda will be his slave."

Gracefully rising to her feet, Saoirse announced, "Then we have learned all we can here. We must leave as soon as possible."

Cynthia followed suit. "It would be well if you made great haste to the elf lands. I know your mother will not be able to keep out of this, Aohdan, but try to caution her. Amaroth may be in need of its queen sooner than we would like. Killkari will swoop down at an unexpected moment to overwhelm us. I hope that you are able to stop his plans before he does so."

"I will tell her your words, dear Cynthia," Aohdan said as he too stood. "Thank you for your wisdom in this matter. My heart is darkened by your words, but I am encouraged to know that there is hope. We shall leave the city as quickly as possible."

With those words they left the small room and hastened back to the main hall. Cynthia spoke quietly, "Farewell, travelers. I hope that your journey is safe. And you, mischief-maker.." here she turned her indigo eyes pointedly on Andrew. "If you are successful in this endeavor you will be forgiven."

Then she gave a quick bow to Aohdan and stalked regally off into the depths of the library. The threesome left the towering building and mounted their horses to return to the royal headquarters.

"Andrew," Saoirse asked, "what in the world did you do to make Cynthia so angry with you?"

Andrew scowled darkly, then turned red. "It was a foolish thing. I wanted to find out more about the history of the Rangers of Arda, specifically the ability of some to converse with animals. I knew that the information I was seeking was in such ancient volumes that only the librarians were allowed to handle them. So I hatched a plot to win the fancy of one of the librarians in hopes that she would take me to the tomes I wished to read.

"I confess that the librarian I wooed was Cynthia. I hadn't meant it seriously, but then as time went on we got along together terribly well. I realized that the relationship that had started out as a ploy had become something very important to me. One day she showed me the keys to the vaults that contained the tomes. She promised that she would take me to them in a few days when she had spare time.

"Rashly, I decided to go on my own to look. It just so happened that the day I decided to read the manuscripts was also the day that Cynthia found out that our relationship was a farce. At least that's what my colleagues told her. You see I hadn't yet acknowledged to anyone that I was now serious about my feelings for Cynthia. When she found out my deception she blew up. She went searching for me and caught me in the vaults. I've never seen anyone so angry before. I deserved her wrath and nothing I could say would sway her. I had made a monstrous blunder. She threw me out and told me to never come back.

"I was so ashamed I didn't even have the courage to go back and apologize to her. Today is the first time I have seen her since."

Andrew finished his tale, face still flushed as he intensely studied the ground beneath his horse's feet.

A small giggle escaped Saoirse. "Oh, Andrew, I'm so sorry! You really know how to stick your foot where it shouldn't go, don't you? You ought to try apologizing. She wouldn't have mentioned forgiving you if she didn't still care about you."

"Andrew, you old rascal!" Aohdan said. "I never realized that you had any other love interests after your wife died. You surprise me! I agree with Saoirse though; go to Cynthia again. Explain your side and beg her forgiveness."

A groan escaped Andrew. "But how do you know she will even see me? The only reason she allowed me today was because of you."

"I will appeal to her. I will ask her to at least grant you an audience. She won't be able to turn me down on that," Aohdan spoke firmly.

"At least wait until we return from the elves. I've had enough humiliation for the time being," Andrew said dryly.

Saoirse and Aohdan laughed for a moment before Aohdan responded, "As you wish, my friend. But you are going to have to reconcile with Cynthia eventually."

Andrew only scowled and spurred his horse ahead of them. Aohdan shook his dark head and a smile played across his lips. He could feel Saoirse's inner struggle to keep her composure in order to not embarrass Andrew further. They rode the rest of the way back through the city in silent merriment.

When they reached the Guard they began to make immediate preparations for the journey to come. Saoirse and Andrew sat down to make a list of supplies while Aohdan went in search of his mother. He found Avana up on the east wall of the city. She was overseeing the practice of a new station of archers who were experimenting with a variety of battle formations in order to find which was the most efficient and effective.

"Archers ready! Turn...draw...release!" Avana barked out commands authoritatively. When she saw her son approaching she gave him a curt nod of acknowledgement never taking her focus from the archers. Twice more she had them repeat the process till it was one fluid movement. Only then did she turn the practice over to the accompanying officer and gave her attention to Aohdan.

"Your eyes tell me that you have learned something valuable from Cynthia, Aohdan. It must be significant for you to come seek me out like this," Avana said, giving him a shrewd look.

Aohdan tilted his head in response. "You know me well, Mother. Is there a place we could speak more privately?"

"Would the East Tower do?"

"Yes. That will suit our needs." Aohdan offered his arm to his mother and she quickly took it.

They walked sedately to the tower door where they gave perfunctory nods to the guards before entering the narrow room. The platform landing served as the base for a winding staircase that led to the top floor of the tower. The upper room was manned by two guards who kept watchful gazes out the windows that looked out over the city and the countryside.

Avana courteously asked the guards to wait at the bottom of the stairs until their return. When the guards had left she turned to Aohdan and said, "Well? What is of such importance that you seek me out alone like this?"

Aohdan paused for a moment, staring at his mother. She was beautiful. Red hair swept in waves to the side of her face while her bright eyes quizzed him trying to fathom his tidings. He knew she was brave, never shirking her duty, but in that moment he wished that she would let him take on this quest alone. He knew Avana would feel responsible, yet he hoped that somehow he could persuade her to stay in Amaroth.

Squaring his shoulders, he launched himself into retelling everything he had learned. Aohdan stayed succinct and factual knowing that Avana would make the best decision hearing the bare facts without his opinions to cloud her judgment. When he told her of Cynthia's true identity, she only snorted softly to herself and muttered, "I always knew there was more to that old librarian than she was letting on." But otherwise she stayed silent for the duration of his account.

When he was finished, Avana crossed her arms and paced across the tight room to one of the tall windows. Sunlight danced along her face and hair illuminating her in a golden glow; her long tresses seemed to be tipped with fire.

"Did you know I never wanted to be Queen, Aohdan?"

Aohdan tipped his head to the side, puzzled. "No, I didn't, Mother. I've heard the tale of how you claimed the throne, but I didn't realize that it wasn't something you aspired for."

Avana gave a short, clipped laugh, breath catching in her throat. "I rule because I love the people. Some days I long desperately for the loneliness of the Wilds, yet I see Amaroth and how I can serve and protect it. Protecting the city is a nobler cause than living an untroubled life."

"You're a good ruler, Mother." Aohdan moved beside Avana and put his arm around her, pulling her close to him. "Amaroth is grateful and thrives with you as their leader."

"And as their leader I now have to make a difficult decision. Should I stay to defend Amaroth from an unknown attack or should

I go to visit the elves? I know your counsel already, Aohdan. Your wish is that I stay with the city. Your face makes that clear! But perhaps the wiser choice would be to go to the elves. Direct contact is always more fruitful than hearsay. I know that my plan was to join you, yet now my heart is divided."

Aohdan rested his cheek on his mother's head. "You are right to say that I wish you would stay here. You are Amaroth's greatest warrior."

"What of this notion that we are *Elestari*? That we could become dragons like Saoirse? I doubt either of us are capable of calling upon something long asleep without strong magic," Avana questioned.

Aohdan sighed. "Part of me wishes to call it nonsense, but I have this strange connection with Saoirse that I cannot ignore. It's a sixth sense that feels like it had lain dormant until I met her. Now it simply hovers below the surface linking us together. Cynthia is not a liar, so as farfetched it may seem I believe it is true. Though I agree that we would need magic to aid us in shifting."

Avana stepped out of his embrace, facing her son. "Then I will trust her. And as much as it pains me to do so, I will stay here in Amaroth. Your grandfather will be happy to spend time with you. However, I would like it if Killian would also go. Though I do not enjoy being separated from him he has a cool head that is not easily swayed."

Unable to hide his relief, Aohdan grinned broadly. "You have brought me great peace of mind, Mother. How soon can we leave?"

"Tomorrow, if Caleb is not out hunting in the Wilds. You would think that I would do a better job keeping up with him," Avana said ruefully.

"Our family is not one to sit by and let others do all the work."

"Once a Ranger, always a Ranger. That's what Aramis told me," Avana said softly, remembering the words of her late grandfather. The pain of his unexpected death from a landslide still lingered in their lives.

"Then tomorrow it is," Aohdan spoke firmly.

Chapter 16

BEFORE THE CITY BEGAN TO STIR in the early morning, the travelers retrieved their horses. Fog hung heavy over the land obscuring the view of the mountains from the ramparts of the city. A lone figure, heavily cloaked, stood on the walls watching as five riders trotted under the arched gateway and out onto the road. The damp ground muffled the clatter of the horses' hooves on the stones. Soon the riders were swallowed up by the mist.

Avana stared after them with a heavy heart. She desperately wished she was riding away with them. Yet she knew that Amaroth needed her more. Hearing footsteps behind her she turned to see Blane, one her most trusted soldiers, walk up next to her.

"They'll be all right, Avana. We need you here. Besides, adventure might come our way sooner than you think," Blane reassured his queen.

Fingering Stelenacht and casting another glance into the fog, Avana replied resignedly, "I know you're right, old friend. It's just not easy."

As Blane and Avana were speaking, the riders were progressing further down the road into the fog. The sun was just starting to peek over the horizon so the fog was still a dense sheet lining the countryside.

Fallon's shape rose from the fog startling the horses. The riders quickly filled him in with the details from the city once they quieted their animals.

"If all this is true, then I must return to the pack," Fallon said thoughtfully. "Father will gather the packs. Danger is in the air. The birds of prey have been circling down from the mountains."

Killian spoke. "I wish you could stay near Amaroth, Fallon. I would feel better leaving my wife knowing you were still here."

"My sister is strong. But I will heed you and hurry my message. I will return with haste," Fallon replied.

Caleb smiled at the wolf. "I doubt you will return alone. Old Finris hasn't seen Avana for several years now. Even adopted fathers grow anxious to visit their daughters."

A rumble of laughter escaped the wolf. "Fathers are all alike. Yes, I expect him to come back with me. His impatience will be a boon to Amaroth. Farewell then. We both have many miles ahead of us."

Fallon sprang away and disappeared into the mist. The sound of his footfalls fading away from them made Saoirse wish she could travel with him. But she had her own journey to focus on. Saoirse rode at the back of the group studying the four men ahead of her.

Caleb and Killian were of particular interest to her. These men had shaped Aohdan's life. Caleb had the bearing of a king with a vigor and suppleness that belied his age. He carried himself with more fire than either Avana or Aohdan. He appeared to be quicker tempered, but clearly had a soft heart underneath.

Killian, on the other hand, was of a steadier sort. Nonetheless, he had a wild air to him. He was witty in speech and sharp-eyed. Very little escaped him to Saoirse's chagrin. Killian had easily discovered her confused feelings for his son. His quiet teasing caused her to reevaluate her previous decisions.

If Killian's banter could send her into such an embarrassing tizzy then perhaps she needed to be more honest with herself. Cynthia's words had also been echoing loudly in her head. The prince and the dragon? What an unlikely match. Yet if she were honest, that was exactly what her heart was clamoring for.

She huffed inwardly, a small note of defiance. Yet she allowed herself to strip away a large part of the self-imposed barrier she had set between her and Aohdan. Instantly, she saw that Aohdan could sense the difference in their connection. He did not turn around, but instead he straightened in the saddle, his posture exuding a new confidence. Saoirse knew that he had a broad grin plastered across his face, though she could not see it.

Though she may have removed some barriers, Saoirse was determined to not let her feelings compromise their quest. The fate of her people and Arda lay in their success. It was not the time to pursue romance. Ahead of her Aohdan was chuckling quietly to himself. Again, he had interpreted her thoughts. With a growl of annoyance she urged her horse into a quick trot and surged ahead of the group. The others exchanged puzzled glances by her odd behavior while Aohdan couldn't help smiling. His patience was winning out with Saoirse.

They traveled a full day's ride and into the evening before stopping. Saoirse knew she needed a good night's sleep to prepare for the flight ahead, so despite her eagerness to continue, she attempted to rest. The others took turns at watch, allowing the dragon woman to sleep. When morning broke over the Wilds they breakfasted and repacked their things for riding Saoirse. Saoirse herself ate a large portion. A side of ham had been set aside for her and she devoured it effortlessly.

They released the horses, removing saddle and bridle, knowing that this close to home the horses would easily find their way back. The moment had now come for Saoirse to shift. Aohdan was still fascinated by the process. Due to the size she intended to grow, Saoirse stood well away from the men. The violet haze surrounded her and her body began to expand. The murky form soon became a silver dragon that grew to an enormous size.

Aohdan realized that he had not truly understood how big a dragon could be. Killkari had seemed massive, yet Saoirse at full size was terrifying. Her head alone was twice his body length and the fangs that curved from her jaws were as long as his legs. She felt his fear and shuddered.

Suddenly he was no longer afraid. Instead he felt ashamed for causing her guilt. He reached out and spoke to her with his mind. "I beg your pardon, Saoirse, for my thoughtlessness. Your form is still foreign to me and takes some getting used to."

With a sigh she responded, "A dragon is a formidable creature. You are right to fear me. I have both the powers of destruction and healing. Let us hope that I will not have to use either."

Walking over to her with the harness he had created, Aohdan placed his hand on her leg and answered, "Indeed. But when the time comes I am glad to have you at my side."

Saoirse did not reply. Instead she thrummed a happy note that rang through him as he worked to fasten the harness across her broad body. Caleb and Killian had not seen Saoirse transform before, yet they took it well in stride. Both were unmistakably impressed by the dragon, but neither seemed fazed by the thought of riding her.

Stretching out with her mind Saoirse addressed the men in her lilting accent as Aohdan finished preparing the harness. "Because of the great speed at which I will be flying I will stay in contact with you through our thoughts. You also will be able to communicate with me now that I have established a connection. It will be helpful that you are touching me as that will maximize our ability to speak with one another. As long as you are in contact with me you will also be able to talk mind to mind with each other. However, once the contact is broken that ability will no longer be available. Does this make sense?"

Caleb spoke up in clarification, "So what you're saying is that as long as we touch you, we can speak without words to the others in the party, correct?"

Saoirse bobbed her great head. "Correct. Just a bit of useful magic so everyone is connected."

Andrew gave Saoirse a wary look and said, "Will we be able to hear the others' thoughts?"

"No. It will be a normal conversation. You may be able to sense the intent behind words more strongly, but each mind is shielded and private."

"Good," Andrew said emphatically.

Saoirse looked over the four men searching for any sign of unease. "Alright then. Time is wasting."

She lay flat on the ground, her legs splayed and neck stretched out. Even so, the men had to clamber up her leg to reach her back. Saoirse waited patiently until they had clipped themselves to her harness. She stood up slowly, giving her riders a moment to adjust.

She stretched her wings and gave them an experimental flap. "Hang on," she mind spoke with a hint of mirth.

Saoirse took a few steps forward and leapt into the air. Her wings powered through the air to bring them aloft. Her riders clutched at her spines, full of nerves. Another few wingbeats and they were coasting on a draft. Adjusting her wings she felt the lift of the air bring her to a hair raising speed. The wind sang as she cut through it.

On her back, Killian gave a wild yell. A war cry filled with the joy of life. His excitement filled Saoirse, inspiring her to let loose a roar that seemed to shake the wind itself. Now all four men were humming with exhilaration. Pushing for even greater swiftness Saoirse found a jet stream that took them streaking across the sky. She could continue like this for hours, eating up miles below them at a breakneck pace, and so she did.

Two more whole days of flying at top speed nearly nonstop left her riders ragged from the extreme force of the wind. Saoirse was famished at the end of each day. She ate whatever she could catch and then curled up to sleep. She left one wing tented for the men to shelter under.

On the fourth day she saw from Caleb's memory that they were approaching the Greenwood. Saoirse found a slower draft and kept an eye on the terrain below her. Far off in the distance she could see a dark green line that faded into the horizon. Her eyesight was better than her companions, so she was unsurprised that it was another twenty minutes before Andrew pointed out the tree line.

Saoirse coasted even lower. The forest was impending and she needed a place to land. She focused on finding a flat space close to the trees. This part of the Wilds was full of gullies and ravines, not an ideal landing site for a large dragon with passengers.

Abruptly, her mind was attacked. It felt like someone had thrown a heavy stone at her and she'd barely had time to put up her shields to fend it off. Looking up she saw a massive gold dragon hurtling toward her. Screeching in surprise she plummeted to the ground to avoid her golden adversary.

She felt the fear from her riders as she hurtled to the ground for an impromptu landing. Saoirse also sensed Aohdan's anger at the attacker. She knew that he feared for her and wanted to fight, but he would be more hindrance than help in the coming battle.

"Run my friends!" she spoke with her mind, "Flee while you can. I will protect you."

She landed heavily halfway down a steep gully. The four men came sliding off her back and raced farther down the draw.

"Come back to us, Saoirse," Aohdan spoke to her, his voice filled with worry.

Her voice burned in his mind. "I will try. Now go!"

Saoirse rose back into the air snarling angrily at the circling dragon. She flew at it letting out an earsplitting roar. Without warning, claws came crashing into her and raked down her side. Another attacker! Spinning away, she howled in pain. Killkari.

There was no time to linger over her surprise at Killkari's appearance. Now the gold dragon was sweeping down on her. She inhaled a deep breath and sent a blaze of flame, not that it would do much good against another dragon. The gold dragon came barreling through the fire. The flames glittered on his scales making them glow iridescently. She was now close enough that she could see the other dragon's eyes. Emerald green, as green as the forest spreading away from them. But something seemed off about those eyes. She couldn't pin down what it was as she made a quick dive to avoid the gold dragon.

Suddenly she had two realizations. The first was that she knew this dragon. His eyes had given him away. This was Markus, one of the youngest recruits to the dragon warrior guild. Saoirse had never seen him in his dragon form before. That's why she hadn't recognized him right away. The second realization was that Markus was being controlled by Killkari.

He flew and pivoted a hair slower than a dragon normally would. Plus his eyes had that strange look to them. It wasn't hard to guess who was in his head. From behind her a furious roar erupted. Saoirse threw herself upwards with powerful wingbeats just in time for Killkari to pass beneath her, clipping her tail and throwing her off balance.

Markus was now upon her. His talons skittered off her shoulder as she rolled beneath him raking his stomach with her own legs. He yowled and snapped at her as she ducked away. Now Killkari was attacking her. He lashed out with his tail, sending her spinning across the sky. Killkari chased after as she banked steeply to face off with him. From the corner of her eye she saw Markus diving for her. She allowed herself to drop but wasn't fast enough to completely avoid him.

Markus seized her right wing with an agonizing crunch as she plummeted. Saoirse screeched in pain, levering herself back up with her other wing to relieve the pressure. Markus shook his head viciously whipping her back and forth as she sought to free herself by battering him with tail and hind talons. She managed to wind her tail around one of Markus's legs and yanked on it with all her might while digging her talons deep into his chest. Being pulled in two directions while in such pain was too much for him and he released her wing.

Just as he did so, Killkari smashed into Saoirse. They fought fang to fang, tooth and claw. They ripped apart the other till the blood rained from the sky. All the while Markus would dive in and heckle Saoirse enough that she could never truly keep a hold of Killkari when they grappled. She was reluctant to go after the golden dragon. Markus was not himself and she didn't wish to harm him any more than need dictated.

Killkari took every advantage of this. He sent Markus after Saoirse without a shred of remorse. The battle was beginning to wear on all three dragons. Saoirse knew she was the weakest. She had been flying at breakneck speed the last four days without truly eating enough to compensate. She sensed that Killkari could feel her weakening. For the first time she let her thoughts shift to Aohdan.

Their connection told her that he was safe in the Greenwood. Relief swept over her. They would find the elves and all would be well. As for herself, the battle was not going to end on such a positive note. Saoirse was tired. There was nothing she could do about it. Using magic would only exhaust her more. Making a gut-wrenching decision, she started sending a flood of images of her fight to Aohdan.

In the meantime, she rallied and brought her fiercest attack to Killkari. She managed to meet him midair again, narrowly avoiding Markus. Letting out a blood curdling roar she tore at her opponent. Killkari was a second too slow and Saoirse bit down hard on his neck. He howled and thrashed in response. Talons came hurtling down onto Saoirse's back and wings, filling her with hot pain.

Still she stubbornly held on. Markus's attack sent Killkari and Saoirse hurtling down toward the ground, spinning and tumbling wildly. Saoirse refused to let go. She could feel Killkari's fear as the ground rose up to meet them at a frightening speed. Saoirse also felt Aohdan's fear from what he had seen. Her heart panged as she mind-spoke to him. "I'm sorry," was all she said.

Impact was imminent as the two dragons fell from the sky, locked in a deadly embrace. At the last second before impact, Saoirse did what she thought was impossible, she severed her connection with Aohdan. If she was killed by the fall, she didn't want him to feel her death. Better for him to wonder.

Saoirse and Killkari slammed into the ground, skidding and rolling apart. A haze of pain like she had never felt before engulfed her and then she knew no more.

Chapter 17

IN THE FOREST AOHDAN CRIED OUT and stumbled to his knees as if he had been struck, clutching his chest. The other three turned to him in alarm as he gasped in pain. Tears streamed from his eyes and his body bowed in agony. A sound that seemed a cross between a howl and yell escaped him.

"Saoirse," he managed to pant out as he writhed. There was a void in his heart like nothing he had ever felt before.

Andrew looked grim. "Something happened to her, didn't it?"

Aohdan didn't answer, but the haunted look in his eyes told the group more than any words. He struggled back to his feet. He swayed, reaching out to one of the rough tree trunks for balance. He leaned against the sturdiness of the tree, comforted by its solid presence. Something had been ripped from him. Aohdan hadn't realized how deep his connection to Saoirse was until it was gone. This must have been how Saoirse felt when she lost Colm.

It was like death itself, a black pit with no up or down. The missing bond left an all-consuming hole in its place. He felt himself drowning in the loss. His vision grew blurry and he seemed to be far from his body.

Suddenly his father was in front of him shaking him. "Fight, Aohdan, fight. If she truly is gone then let the pain turn into something else. Avenge her and protect Arda!" Killian's eyes glistened with unshed tears for his son.

Killian's words acted as a shock to Aohdan. He felt the pull of despair recede enough for him to regain his senses. Words were still beyond him, but he nodded in reply.

Caleb eyed their surroundings and said seriously, "If Saoirse is dead then we must go on. Time is short. Reaching the elves may be our only hope."

Taking his bearings again, Caleb led the group at a swift pace. Aohdan tramped dumbly after the others as they filed further into the forest. Their speed was enough to keep Aohdan distracted from thinking too much about his shattered heart. As they went deeper, the forest changed around them. The last time he had been in the Greenwood he had been a teenager. He remembered being captivated by the forest then. It was such an oddity compared to what he was used to. Now he barely registered the ethereal beauty that grew around him.

A strange glow came off the plants and trees illuminating their path. Florescent yellow slime dripped from the tree trunks. Tiny fiery red hummingbirds and lime green butterflies flitted over their heads, flying around sampling nectar from flowers that bloomed in shades of magenta seen nowhere else in the land. The air thickened with a heady scent of the exotic flowers and leaf mold. Vines hung down in swaying curtains from the trees. Enormous ferns brushed their shoulders as they passed. Beneath their feet the ground was dotted with white and azure flowers supported by a soft mulch that squelched from years of buildup. They had now crossed into the only rainforest in Arda.

Without warning Caleb stopped, nearly causing Killian to run into him. Andrew and Aohdan froze in place. From the heights of the trees and the thickening underbrush a phalanx of elves stepped forth. They were heavily armed with all manner of weapons. The trees seemed to bristle with swords and spears, accompanied by a bow on the back of every elf. The elves were dressed in the same bioluminescent raiment as the trees. Their close-fitting armor, formed to each wearer, seemed to glow and pulse, rippling with their movements making them blend in perfectly with the treetops.

"Welcome back, Caleb, son of Aramis," a tall dark-haired elf called in greeting.

His armor was inscribed with a bright silver stag, the mark of a royal guard, Aohdan remembered. The elf's eyes were emerald green, clearer and brighter than any human. The elf sheathed his sword and offered his hand to Caleb with a smile.

Caleb returned the smile, looking relieved. "Bentaris. I am glad to see you. We need to see Valanter and speak to your lore masters. It's urgent."

Bentaris gave a sharp, sad laugh. "It must be, to get most of the royal family to enter our realm. We saw the brawling dragons. I have my own guesses as to why you are here, but now is not the time for discussion. We have horses and zeeback waiting. We will take the zeeback to Mirava since they will be faster."

Questions welled within Aohdan. Could Bentaris tell him more about Saoirse? How had she lost the battle? Was there any chance she was still alive? Though the void inside him said otherwise, a part of him couldn't believe she was dead. He struggled to keep from shouting out everything he wanted to know. But even if it galled him to do so, it was far better to wait until he could get answers for the whole picture.

He followed the elves as they led them to their promised steeds. Through his haze of grief Aohdan was curious to see the zeeback. He had heard about them, yet never had the chance to see one of the rare creatures. He was even more intrigued that he was going to have the opportunity to ride one.

They entered a clearing that held dozens of horses and zeeback alike. The horses were straight-limbed and tall mostly all in grays and blacks. They whickered softly at the new arrivals. None of the animals were tethered. They simply grazed freely on the short grass. However, it was the zeeback that Aohdan found captivating.

They were comparable to the horses in size, but their two heads and necks combined with unique coloring made them stand out. Their hides were a deep chocolate, striped with white. The white seemed to almost glow and ripple with their movements similar to the elven armor. The zeeback had soft violet eyes that caused Aohdan to lurch as he thought of Saoirse. They had deer-like faces, but their eyes were ringed with white and their pointed ears boasted silky tufts. The zeeback's necks were thin, but each had a heavy striped mane while their hindquarters possessed thick tails that put the horses to shame.

The animals came forward to greet the elves, nosing them gently. They gracefully avoided the strangers, careful not to touch them. Bentaris spoke quietly in elvish to one of the zeeback that approached him. It nuzzled his shoulder with one of its heads and let out a low bleat. Four more zeeback drew from the herd. They ringed Bentaris and he pointed out the strangers to them.

"The zeeback will carry you. They understand where we are going so there is no need for saddle or bridle. Speak kindly to them and they will be faithful to you. They will not let you fall unless you do something foolish," Bentaris said, making eye contact with each of the royal party.

The group nodded in response and went to meet their new steeds. Aohdan was relieved to have a true distraction from his broken heart. His zeeback gazed at him with two pairs of intelligent eyes. He offered his hand palm up in way of greeting. Each head snuffled his hand, then stepping closer, they nosed him from head to toe. Looking around, Aohdan noted that the other three were getting the same treatment from their zeeback.

Finally after inspecting him, Aohdan's zeeback turned so its side was facing him. It curled one head around to him with an expectant look. Reaching out, Aohdan gently placed a hand on the glossy hide that was soft as the finest silk. Warmth and life radiated under his palm. He ran his fingers along the zeebacks' shoulder and back in the same soothing motion he often rubbed his horse with. The zeeback arched into his touch in response, letting out a breathy sigh.

"What's your name, I wonder?" Aohdan questioned the zeeback.

Bentaris answered him. "Josisis is yours, Aohdan. Caleb, you ride Miishalle. Killian, yours is called Cassi, and Andrew is on Tyber."

Killian growled as he pulled himself up onto the zeeback who stood patiently. "Dwarves were not meant to ride four-legged beasts," he commented to his son as Aohdan suppressed a smile.

"And yet you now can add zeeback to the list of animals you have ridden," Aohdan replied, desperate to feel the lightness of his words. He vaulted easily onto the zeeback taking up a handful of the thick black mane to steady himself. He saw his father watching him closely and knew that he wasn't fooling Killian with his false cheer.

"Don't give up yet on Saoirse," Killian spoke, his eyes full of worry for his son. "Remember that Avana found Caleb even after it seemed all hope was lost."

Aohdan's heart twisted. He guided the zeeback next to his father using his knees. "I can't feel her anymore. There's nothing. Either she is dead or in a state of the deepest unconsciousness. You saw her fighting. I can't help but fear the worst."

"Yes, we saw her battle. Yet there is always a chance until you know for sure she is gone. How do you know she didn't cut off the connection herself? Give her credit, she knows that the enemy could access you through her. What if she knew she would be captured? Do you really think she would put you in danger?" Killian reasoned.

His logic cut through Aohdan's pain bringing sudden clarity. What if his father was right? Though Saoirse had said that a bonded pair could not be separated, perhaps she was wrong. "You're right, Father. I should trust her judgment. I'm sorry for giving up so quickly."

Killian snorted. "If I knew that something terrible had happened to your mother I would be going crazy too. Don't beat yourself up. Worry makes you lose your good sense."

For the first time since he had lost his connection to Saoirse, Aohdan felt hope. He gave his father a grateful look. Killian nodded in return with a small smile. Bentaris was leaving the clearing on his zeeback with Caleb and Andrew following so father and son urged their steeds forward.

Bentaris called out to the group, "Hold on tightly, my friends. The zeeback will start out slowly, but we are in a hurry so they will not stop."

With those words his zeeback broke into a trot that quickly morphed into a long striding gallop. Aohdan took a firmer grip on the mane twined between his fingers and he leaned forward over the long necks. Josisis responded by taking off in a rocking lope. Soon the zeeback was galloping swiftly through the forest with effortless strides.

Aohdan marveled at the smoothness of the beast. It kept up such a steady cadence that Aohdan was tempted to let go his hold on the thick mane. He was glad he didn't when Josisis leaped gracefully over a fallen log without faltering. The zeeback stretched out and lengthened their strides. They were flying now. Aohdan knew that this was faster than any horse could travel. The zeeback kept up the pace so effortlessly, he got the feeling that if they were not weaving through the forest their speed would be even greater.

They sped through the trees till the forest began to thin around them. Aohdan was surprised to see that there seemed to be an abundance of purple spruce. They were normally only found in the heart of the Greenwood. Yet it seemed that they also grew here in the elf kingdom. As the trees grew fewer, they also appeared to get taller. The purple spruce rose to towering heights above them as the space between them broadened. Each tree itself was a living forest with limbs spanning many lengths. The air had become less humid and a heady scent of vanilla permeated the air. Aohdan knew that was part of what made the purple spruce dangerous.

Their inviting fragrance enticed unsuspecting travelers to brew the needles into a tea. The tea from the poisonous needles would taste as sweet as the scent promised, but death was swift. On the other hand, Aohdan kept in mind the healing properties of the dried roots of the spruce, one of the greatest treasures in Arda. They could cure any malady except the one caused by the poison of the tree's needles.

He imagined that the large number of purple spruce this far from the center of the forest had something to do with the citadel of the elves. *Magic draws magic,* he thought to himself though he wasn't sure what sort of magic a tree held.

Ahead of him Bentaris slowed down on his zeeback. The group slowed with him, their animals barely breathing harder than when they had left.

"Welcome to Mirava," Bentaris said, waving to the land in front of them. As he spoke a great city seemed to spring up from the forest.

Its walls seemed to shift and shimmer in the same way the elves' armor did. Great spiraling houses that were built around the trunks of the purple spruce peeped over the wall. Blue flags with the white running stag emblazoned on them snapped lazily in the breeze from the ramparts. The gates of the city rose up before them with only one guard per side. One would think they were made of glass, but the streaks of purple and gold running through them told otherwise. Aohdan wondered what they were made out of. However, the question could wait.

Bentaris quickly answered the question that had been forming in Aohdan's mind. "Mirava is shielded not only with magic, but the mirrored walls create an optical illusion that everything is the same as the forest around it. You would never know it was there until you touched the structure. Only then would it reveal itself to you. I'm sure you also notice how few guards we keep. Very few creatures make it to the gate without our knowledge so there is little reason for us to keep a heavier watch."

Caleb laughed. "Your guards are scattered throughout the forest. You track anything and everything that enters or leaves the Greenwood. That's the real secret."

The elf returned the laughter with a smile. "Well said, friend. I remember the days when you were a Ranger and you would try to sneak through without us noticing!"

"And I succeeded! But only once. It was the most miserable crossing of the Greenwood I've ever experienced." Caleb shook his head ruefully.

"You'll never let us forget that, will you?" Bentaris teased. "Even elves are fallible."

Andrew gave a haughty sniff. "It's a good thing too. Otherwise you would all be insufferable."

"Like old retired Rangers?" Bentaris quipped as he rode toward the city gate.

Killian was unable to muffle his snort of laughter at this comment and Aohdan found it difficult to contain his own chuckle. Andrew sputtered for a moment. Then he drew himself up indignantly on his zeeback and let out a muffled harrumph.

Aohdan could see that Bentaris was smiling to himself, though he was pretending to be unaware of Andrew's reaction. Aohdan was pleasantly surprised by Bentaris. The elves in Amaroth tended to be more reserved, but Bentaris, on the other hand, seemed open with a good sense of humor.

They rode through the gates and into the city.

Chapter 18

AVANA PACED THROUGH THE TRAINING GROUNDS of the Guard. She had her soldiers on high alert after their enlistment call had gone out. Avana dropped the age to join the Guard to 17 years old because they would need every able-bodied man and woman willing to answer their call. War was approaching.

In the five days since her family and Andrew had left, Avana's scouts and spies had begun to bring in frightening stories. Goblins were on the prowl again. They were rumored to be armed with bright silver and seemed to have no fear of death. They pillaged villages, killing wantonly, burning down every building. They were also taking no prisoners. This was very different than their normal hit-and-run tactics. And to top it off, there had been a sighting of a large black dragon. King Halfor, the dwarf king, had sent her a warning about it.

Avana felt the drive of any good commander. Protect and encourage. Keep the people safe. Spread peace in the face of fear. All of this was her burden. She missed the steadiness of Killian. He had been her rock in the storms. Now she was alone.

Well, not alone, she thought to herself. *I have another old friend to rely on.* Avana quickened her pace. She strode through the barracks till she reached a familiar apartment. Reaching out she knocked loudly on the door. From the other side she could hear the now familiar shuffle of a chair being pushed back and the steps coming to the door.

Captain Grayson opened the door. His stature wasn't as proud as it once was. Avana knew he was approaching his ninetieth year. His face was lined from years of exposure to sun and weather. His thick mane of hair and long beard were now completely white. But his gray green eyes still twinkled with life.

"My dear girl! To what do I owe this pleasure?" he exclaimed, pulling her into a fierce hug.

Avana hugged him tenderly. "I need someone to talk to, Uncle. I'm sorry I haven't visited sooner. I've been so busy recently. I'm sure you've heard the rumors floating around."

"There have been fascinating things going around, Avana. Come inside and you can tell me more about them." Grayson stepped from the doorway.

Avana walked inside to the comfortable living room. A fire crackled on the hearth while Grayson's rocking chair sat in front of it. Avana settled onto one of the three high-backed couches that lined the room. The smell of fresh bread wafted from the kitchen.

"Been baking much, Uncle?" she queried with a raised eyebrow.

Grayson laughed as he settled into the wooden rocker. "Keeps me busy. Never knew I liked baking bread until I retired from the Guard. It requires patience and a pinch of talent for a good loaf. Don't worry, I've been talking to your captains though. Your planning is coming along just fine. Now what are all these rumors about? I know from the captains that the goblins are rising, but there's more going on than what they know."

"Perceptive as ever, Uncle." Avana shook her head as she smiled. "You had better hang onto your beard. It's a bit unnerving."

Then Avana told Grayson everything she knew about Saoirse and the *Elestari*. She finished her tale with the information that they had learned from Cynthia.

When she finished, Grayson gave a sharp snort. "I always knew there was something different about that old bird. Good old Cynthia. Glad she's on our side mind you. But it is a bit unsettling to learn we've had dragons living among us without our knowing it."

"I'm more worried about what the future will look like. Are we prepared for an influx of refugees if the *Elestari* are really in captivity? They have to stay somewhere before they can rebuild," Avana said, biting her lip.

"The citizens of Amaroth are willing to help. We have the greatest mix of peoples of any city in all of Arda," Grayson replied with a smile.

Suddenly they were interrupted by a knock at the door.

Grayson's smile turned into a frown. "Who could that be? I don't recall scheduling any captains to come at this time of day."

He stood up from his rocking chair and headed for the door. His deep baritone mingled with a female voice that floated back to Avana. In a moment he was back with the unexpected guest. It was Cynthia.

For once her usual regal, demanding demeanor looked harried. Her eyes were full of worry. She lost no time in speaking.

"My Queen, I am so glad to have found you. You were not in your usual haunts. I feared you had left the city. I have pressing news for you and a request."

Avana felt a stab of worry touch her heart. "Then by all means get on with it!"

"Something has happened to Saoirse. I'm afraid I wasn't completely honest with them the other day and put a tracking spell on the three of them when they came and visited me. I wanted to keep an eye on their progress and make sure they were well."

"Is Saoirse dead?" Avana asked heavily.

Cynthia shook her head. "I don't think so, but she is very close to death. Her consciousness is in the deepest form of retreat. Only a step from death's door. It happened instantly. One moment she was there and the next I could barely sense her. To top it off the group is separated. The others all seem to be fine though," Cynthia spoke, answering the next question Avana had been about to ask.

"So what happened, do you think?" Grayson stroked his beard.

"I believe Saoirse was hurt. I didn't sense any magic causing her to stay unconscious. However, I suspect she is captured. Aohdan and Andrew have made it to the elf kingdom while she is going further into the Wilds," Cynthia said.

Avana let out a deep sigh. "I am glad to hear they reached the elves. And it certainly sounds plausible that Saoirse may have been captured, but is there any chance they would have split up on their own for some reason?"

Cynthia smirked slyly at Avana. "Your son is head over heels for that girl. He wouldn't leave her side unless he was forced to."

"And you would probably be right." Avana allowed a small smile to shine through her concern. "Now that you have told us your news, what is the request you wanted to make?"

Cynthia stepped closer to Avana and took her hands between her own. "Aohdan told you about the *Elestari* and how you are both descendants of them, correct?"

"He did. It was a lot to take in," Avana said.

"It wasn't something I did lightly. And what I'm going to ask you I do with the utmost gravity." Cynthia's eyes gazed at Avana with an intensity she had not seen before. "My good Queen, I want you to shift."

Avana could feel puzzlement cross her features. "What do you mean?"

"I mean you must wake your dragon," Cynthia replied.

A tremor of shock went through Avana that shook her from head to toe. But along with it came a new awareness. Something inside her that had long been asleep, wakened. It felt foreign and familiar all at once.

Her heart pounded at the revelation and she clutched Cynthia. "I feel it. It's waiting for me. It's always been there, hasn't it?"

"Yes. Though you won't have the same strength of magic as a full blooded *Elestari* you will at least be able to shift. Your level of power will probably be limited to that of a normal dragon like the noble Zellnar."

Avana snorted. "As if any dragon is ordinary."

"True, but you will notice a difference," Cynthia answered. "I would ask that you go to Zellnar and ask him to help you. You won't master your dragon form overnight. You didn't grow up with it."

Tilting her head Avana asked, "Why can't you help me, Cynthia?"

Cynthia's eyes filled with tears and she laughed. It was a sad laugh that didn't fit with her strong character. "I can't shift. I had a curse placed on me for wanting to leave the Blue Fire Mountains. They granted me my wish and let me go, but I no longer have the ability to access my dragon."

"They feared the world that much?" Avana said in surprise, seeing the pain in Cynthia.

"They have grown soft, my dear. Though you wouldn't know it from the outside. But the goblin attack is proof that they had buried their heads in the sand for too long. Saoirse in her youth hadn't yet been exposed to the true depth of the *Elestari* fear. For the young if everything is well, then what is there to question?" Cynthia released her hands and gestured to the house around them. "How many of your young soldiers ask why you are choosing to strengthen your forces on only rumors?"

Avana nodded, seeing the sense in her words. "You make a good point. There are always the few exceptions, but what you say is true."

"Enough about youth. Surely you have questions of your own about your dragon," Cynthia pressed.

"Well I certainly do," Grayson interjected. "How's she supposed to turn into an enormous dragon without the entire city finding out? And is it really something we want Amaroth to know of? It might take some getting used to if they find out their Queen is a dragon lady. The Elders are certainly going to have a fit."

"The Elders can get stuffed," Avana said in annoyance at the mere mention of the prickly old men that monitored each of the districts.

Cynthia smiled at their reactions. "You will have to practice under cover of darkness. Zellnar will help you. I can provide cover if necessary. It would be awfully hard to see a dragon if the city was covered in fog. Even if I can't shift, I am not helpless."

"But is this something that the citizens of Amaroth should be privy to?" Grayson pressed.

"Until I know more, I don't believe this should be public knowledge. In fact, I don't think the majority of the Guard even needs to know. I trust the both of you to be discreet." Avana studied them for a moment thinking hard. "I suppose that I should go tonight to see Zellnar. I haven't spoken to him in six years. I believe he has retreated back to Lonrach Lake to sleep."

Cynthia nodded in response. "He is indeed in the lake. He will be delighted to help you. Zellnar has been faithful to your family line for many years."

"I am forever indebted to him for what he has done. Zellnar is the reason Amaroth is still standing. He was the real hero," Avana said remembering back to the terrible battle against the goblins so many years ago.

"Now you know that's not true. You were the one who called upon him. He would never have woken without you. You deserve as much credit as him. You led the troops, Avana. Zellnar simply finished the battle for you," Cynthia said.

Avana allowed a smile to cross her face. "I only did my duty and what was right."

"And now stand up and do it again," Cynthia encouraged. "Go now to Zellnar. The sooner you begin to learn how to shift the better."

"I'm not going to win this argument, am I?" Avana said.

Grayson harrumphed. "I think you best do as she says. I don't totally believe this mumbo jumbo, but I'm guessing we don't have much time, my dear."

"Alright. I'll go now. It's still afternoon though. Will you provide me cover, Cynthia?"

Cynthia tilted her head and crossed her arms. "With pleasure."

Avana turned to Grayson, "I'm sorry for running off so soon. I will be back. I trust your judgment and I will need your advice as I proceed. Farewell."

With that she paced quickly from the room and out the door.

Grayson let out a deep sigh as he watched his niece leave.

"She never was one to turn away when adventure called. Would that I could follow her."

Cynthia's eyes glittered in the firelight. "That is why she is a great queen, old captain."

"Avana won't be forgotten. And speak for yourself about age! If I understand correctly you're no spring chicken either," Grayson harried.

This earned him a ferocious glare from Cynthia. "I happen to be middle-aged among my people, thank you very much."

"Is it true that you and Andrew were once seeing each other? I know you have a deep dislike for him, but I remember a time he could often be found at the library," Grayson asked. He was curious, but also enjoyed needling Cynthia.

Now it was Cynthia's turn to sigh. "Once we had feelings for each other. But he betrayed my trust. I may have been a bit harsh in my anger."

"A bit harsh? The poor man's been terrified of you ever since!"

Cynthia let out a decidedly dragon-like growl. "When I was but a small child my promised life mate was killed in an accident. He was my best friend. At the time I didn't fully comprehend what had happened, but I found that I could love no one else as I grew up.

There are other *Elestari* like me who for some reason or another are alone. We are not meant to live solitary lives. That's why I wanted to explore the world. It would distract me from my loneliness. When I met Andrew I no longer felt alone."

"And his betrayal was something you couldn't bear," Grayson guessed as he watched emotion cross Cynthia's face.

Cynthia winced. "It was as if he had run his sword through me. I was furious. Yet now I regret my anger. But I'm no good at apologies." She shrugged in a philosophical manner.

Grayson shook his weathered head and laughed. "You are looking at the king of failed apologies and regret. I never got a chance to right the wrongs with my sister. At least I was able to with Caleb. I know you are proud, Cynthia, but don't let pride take the place of what's important. People are what matter. If Andrew ever truly cared for you then he will accept your apology. He might even have one of his own for you."

Cocking her head to the side Cynthia said, "I see why Avana comes to you for advice. You are wise. I will think on your words. For now, I have a fog to raise. Thank you for your hospitality. I will show myself out."

Cynthia gave Grayson a small smile in parting and left. Grayson sat in his rocker pondering the events. There was much to think over if he was going to be any use to Avana.

Chapter 19

AVANA STRODE THROUGH THE CITY WITH fierce determination; Stelenacht was strapped to her back. Not that she would need her sword, she imagined, but wearing it made her feel complete. When she reached the city gates she was gratified to see a heavy fog begin to roll in from the mountainside behind them.

The guards nodded to her respectfully as she passed under the arch and out onto the road. Avana often went out alone to meet with her wolf friends, so they were not concerned by her departure. She kept up her long strides till she had reached the edge of Lonrach Lake. The fog now lay densely over the ground. The lake was dark and the quiet slap of the water on the shore was the only noise to be heard. Everything else was muffled in the thick blanket that spread across the lake and the city.

Drawing Stelenacht, she breathed out the sword's name. At the sound of its name the sword glowed a fiery blue in response. Avana reached out with the tip of the sword and touched the water in front of her. Immediately, she could feel the pulse of energy it sent out.

The water of the lake seemed to boil and seethe. In a moment the dripping head of a huge cobalt dragon appeared out of the lake before her. Its eyes flashed emerald green and it gave a toothy smile when it saw her.

"Greetings and salutations, Queen of Amaroth. It is good to see you again."

Avana smiled in return. "It is good to see you too, Zellnar. We have missed your watchful presence."

The dragon gave a rumbling laugh. "When I went to sleep you had little need of me. Your kingdom is strong and you are a good ruler. But I don't think you have woken me to ask again for my protection. I sense you have a question for me of another kind."

"Indeed. I need your help. I need you to help me shift." Avana came straight to the point.

Zellnar's eyes widened a fraction. "So you have learned of the *Elestari*. My distant brethren. And you must have learned more about your heritage. There must be more to it than this though; surely you do not wish to shift because you learned it was possible."

"No, there is much more." Avana rapidly outlined everything that had occurred.

Zellnar gave an earth-shaking growl when she finished speaking and it caused Avana to step back.

"I see why you came to me. Yes, you must shift. And I must wake from my slumber and protect the city. I will help you. It won't be easy at first, you know. You're a bit old to be trying such things."

Avana nodded. "I had guessed as much. Nonetheless I am prepared to try my best."

"Good. Then we shall begin." Zellnar pulled his heavily armored body out of the lake spraying water all over Avana.

He stretched languidly, partially covered by the fog. Water plants hung off of his wings and scales. Zellnar rolled his shoulders, then lay down with his head outstretched so he was on eye level with Avana.

"I take it you feel your dragon?" he asked.

Avana felt a frown cross her face. "Yes...but I don't really understand it."

Zellnar chuckled, a deep, gravelly sound. "Nor will you for some time I suspect."

"Then how am I supposed to turn into something so foreign?"

"It will grow less strange with practice. Now, reach for the dragon," Zellnar commanded, fixing a bright green eye on her.

Avana closed her eyes and felt for the strangeness inside her. When she touched it, the strong feeling threatened to engulf her. She threw her eyes open and gasped, clutching her chest.

"I see you found your dragon," Zellnar said. "Good. It will feel overwhelming. Don't be afraid of it. It's part of you. Try again. Let it take you and you will shift. But I will warn you the first time you do, don't try and hold the form for long. You will want to try everything immediately, yet you will do better to take things one step at a time. Even birds must learn to fly."

"Alright. I will try again," Avana said as she shook from nerves and the water she was soaked in.

She plunged within herself again. This time when she found the dragon she did not flee when it came over her. A pleasant tingling filled her body. Suddenly she realized she was changing shape. Stretching, growing, wings burst forth from her shoulders. Her body elongated and she felt a sense of strength like nothing she had ever known before. Finally, the shift was finished. Avana opened her eyes.

She could see much more than before. She discovered her eyesight could pierce the fog. The colors of the world around her were much more vibrant. She stood on four legs instead of two. Something shifted behind her and she craned her sinuous neck to see what it was. Her wings. They rippled and shuddered with her movements. Avana looked down at her body. She was covered in shimmering, light blue scales the same color as Stelenacht when it was glowing.

She took a wobbly step forward, throwing her wings instinctively out for balance. As she flared her wings she was seized with a desire to fly. It was an urgent need full of desperation. Avana reared back onto her haunches with her wings spread wide.

Zellnar called out to her, "Wait, Avana. You are not yet ready!"

But it was too late. She had already launched herself into the air, her wings pumping strongly. Upwards she spiraled until she pierced through the layer of fog into the open air. When she did so, she was suddenly caught by an unexpected wind. It buffeted her, sending her spinning through the sky. Panic filled her chest as she fought the strong gusts.

"Relax! Stop fighting it. Soar with the wind instead of against it." Zellnar came rocketing up through the fog to fly beside her. His deep voice rattled through her fear.

Gritting her teeth she ceased her frenzied wingbeats and tried to simply glide along. The wind seemed to surround her. This time it cocooned her instead of dragging her every which way. Avana leveled out. Her heart galloped madly as she let the wind embrace her. Flying was intoxicating. She never wanted to leave the sky.

Dimly she could hear Zellnar speaking to her, coaxing her back to the ground. Reluctantly she followed him back into the mist. As they neared the ground, Avana again felt a bolt of panic. She didn't know how to land. She stalled sharply mid-flight only to find herself tumbling towards the ground. Her wingbeats were ponderous and awkward as she attempted to correct her descent.

Now the ground was so close she could touch the blades of grass. She landed with a heavy thump, staggering under the force from her own wings. She tripped over her forepaws and went sprawling out across the grass.

For a moment she lay still. Then with a sigh she pulled herself upright giving a shake like a dog. Zellnar landed nimbly beside her.

"I see you are as fearless as a dragon as you are a human," he said with a note of humor in his voice.

Her shoulder and wing ached from her fall. She looked at him realizing with a start that they were eye to eye. She must be very large indeed if she was at head height with him.

"I am impulsive, good Zellnar. Even after years of learning patience I can't resist."

He gave a languid shrug. "You learned your lesson. Now it's out of your system, I can trust you to follow my instructions."

"You are correct. I will not allow instinct alone to drive me."

"Good. You have much to learn in a short time. Since you already have shown a propensity for flight, let us try it again. This time take it slowly," Zellnar commanded. "Your take off was clean. Practice will improve it, but since you did not seem to struggle with it, we will focus on other areas."

"Like actually flying and landing?" Avana winced.

Zellnar let out a guttural laugh. "Yes, the wind is your friend. Don't fight it. Flying should not be exhausting unless you are trying to achieve great speed. Let the wind do the work for you. Use your tail as a rudder. Follow me."

The cobalt dragon bounded into the mist, leaving Avana speechless. With a growl she leapt into the air after him. She again was seized by the fierce desire to fly until she could go no further. This time she was ready when she pierced, streamlined through the mist. She let the wind take her, stretching her neck and tail out to increase all her possible surface areas.

Zellnar swooped over her gracefully. "Follow me!" he called out again.

He began a series of zigzags across the sky. Avana watched him carefully and tried to imitate his maneuvers. At first it was difficult to tack back and forth. Then she remembered Zellnar's words about using her tail as a rudder. She tried it and was pleased to find that she was successful. She lacked the refinement of Zellnar's movement, but she was able to keep up.

She followed him as he crisscrossed the sky with a variety of turns and swoops. Periodically he would sweep back and watch her as she practiced. He was patient allowing her to ask questions as she slowly grew comfortable in the body of a dragon. The sun was beginning to set by the time he had deemed she had done well enough to quit for the day.

"When you land, use your wings to backpedal. Arch them so they catch the air to slow you down. Try to set your hind legs down first. Use your tail to keep balanced. If it's particularly windy you would do well to snap your wings closed right away when you land. Otherwise the wind will make you unstable and you will possibly be pulled over," Zellnar lectured her as they neared the ground.

Avana listened carefully to his words. Focusing hard, she gave a few back sweeps with her wings arching them just as Zellnar had said. However, she was so bent on her flight she forgot to set down her hindquarters first. Avana landed awkwardly on her forehand, and barely escaped another tumble with a frantic wingbeat to right herself.

To her surprise Zellnar looked pleased. "That was better. You learn quickly. Tomorrow we will work strictly on landing, till you are comfortable, I think. After you have mastered that you will be ready for more difficult flights."

Avana cocked her head, "Thank you for teaching me. That was exhilarating."

"Flying always is. But we are not finished yet with our lesson."

"What do you mean?" Avana asked.

Zellnar stretched his wings and then lay down. "We must work on your magic. You will have an easier time accessing it in your dragon form at first."

"Magic?" Avana said, sitting down and curling her tail around her. "Cynthia told me I would be limited in that area."

"And she is right. However, you may be stronger than she suspects so we must test it," Zellnar replied. "The first thing I wish you to try is establishing a connection to Killian. You are familiar with Saoirse's ability to mindspeak, correct?"

Avana nodded.

"I believe you should also be able to do so. But first I want to see if you can bond with Killian. If you are able to, then I think you will be stronger than Cynthia predicted."

Avana studied Zellnar who gazed back at her seriously. "What shall I do then?"

"Normal dragons do not form bonds the way *Elestari* do, so I'm not going to be able to guide you like before. However, I have some ideas of what to try," Zellnar answered. "First, simply try feeling for him."

Drawing into herself Avana searched for the familiar feeling of Killian's presence. Nothing came to light. She shook her head and sighed.

"Try picturing him while you search," Zellnar pressed. "I will add a searching spell to assist you." He began a low melodic chant that made Avana's scales tingle.

Avana tried again. This time she thought she sensed a distant glimmer of Killian, but as soon as she grasped at it the sensation was gone. "That was better. I thought I had found him for a moment," she commented.

"Excellent." Zellnar closed his eyes thinking. His fiery green eyes opened, "Picture a moment of great importance between the two of you. Keep that in your vision as you search for him. I'll keep up my spell."

She let a smile cross her scaly features. She closed her eyes. Her thoughts ran over all the years with her husband. She remembered back to the moment when he had first kissed her. He had been comforting her after their first attempt at searching for the dwarf prince Halever which had been an abysmal failure. Killian had smelled of woodsmoke and leather. His eyes had been bright in the firelight. Without warning, her eyes flew open.

Avana gasped and trembled. She could feel Killian.

Chapter 20

FAR AWAY IN MIRAVA, KILLIAN STOPPED dead in his tracks. He thought he had felt Avana with him. But that wasn't possible. She was hundreds of miles away. He shook his head. All his traveling must be getting to him.

He stepped forward only to grab his chest much like Aohdan had done earlier. Avana. She was here! She had to be! He could sense her. She was in his heart and his head. With a jolt he heard her voice calling out to him.

"Killian! I have found you!" Her voice was full of delight.

He suddenly realized that he was hearing her in his head. No one else around him had heard her call out to him. Her *Elestari* blood, it had to be. But how had she done this?

Her voice called his name again. "Killian!"

Feeling overwhelmed he answered her hesitantly with his mind. "I hear you, Avana. But I don't understand. Yet I am so glad to hear from you."

"It's my dragon, Killian. I've woken it! Zellnar is teaching me to use my magic and how to shift," she answered, full of excitement.

Killian was speechless. Avana had never been ordinary. He had known when he married her that life would not be dull. He hadn't even been that surprised when he learned she was descended from the *Elestari*, but he had never imagined she would attempt to shift.

Thinking of his wife as a dragon like Saoirse was something he couldn't even picture.

"Are you alright, my love?" Avana asked anxiously in his head. "I promise you I am fine. I am not used to this body, but with Zellnar I am learning to master it."

"You're a…a…dragon? Right now? At this moment?" Killian stuttered out.

A thrill from Avana's enthusiasm went through him. "Yes, at this moment. I will shift back soon, but for now I am dragon."

His mind still could not grasp her words as truth.

"Let me show you," she said.

Abruptly he was seeing through a different pair of eyes, disorienting him. He looked around. Behind him were a pair of sky-colored wings that attached to a spine-covered back that bled into a long, sinuous tail. Then in a gut-wrenching jump, he was back in his own mind seeing with his own eyes.

"I..I believe you, Avana. Though I still struggle with the idea," he said.

Avana's words were a comfort. "I don't yet understand either. But my dragon feels right, if there is any solace in that knowledge. I admit it is quite a temptation to not go flying after you. Wings certainly help get you places."

Killian gave a faint chuckle. "Yes, they certainly do. Riding Saoirse was incredible. I still am in awe of how fast we made it across the Wilds."

"I can't wait till we can fly together. But I am glad you have at least tasted the joy of flight." Avana sent him an image of her smiling. "However, I am digressing. Please, tell me what has happened. Cynthia told us that some ill has befallen Saoirse."

"How did Cynthia know something had gone wrong?" Killian asked, feeling confused.

Avana's voice echoed with a grin. "She put a tracking spell on you. She wanted to make sure you made it to Mirava."

"Of course she did," Killian said, shaking his head. "But back to Saoirse. We had an excellent flight till we reached the edge of the Greenwood. In fact it was just as Saoirse was looking for a place to land that we were attacked."

"Attacked!" Avana said in alarm. "By whom? Goblins?"

Killian felt a surge of anger. "No. Worse, I'm afraid. We were attacked by Killkari and another dragon. It was gold in color. I'm not sure of this, but I got the impression the other dragon was being controlled by Killkari. It moved strangely. Not as fluid as the other two, I suppose."

"Mmmm. That would fit with what Cynthia told us," Avana said. "But what happened to Saoirse?"

A heavy sigh escaped Killian. "I don't know exactly. I think she recognized the gold dragon because she was holding back as she fought with it. Killkari seemed to be using that to his advantage. I think that she could have easily beat them if she wasn't worried about the other dragon. I also imagine she was tired. When we made it into the forest, Saoirse appeared to be holding her own. However, something happened to Aohdan when we got a good ways in that made us think that she was grievously hurt."

"What happened to Aohdan? Is he alright?" Avana asked. Killian could feel the anxiety lacing her words.

"Somehow the connection that they shared was severed. Aohdan thought she was dead. It nearly drove him mad for a bit. I too fear the worst, yet I have hope. For some reason I do not think she is dead. I'm not sure why...." Here he trailed off.

Avana answered him. "You are right. Cynthia told me that she is alive, but barely."

Killian's heart leapt at her announcement. "I am relieved to hear your news! I was barely able to persuade Aohdan to not give in to the blackness that overwhelmed him. He will be overjoyed to find that she survived the attack."

"Our son is madly in love with her, isn't he?" Avana said affectionately.

Killian laughed. "As much as I am with you. She is good for him."

"I'm glad I have good tidings for his sake. It is not easy for him to live in our shadows."

"But he does not live in our shadows. He is his own man. Already he is a strong leader and Amaroth loves him. He has proved himself on countless occasions," Killian countered.

"Yet that is not how he sees himself," Avana gently corrected.

Killian knew she was right. Through this new bond with Avana he was able to express without words his love for his son. How much he wanted Aohdan to see the truth. Avana shared the emotion with him. The closeness of these feelings helped him begin to understand how Aohdan had felt when Saoirse had been cut off from him.

Avana shared his sentiment. "It must have been extremely unpleasant to lose a bond like this," she said.

"It is the only time I've ever thought he was going to completely give up. You know how strong his spirit is. But that nearly broke him."

"We shall have to be very careful ourselves then," Avana replied.

The bitter taste of fear came unbidden to Killian at the thought of losing his wife. "I can't imagine life without you. Yet my greater concern is that I could be used against you."

Avana let out a deep growl, a foreign sound to Killian, bringing the truth of her current form into reality.

"We have been through much so far. Let us not worry about what might be. Instead let us each focus on the task at hand."

Killian let out a sigh. "Truly we must. I suppose this is goodbye then. I ought to go and tell Aohdan before we meet with Valanter. We were settling into our quarters when you reached out to me."

"Yes, I should let you go. We both have pressing agendas. I love you, Killian. I'm not sure exactly, but I think I will be able to contact you whenever I want from now on. You might also be able to speak to me; however, I'm not sure how strong our bond has to be before you can do so," Avana said with a sad note in her voice.

Killian smiled. "Then we must practice this mindspeaking often. I love you too. Farewell, my dear."

A wave of sadness crept over him as he felt Avana's presence recede. But in its place he noticed that there was a connection to his wife that he had never had before. It felt like she was somehow near him, yet not. He didn't have time to mull over this new bond, so with an internal shrug he went off to speak to his son.

Aohdan sat in his room sharpening his sword, brooding over the loss of Saoirse. He barely registered his father entering.

"Aohdan, I have news for you. It's from Avana. She says that Saoirse lives." Killian went straight to the point.

"WHAT! How do you know this?" Aohdan exploded as hope rushed into his heart. He gripped his sword tightly.

Killian took a deep breath with a look on his face that caught Aohdan off guard. "I spoke to your mother."

Shock bloomed in Aohdan. "What do you mean?"

"She was able to communicate with me through her mind the way Saoirse did with us on our flight here. She…she's a dragon, Aohdan," Killian said slowly.

Aohdan dropped his sword with a clatter. "You're saying she shifted? That the *Elestari* blood was strong enough?"

"Apparently so. I saw through her eyes. It was incredible. Also, Avana believes that she and I will create a bond similar to what you have with Saoirse." Killian's voice was full of emotion.

Collecting his sword from the floor, and his thoughts at the same time, Aohdan asked, "What do you think about her new ability?"

"It's hard for me to take in," Killian admitted. "But if it strengthens our relationship, I'm all for it…even if I do have a dragon for a wife." He let out a quiet laugh.

"Not that long ago I would have thought all of this was impossible, but now I've seen things I couldn't imagine. It gives me hope that we can defeat Killkari," Aohdan replied.

Killian put a hand on Aohdan's shoulder. "There is always hope. I am glad to have brought you some, yet it is not really me you should thank. It was Cynthia who told Avana that Saoirse was alive. She also is responsible for encouraging Avana to shift."

"Ah, Cynthia. She's full of surprises. I am grateful though. I will not forget her when we return." Aohdan smiled.

"Speaking of our return, we ought to go meet with Valanter now that we are refreshed from our journey. The sooner we speak with him the sooner we can go home," Killian said with a serious air.

Aohdan nodded and stood up, sheathing his sword. "The others are ready?"

"Andrew was eating of course, but he should be finished by now. Caleb did little more than wash up before he began prowling around his room," Killian stated.

"Then let us go," Aohdan said.

Chapter 21

THE KING SAT AT A TABLE surrounded by intricately carved high-backed chairs. Valanter motioned for Aohdan and his group to join him and the few other elves, such as Bentaris, who was already seated. Men and dwarf sat down with worry in their eyes.

As Aohdan sat down, he studied the king of the elves. He only recalled meeting Valanter once, and that had been when he was a small child. The two things that stood out to him most between then and now was the king's height and he was surprised that even as an adult, Valanter was still an imposing figure.

The elf king had piercing eyes and hair so blond that it was nearly white. Even sitting, he was nearly a head taller than his brethren at the table. Yet he was not dressed ostentatiously like Halfor, the dwarf king, was prone to. Valanter was clad in the shimmering bioluminescent colors with the silver stag emblazoned on his chest similar to his palace guards. He could easily have passed as one of them. The only sign of royalty he bore was a light circlet of twisted bright silver that he wore as a crown.

"Welcome to my city," Valanter said, his voice ringing throughout the room though he had barely raised it. "You have come in grave need. One of your number is missing and for that I am deeply sorry."

Killian spoke first. "Do you have any news of her? We feared she was dead but have learned otherwise."

Andrew broke in. "She is alive? That's wonderful!"

"Your *Elestari* companion was taken by Killkari. We think we know where. There has been much goblin activity in the far Northern mountains. In the mountains there is hidden an ancient stronghold that once belonged to the King of Amaroth," Valanter replied, making eye contact with each one of them.

Bentaris continued where Valanter left off. "This stronghold has been one of the greatest secrets that the elves have kept since the battle that nearly destroyed all of Arda. Even the Great War that you fought in, Caleb, was nothing compared to what we fought against the *Elestari* king."

Caleb's blue eyes flashed. "Then it must have been a terrible battle indeed."

"The Tiered Mountain was the logical choice to attack since it stood between Amaroth and the stronghold. The dwarves were nearly lost by the time we arrived. We drove the king's army back, but the *Elestari* were strong. The mountain streams ran red with blood before we finally defeated the king," Valanter said with bitterness in his voice.

"When the battle was over the *Elestari* worked with our people to eradicate any record of the stronghold or of the *Elestari* themselves. Then they went into hiding. Their guilt was something they could never forget," Bentaris said sadly.

Andrew let out a frustrated huff. "But how did you defeat the king? That's what we need to know! You say it was a terrible battle, but that doesn't help us any!"

Valanter and the elves at the table exchanged grave looks. Valanter bowed his head and steepled his fingers.

"We will show you, though it is not something we do lightly. Come with us."

Standing regally, Valanter rose from the table followed by the other elves. Aohdan saw surprise written on the faces of Andrew and Killian. Only Caleb seemed to know what was going on. They strode silently after the king as he led them deeper into the palace.

As they walked the air seemed to take on a different quality than it had before. It sparked and crackled with magic. Aohdan felt the hairs on the back of his neck stand on end in response. Soon Aohdan found they had entered a huge green lawn. Somewhere along the way they had passed from walls to open space, but he couldn't place where that had been.

Ahead of them a light began to shine, growing brighter and brighter as they walked toward it. As they drew nearer Aohdan realized that the light was coming from a massive purple spruce. It was bigger than any other he had yet seen. It dawned on him that the trunk was so large that he could barely see around it. Each individual needle from the branches glowed like it was on fire.

Everyone except Caleb was stunned, which Aohdan didn't quite understand. Suddenly something moved at the base of the tree. At first Aohdan didn't comprehend what was happening. Was the tree itself coming to life? No, it was something entirely different. It was a dragon.

The gigantic dragon was wrapped around the tree nearly the same color as the bark. Its scales shimmered and changed with each sinuous movement. The dragon shook its wings causing the tree itself to shudder. This dragon made Saoirse seem like she was the size of a child's toy. Then a voice vibrated through them. An ancient voice, full of wisdom and years. Flowing as a river but with a rumble that Aohdan felt pierced the very ground.

"Hail Valanter, elf king. Hail Caleb, son of Aramis. You have aged; time must be going by faster than I thought," the dragon said slowly. "You have brought friends with you. One who is of royal blood and related to you no less."

The dragon fixed an enormous golden eye on Aohdan.

Valanter replied, "Hail, great Nokoa. Long have you protected the elf kingdom and the Greenwood Forest. These men have come from far away to learn your secret. An evil has again descended on Arda that threatens us all."

Nokoa answered, "Very well. For over two thousand years we have kept this secret, Valanter. Even you, Caleb, who knew of my existence, have not been privy to what I am about to share with you."

"I am honored that you would choose to now share with us," Caleb replied with a deep bow.

Deep laughter shook the ground from Nokoa. "Beware. Secrets are not easily kept." With a sigh that Aohdan felt to his core, Nokoa said, "What you seek is called a heartstone. A heartstone is the core of a great entity like a mountain or this forest. At the base of this tree lies the heartstone of the Greenwood. That is why I guard it. Heartstones are extremely powerful. No mere mortal can wield one. They must be imbued with magic."

Valanter said quietly, "Heartstones are very rare. It is nearly unheard of to find one. Yet, when they are uncovered they can either be used for great good or great destruction. A heartstone is also impossible to destroy."

"What do you mean, impossible to destroy?" Killian asked with a note of defiance in his voice.

Nokoa answered him. "Only another heartstone can be used to defeat one. Really it is more of a cancellation of powers and they must touch each other in order for this to work."

Aohdan spoke for the first time. "So that's how you defeated the king all those years ago. You used the elven heartstone to stop him."

"Yes. It was our only hope," Valanter said as a frown marred his beautiful face.

"Nathan was the greatest king Amaroth has ever had. He found a heartstone and with it great temptation. When his son Brandon died, Nathan delved into necromancy, trying to bring him back. He became the most powerful wizard to ever walk the land, but he could not bring his son to life. There are some things that even magic cannot fix. Death is one of them. He couldn't live with that reality and he slowly went mad," Nokoa said solemnly.

Aohdan shuddered as he thought of the grief Saoirse and Andrew had suffered. He felt keenly the loss of his connection to Saoirse. Nokoa seemed to sense his thoughts and looked at Aohdan again.

"Someone has again discovered a heartstone, I presume," Nokoa said, still looking at Aohdan. "Otherwise you would not be here looking for answers."

"An evil dragon named Killkari is behind the recent thefts of bright silver. He also took captive the entire *Elestari* nation. He and another dragon attacked us on the way here. The other dragon was being controlled by Killkari," Aohdan stated. "He has taken up with the goblins."

Nokoa growled a low note that reminded Aohdan achingly of Saoirse. "Then he must have a heartstone. No ordinary dragon could bend the *Elestari* and the goblins to their will. This is truly dire news."

"If what you told us is true, then it is the only possible answer," Caleb said.

"Do you know how old I am, son of Aramis?" Nokoa asked with a note of reproof in his voice. "I am as old as this tree. As old as the forest. I was here before the elves. I would not lie to you."

Caleb bowed gracefully. "Forgive me, ancient one. This has been a tangled maze of information to follow."

Nokoa inclined his massive head in return. "I understand, brave one. You have always had the heart of a warrior. Now we must attend the matter at hand. You will require the elven heartstone to defeat your enemy."

Valanter's proud form slumped at these words. "I knew this was to be your answer, Nokoa, but I had hoped against it. I had not wanted to go to war again so soon."

"You will not need to. I do not see a battle of the nations as the answer. There may indeed be bloodshed, but not at the cost of your people," Nokoa said.

"What do you mean? Surely you are not implying that we should send the heartstone with these men! They have no magic. It would kill them. It took our strongest elves to wield it before," Valanter protested.

Nokoa raised a scaly eyebrow at Valanter. "No magic, you say? Do you not forget who they are descended from? The line of kings is steeped in it!"

No longer able to keep silent Killian burst out, "My wife Avana has already called upon her dragon and successfully shifted, Valanter. Truly the royal family has magic in their blood."

Shock crossed Valanter's face at this news. "Why did you not speak of this before?"

"Avana contacted me shortly after we arrived in the city. Right before our meeting. She mindspoke with me," Killian said.

Laughter again rolled from the great dragon. "The Queen is daring. She is not afraid to defend her people. Take heart at her initiative, Valanter. You yourself had high hopes for her as ruler of Amaroth."

"I suppose that is how it must be then," Valanter said quietly. "I do not like it, but you have shown me my fears are invalid."

"Not invalid. You are wise to fear. And you are partially right. They are not yet ready to wield the heartstone," Nokoa replied. He stared directly at Aohdan. "But they will be."

To Aohdan the dragon's words seemed to emanate from inside him. Nokoa was in his head. Reading his mind. Probing his heart. Part of Aohdan knew he should be afraid of this ancient creature, but there was no malice on the part of the dragon. Only curiosity.

"Young Aohdan, you are the key. You are a unique combination of human, dwarf, and *Elestari*. You too must shift. Only after you have mastered your dragon will you be strong enough to carry the heartstone and wield it," Nokoa stated to the group, but addressing Aohdan.

Aohdan's heart began to pound, trying to escape the confines of his ribs. He found that his traveling companions and the elves were staring at him. Aohdan sought his father's eyes that conveyed courage and pride. Then his gaze flicked to Valanter. The elf king was expressionless. Yet something like hope lurked behind the king's gaze.

Turning, Aohdan was met with the bright eyes of Nokoa. "I do not know how to shift, but I will learn."

"I will teach you to shift and as much about magic as I can in the limited time we have," Nokoa said. "The sooner you can set this evil to right the better."

Caleb stepped toward his grandson and put a hand on him. "Nokoa is a good teacher."

"And we must leave him with his pupil," Valanter said. "The less distractions the better. Come now. Bentaris will retrieve Aohdan after his first lesson is over."

Wordlessly, the group returned the way they had come leaving Aohdan alone with the ancient dragon.

Chapter 22

STANDING IN FRONT OF NOKOA, AOHDAN felt exposed. The dragon seemed to know everything about him and he knew nothing of this great creature. In order to learn from him, he would need to set aside his fears and trust Nokoa.

Breaking the silence Nokoa spoke, "You have an extraordinary advantage, Aohdan. You are still young. You are familiar with the *Elestari*. Most importantly you already have a bond."

Aohdan flinched. He couldn't help it. Saoirse's loss was too raw. He swallowed hard. "The bond was broken."

"Really? Is she dead?"

"Well no… at least that is what we were told," Aohdan said, frustration and confusion welling inside him.

Nokoa brought his house-sized head closer to Aohdan. "Then it is not truly broken. Saoirse cut you off, but you will be able to find her."

"How shall I find her?"

To Aohdan's dismay, Nokoa replied, "You will find her by shifting."

This was not the answer that he wanted to hear. Nokoa spoke in riddles. What did shifting have to do with his bond to Saoirse?

With a silent growl of frustration, Aohdan threw back his shoulders and crossed his arms. "Then I am ready to shift."

"Good." Nokoa chuckled. "Then we will begin."

The dragon slid closer to Aohdan, carefully uncoiling the front half of his body from around the tree.

"Place your hand on my leg and close your eyes. I want you to feel my magic," Nokoa instructed.

Taking a deep breath, Aohdan walked up to Nokoa. He was an ant compared to the dragon. Reaching out he placed his hand on the iridescent scales and closed his eyes. Instantly a surge of powerful magic flowed through him.

He went rigid from the shock. Nokoa's mind was a completely different universe. At first it was unfathomable. He was drowning in magic and dragon. Then he felt something inside him stir. It responded to the vastness of Nokoa. Gasping, he grabbed onto the thing. He let it overwhelm him. Whatever it was, it understood Nokoa in a way that Aohdan did not.

Suddenly, Aohdan was attacked by a blast of magic nearly dropping him to his knees. The thing inside him responded with a roar and it raised up a shield for his mind. Without warning, Aohdan realized that his body was changing shape. Elongating, growing new sinew and muscle that had not been there before.

His eyes flew open and the world had changed. Everything was clearer. He was amazed at the myriad of colors that he could now see. Some things appeared to shimmer with their own light. He realized that it was magic emanating from them that caused them to glow.

"There is a pool nearby where you may see your transformation," Nokoa said in a pleased voice.

Taking hesitant steps in his new body Aohdan walked to the pool. Though he knew what was coming he was still astonished by the figure that met him in the pool. He had become a glittering black dragon! At first, he was repulsed that his dragon was so similar to Killkari, but upon closer inspection Aohdan realized he was nothing like him.

Killkari had red eyes that sparked with anger whereas Aohdan's were still his own. The bright blue of a summer sky. Next, he noticed that his scales seemed to glitter a black so dark that they were nearly blue. Killkari was a matte black. His scales sucked in light and did not reflect it. Aohdan's on the other hand shimmered where the light touched them.

Trying out his voice, Aohdan spoke, "I...I did it. I shifted!"

He stretched his long body and shook out his wings as Nokoa replied, "You did well young one. You have found your dragon. It will help you use your magic to handle the heartstone and reach Saoirse."

"It feels strange, but somehow I know my dragon has been part of me my whole life," Aohdan murmured to himself.

"It has lain dormant until you called on it," Nokoa said. "Now you must let it become as much a part of you as your other shape."

Already Aohdan could feel this was becoming true for him. Abruptly, he found his mind again under magical attack. He scrambled to block the foreign entity, barely able to raise a shield in time. Panting heavily, he looked up to see Nokoa smiling at him.

"You learn quickly, but there is an easier way to protect yourself," Nokoa stated.

Shaking his head to clear his mind Aohdan asked, "What should I do?"

"You must build a barrier around your mind. Visualize yourself building an indestructible wall. Identify your weaknesses and fortify those places with extra care. Once you have your wall built it will be there permanently. However, it requires tending. Every night you must check it for signs of wear. Especially after a mind battle with another. It will be your first line of defense and should keep out all but the most skilled," Nokoa explained.

Aohdan spent the next hour carefully crafting a ward around his mind, which Nokoa swiftly probed for defects and lectured him on how to improve it. Finally, he created a barrier that met with the old dragon's approval. Then they took a short break.

Closing his eyes, Aohdan lay down his head stretched out on the ground. He curled his tail around his body and folded his wings back. The grass was a soft velvet against his scales. His sense of smell was heightened and he breathed in all the new scents.

Aohdan could smell the musty scent of tiny mice that scurried through the grass around the base of the spruce. Then there was the gingery smell of the trilling crickets. These scents were overlaid by the dozens of different flowers and plants that each carried a unique smell, varying from sweet to spicy. The purple spruce itself had become even more attractive. The scent of vanilla it carried was much stronger, but now it held undercurrents of honey, almond, and cinnamon.

For Aohdan it was overwhelming. His dragon seemed to be familiar with and able to identify each new smell, while his human side was barely able to guess what it was. Even the grass smelled different. It was as if he could smell the very life of the things around him.

To add to all of this, his hearing had improved. Not only could he smell the mice, but he could hear them rustling. And the crickets had been amplified to a level where he could pinpoint the exact location of each tiny bug. All of the sensory input was enough to make him want to put his paws over his ears.

"Use your barrier, Aohdan."

Aohdan pulled his head up abruptly, tilting his head to look at Nokoa.

"Everything that overwhelms you can be moderated by using your ward to shield your mind," Nokoa explained.

Feeling too inundated to answer, Aohdan simply concentrated on toning down the distractions as Nokoa had instructed. He was relieved when he was successful after a few tries. He enjoyed a long minute of peace before Nokoa broke in again.

"You're ready to reach for Saoirse. You have sufficiently protected your mind and shown me that you can weed through distractions."

This news got Aohdan's full attention and he nearly jumped up, when Nokoa again cut him off.

"Being relaxed will aid you in your search. Stay where you are. Picture her and reach for the bond."

Aohdan closed his eyes again. In his mind he pictured Saoirse. The way her silver hair floated around her shoulders. Her violet-colored eyes that sparked with life. The graceful way she handled her sword. Her laughter and most importantly her voice. The trace of accent it held that always managed to make her sound exotic. He concentrated on all of these things.

Aohdan let his newfound magic flow through him. Saoirse was out there. He knew it. He searched for her letting his heart take him farther and farther away from the forest. Across the Wilds and into the mountains. Through woods and caverns he sought her. Then he found her.

His heart somersaulted with joy. Saoirse was far, far away, but she was alive. Pinpointing her location would be very difficult. Mind-speaking, he called out her name, "Saoirse!"

He waited to hear from her. There was nothing. He cried out again, "Saoirse!" Still nothing in response. Aohdan reached out for her mind, trying to reform their bond. To his alarm he could feel nothing. Over and over he tried to reach her, yet she did not hear him. A wave of frustration crashed over him. He withdrew his mind and brought himself fully back to the clearing feeling utterly spent.

Nokoa appeared to understand what had transpired. "You have reached her. You are making progress, but you must regain your former connection."

Aggravation welled up from Aohdan. "Why won't she respond to me?"

"Because your magic is not yet strong enough," Nokoa answered with infuriating calmness.

"Then what is the point of seeking her out if I can't properly reach out to her?" Aohdan questioned.

Nokoa growled softly, "You need practice. She gives you purpose."

Aohdan ground his teeth and dug his claws into the soft soil. This was not the answer he wanted to hear, but it was logical. He was exhausted. Though time was critical, he wanted to stop and sleep. He was sure Nokoa knew this, but he wasn't going to give the ancient dragon the satisfaction of seeing him give up.

So Aohdan tried again. Over and over he tried to regain his deep connection to Saoirse. Each time he failed. He'd have better luck talking to a brick wall, he decided. To add to the strain Nokoa wanted him to begin practicing flying while he continued to hammer at the link between him and Saoirse.

Flying was reviving for Aohdan. It was addictive. His instincts were strong and he was able to master many of the maneuvers Nokoa called for. But on the other hand, he still felt unfamiliar with this new body and multitasking had never been a strong suit for him. When Nokoa finally declared the lesson over, Aohdan transformed back into a man. He nearly fell over from exhaustion.

He was grateful that Bentaris could help him back to his room. When he did, he collapsed onto the bed and immediately fell deeply asleep.

Chapter 23

FOR THREE DAYS AOHDAN WRESTLED WITH his connection to Saoirse. Nothing he tried seemed to work. Without his dragon he knew he would have gone crazy over his inability to reach her. He practiced shifting constantly. There was much to be learned about his dragon form. Being a dragon came naturally compared to the magic that Nokoa wanted him to work. Nokoa knew just how far to push him before reaching the breaking point.

Aohdan flew for hours on end while performing complicated spells. Nokoa taught him how to attack another simply by using his mind. Nokoa constantly forced him to think on the go all the while pestering Aohdan to connect with Saoirse.

Early on the fourth morning he woke up to a knock on his door. It was Bentaris.

"Good morning, Aohdan. Nokoa requests that you have a change in your schedule."

Aohdan sat up and rubbed the sleep from his eyes with the back of his hand. "What does he want from me now?" he replied. His mind was still fogged over from sleep. His body ached from the strenuous training it had been through the last three days.

The elf grinned, knowing full well the ways of the old dragon. "Nokoa requests that you go to the smithy to forge a sword."

"But I have a sword." Aohdan frowned.

"Not like this. You need a stone to help store your magic in. Since you're a warrior, the logical choice to place a stone is in your sword," Bentaris answered, handing him his boots to pull on.

Aohdan yawned as he pulled his tunic over his head. "What if I go back to bed instead of going to the smithy?" he growled at the elf.

Bentaris laughed, his eyes flashing. "Then I'll have to carry you."

Aohdan raised an eyebrow at him. "You wouldn't."

"Oh, yes I would! I would do whatever it takes to keep you on task. Because the alternative is to risk the wrath of Nokoa. And that is not something I would wish on my worst enemy." Bentaris suddenly became serious.

Groaning, Aohdan glared at the elf, but stood up and followed him through the palace. The smithy was located outdoors in a rocky outcrop to minimize the chance of anything catching fire. When they reached the smithy, the first thing Aohdan noticed was the heat. An enormous furnace glowed and sent sparks into the dark early morning sky. He saw two figures outlined in the darkness.

One he recognized was his father, the other unfamiliar.

"Good morning," a strange voice reached out. "Welcome, Aohdan. I have heard much about you, but we have never met. My name is Nedanael."

Recognition ran through Aohdan. "I know your name. You are the great elven smith who my mother rescued and a friend of my grandfather."

Nedanael let out a quiet laugh. "At least you have heard of me. I'm ashamed that we have not met before, but my appetite for traveling was lost after my capture. I was heartened to see Caleb with you. I have not seen him since the battle against the goblins before you were born."

Killian interjected, "We don't fault you for keeping to the Greenwood. Avana and Caleb know why you are content to stay within the elven realm."

Bentaris interrupted them. "I'm sorry to hurry you, but Nokoa specified that you start work on a sword as quickly as possible. That's why he wanted you to start so early. I have other duties to attend, but I wish you the best of luck, Aohdan."

"Then let us begin," Nedanael replied with a smile in his voice. "I shall enjoy a challenge."

Bentaris bid them farewell as Nedanael spoke over a glow orb and a soft light lit up the smithy. "Young Aohdan, you must first choose a stone that best fits your magic. I have many that you can choose from."

He gestured to a bench covered in stones in all shapes and sizes, from semiprecious jewels and rare diamonds to smooth river rocks. Aohdan walked to the bench and stared at the stones. How was he supposed to choose the right one? He picked up an emerald that caught his eye. He tried to imagine storing some of his magic inside of it. For some reason it didn't feel right to him so he put it back. Next, he touched an amethyst that reminded him terribly of Saoirse. This stone was closer, but still not right. He looked over the bench again.

This time he noticed a medium-sized black rock resting on the far corner of the bench. It was nondescript and seemed to lack the luster of the other stones around it. Aohdan picked up the black rock. Two things happened when he touched it: first, a spark of magic ran through him from the stone; second, the stone began to glow in his hand.

"What's the meaning of this?" he asked, nearly dropping the stone in surprise. He looked over at the elf who was smiling at him.

"An interesting choice, Aohdan. That is what we call a sister of a heartstone. It seems to have chosen you as much as you have chosen it," Nedanael replied.

"A sister stone?" Aohdan and Killian both asked at once, causing them to laugh.

Nedanael smiled with them. "For whatever reason a heartstone seems to only be able to contain so much magic. A sister stone is what it creates when its magic overflows. They are not nearly as powerful as a heartstone but have the characteristics of one. They are nearly indestructible and can also nullify each other when touching."

Aohdan held the stone out to Nedanael. "But why is it glowing?"

"It glows because it is reacting to your magic," Nedanael said.

"May I see it?" Killian asked, holding out his hand.

Aohdan nodded and carefully dropped the stone into Killian's outstretched palm. To his surprise the stone continued to glow. He noticed a shiver ran through his father as he cradled the stone.

"Fascinating," murmured Nedanael. "You both have an affinity for the sister stone. How unusual."

Killian's eyes went dark. "What does that mean?"

"It means you have magic in your blood, Killian. Also, that you are able to use the sister stone," Nedanael replied thoughtfully.

"I don't quite follow…" Killian said.

Nedanael frowned slightly as he puzzled over the matter. "I believe it has to do with your heritage. You are of the royal dwarf line."

"Yes, but the crown would never reach me. Halfor is my uncle," Killian answered. "Besides we are not wizards or sorcerers."

"That may be true, but all royal blood has traces of magic in it," Nedanael stated. "Your magic clearly awakens the stone. Why it responds to both of you, I have no idea. I will have to look into this phenomenon further."

Killian gave the black sister stone back to Aohdan. The stone kept its glow as long as one of them was touching it.

With a sigh Nedanael said, "But as much as I would like to pursue this further, we have a task at hand. Let us begin."

The master smith and Killian worked tirelessly with Aohdan. Another three days went by as they hammered and shaped the blade. Nedanael taught Aohdan the strongest spells to weave into the bright silver to strengthen it. They set the sister stone into the pommel. For the final task Nedanael had Aohdan shift to his dragon form.

"Breathe your dragon fire over the blade. This will give it an added protection. Then only someone wielding another sister or heartstone will be able to shatter it," he instructed.

Aohdan was nervous that he was about to melt all of their hard work into a bright silver puddle on the anvil it was sitting on. But he kept his reservations to himself. He did as he was instructed. He shifted to his dragon and bathed the sword in flame. To his relief, the sword did not melt. Instead it appeared to take in the flame. When he ceased his fire, the sword continued to flicker. It glowed with a soft blue light that reminded him of his mother's sword, Stelenacht.

He shifted back to his human form, eager to take up his new weapon, but Nedanael stopped him.

"You must name your sword. Only then will it be properly yours."

Aohdan skimmed over names in his head. He did not want to misname this sword. Finally, one stuck out from the others. "Illista," he said quietly.

Killian smiled tiredly at him. "Strength. I think that is an appropriate name."

"Illista is a good name," Nedanael agreed. "Now you may take up your sword."

Reaching out, Aohdan picked up the newly christened sword from where it lay on the anvil. He spoke its name as he touched it and the sword lit up with a blue flame. The black sister stone in the pommel pulsed with energy. He swung the sword experimentally feeling the weight of it. It was perfectly balanced. Illista moved in tune with him. He looked over at his father.

Killian beamed with pride, his dark hair and beard a wild mess from their exertions. Looking at him, Aohdan realized that he was probably just as much a mess as his father, but somehow it was fitting. Their effort had been grueling, but the prize was worth it. Feeling exultant, he offered Illista to his father.

Killian took the sword reverently from his son. He too swung the great sword, feeling it out for imperfection. Aohdan watched as his father began a series of complex cuts going faster and faster with each swing. He could see the wild light of mischief in Killian's eyes grow to a blaze. With a mighty yell Killian brought Illista down with a ringing clang on the anvil, neatly splitting it in half.

Dazed, Killian looked over at Aohdan and Nedanael. "I got a bit carried away..." he trailed off with a sheepish grin.

Nedanael had a bemused expression as he studied the broken anvil. After a moment he said, "Well at least we know the sword is strong."

Aohdan couldn't help but laugh. "I think you're right. Actually, this will be an excellent test for me. I'd like to see if I can repair the anvil."

"Very well," Nedanael said, crossing his arms.

Aohdan crouched down next to the two halves of the anvil. He put a hand on either piece. Closing his eyes he pictured the anvil whole again. He felt the magic begin to well within him responding to his call. He opened his eyes. Blue flames ran down his arms and over his hands. Carefully, he pulled the two pieces together. When they met, the seam was engulfed in his flame. Aohdan envisioned the split sealing. In another few moments the glow of his fire began to die. When it had completely faded, he stood up. The anvil was whole again.

"Well done!" Nedanael complimented him. "You have learned a great deal in a short time. Nokoa will be pleased. I know you are tired, but I think you should go to him immediately."

Aohdan agreed. He hoped that the dragon felt he was ready to carry the heartstone so they could continue their journey. Killian handed him Illista. Removing his old sword from its scabbard, he replaced it with Illista. He left his old sword in the care of his father before he hurried to meet with Nokoa.

When he reached the secret clearing, he found Nokoa stretched out across the lawn with only his tail wrapped around the tree. The old dragon did not appear surprised at his arrival.

"You have succeeded, young Aohdan," Nokoa rumbled, shaking the ground beneath Aohdan's feet.

Aohdan pulled out Illista and held it up for Nokoa to inspect. The great hoary head bent over him, examining the blade.

"It is well made. What did you name it?" Nokoa asked and Aohdan told him.

Nokoa gave a toothy grin. "A sword named strength. It fits you. Now, young one, call Saoirse."

Aohdan sighed. He had been afraid that Nokoa would ask him to try again. A streak of stubbornness suddenly flared in him. He knew Saoirse would not give up on him if the situation was reversed.

He sat down on a large stone. Unbuckling his sword, he set Illista in its scabbard across his lap. Taking hold of the hilt, he let his mind seek out Saoirse. She was still far, far away. He came in contact with her mind shield. It was as unyielding as before. With every ounce of will he battled against it. Aohdan sweated and strained as he tried to break through.

As he wrestled with Saoirse's conscience, Aohdan had a revelation. Why not try to reach her heart? All this time he had been trying to open her mind to him, but it was her heart that held their bond. Aohdan withdrew his fierce assault on Saoirse's mind.

The response was immediate. When his mind touched her heart, their bond was re-forged as though struck with lightning. A tremor ran through Aohdan. The hole inside him filled with Saoirse's heart. Their two magics crashed together and he sensed the shock from Saoirse over being reunited. Even more strongly he felt her dragon respond to his own.

It roared in astonishment, that changed to delight. "Aohdan! Oh, Aohdan we are not separated….and you're a dragon!"

"Yes, I am a dragon. I had help learning to shift from the elves and a friend," Aohdan replied feeling overcome now that he had finally reached Saoirse. He sent her a rapid series of pictures of the events that had led up to their reconnection. When he finished, he quickly asked, "Are you alright? Where are you?"

Saoirse shuddered as she responded, "I am chained to the rocks in a hidden fortress deep in the Cascade Mountains. The place is crawling with goblins. But it gets worse." She paused, taking a deep breath. "The *Elestari* are here too. They are under the sway of Killkari. The few who are too strong for him are kept chained like I am."

Through Saoirse, Aohdan beheld over a dozen men and women along with several dragons manacled to a towering stone wall. As he did so, he realized that Saoirse was badly injured. He had been so elated at breaking through to her he hadn't noticed the buzz of pain that filled her.

"You're hurt," Aohdan growled.

"Yes. But I am alive," she replied, dodging his question.

Ignoring her answer, he inspected her injuries. He was horrified when he finished. Saoirse's wings were a tattered mess. One was broken while the other had been twisted so badly it might as well have been broken. She was covered in deep gouges from claws and teeth. She had ribs broken on both sides. And to top it off the tendons in her right hind had nearly been severed.

Anguish and rage clouded his mind. He wanted to rip Killkari apart. His grip on Illista tightened.

"Please, Aohdan," Saoirse's voice pierced his anger. "Don't be rash. The time will come for revenge."

Aohdan let Saoirse's words quiet his rage though it galled him. Instead he focused his energies on her wounds. He started with her wings. She would be the most mobile if he could heal them. Saoirse hissed when she realized what he was doing.

"You will overtax yourself, Aohdan," she said with deep worry in her tone. "The distance is too great."

Again, Aohdan ignored her. He kept his attention firmly on healing her wounded wings. It took him several minutes, but when he finished he could tell a difference in her pain level. Next he moved on to her ribs and then her torn tendons. As he repaired the last of the injured leg muscle he sensed he had reached his limit.

Her cuts and scrapes would have to wait. He felt the flood of relief from Saoirse as she was released from the stress and pain of her major injuries.

"Thank you," Saoirse thrummed. A shy gratitude emanated from her along with a hint of something more. Aohdan now was endlessly tired. Nonetheless, Saoirse's feelings were not lost on him. Before he could let his heart run away with him, he said, "I must go now. We will come for you and your people."

"Farewell then," Saoirse answered. They each keenly felt the lessening of the other's presence as they broke off their conversation.

Coming back to himself, Aohdan felt whole for the first time in days. He looked up to see Nokoa eyeing him with a smug look. "You figured out the secret to reach her. You have done well. Now you are ready to take the heartstone."

Elation at this pronouncement recharged Aohdan's exhausted body. Standing up he buckled Illista to his side. "I am pleased to hear you say so."

"Go to the base of the tree. I will call the stone from beneath the roots. Then you may take it and be on your way," Nokoa ordered.

Aohdan did as he was instructed. He stood at the foot of the great tree suddenly in awe again of its vastness. The bark shimmered, while the grass growing around the tree moved with a life of its own though there was no wind. Nokoa began to thrum a low ringing note that slowly grew louder till it filled every part of the forest. As he did so, the ground at Aohdan's feet vibrated and rippled. He stepped back in surprise.

The roots of the tree came pushing up from the ground in a churning, writhing ball where they wrapped around something. Nokoa's thrum took on a different tone and the seething mass slowed. It split open to reveal a fist-sized blood red stone. The stone echoed Nokoa's thrum with a humming of its own.

Cautiously, Aohdan picked up the heartstone. It let out a burst of white light when he touched it momentarily blinding him. The power that ran through him from the stone was almost too much to bear, but instead of fighting it, he let it replenish his spent stores of magic. The stone responded by quieting down, appearing to be satisfied.

For the first time, Aohdan realized the true power and danger of carrying the heartstone. To hold it was intoxicating. He was instantly stronger than any other being in the forest, except for Nokoa. Aohdan knew that if he wished, he would be unstoppable.

But the sway of power and magic was only alluring for a moment. He did not want to conquer the world. All Aohdan wanted was to be a good king when the time came. He also knew that he would never win Saoirse with magic. That thought made it all the easier for him to turn away from the supremacy the heartstone offered.

"You have passed the test," Nokoa said.

With senses heightened from the magic, Aohdan turned to the dragon. "I understand now why you pushed me. I will carry the heartstone, but I promise to return it."

"I have faith that you will succeed," Nokoa replied. "If you ever wish to return and study more, I have not had an apprentice in a thousand years."

"I am honored, Nokoa," Aohdan said humbly. "If my path takes me to a place where I can do so, I will study under you."

"Farewell then, young prince. You must away on your journey. Make all haste. I shall not rest easy till you have returned the heartstone," Nokoa intoned.

Aohdan bowed respectfully. "Farewell, Nokoa. I shall return when the task is over."

Turning on his heel he left, his heart full of confidence for the first time since reaching the elven kingdom.

Chapter 24

NOW THAT AOHDAN COULD CARRY THE heartstone, it was time to return to Amaroth. Valanter gave them a map leading to the hidden fortress. When they saw the map, the location of the fortress struck fear in their hearts. It was far too close to the Tiered Mountain. Killian was especially upset. He immediately spoke to Avana, asking her to warn King Halfor.

At first, Aohdan wanted to fly them back to Amaroth as Saoirse had. However, he was voted down by the elves and the other members of this traveling party. Valanter in particular was against the idea.

"If you were attacked on the way here, there is a high probability you would be attacked on the way back. A dragon is an unusual sight. Carrying the heartstone you will want to draw as little attention to yourselves as possible," he said.

The others agreed with him. Instead Caleb had a different idea. "What if we call Finris and Fallon? Wolves can still cross quickly, but they are a normal part of the Wild. No one will think different of them for being on the move."

"But don't forget that Finris was supposed to be protecting Amaroth," Killian added.

Caleb nodded. "True. But he is High Chief over all the packs. He can send others to come and carry us." He looked over at Aohdan. "Do you think you can reach out to Fallon? Since he is familiar with Saoirse, I believe he would respond better to your mindspeak."

"Yes, I believe so," Aohdan replied.

Stepping away from the group, Aohdan focused on searching for Fallon. He started near Amaroth, guessing that the wolf would be with his father Finris. He was not wrong. He found Fallon a few leagues away from the city, prowling in search of lunch.

"Fallon," Aohdan called out to the wolf.

He felt the wolf jump in surprise at the voice. Fallon let out a fierce growl.

"What are you doing in my head, Aohdan? How is this possible?"

"I have learned to shift, my friend. And I have magic," Aohdan said.

Aohdan sensed Fallon shaking his head in wonder. "Your magic is very strong. I feel it through every bone in my body. But not all the magic is yours. This is a strange puzzle."

"You are right. But I do not feel comfortable telling you everything till we meet face to face."

"That is wise. I do not wish to endanger you. Besides there is trouble here. Goblin hordes are coming down from the mountains. They carry bright silver weapons. We have kept them away from the city for now, but they are increasing their numbers," Fallon growled.

"You bring ill news! This makes my request all the more urgent," Aohdan said.

The wolf replied, "What do you ask of me?"

"We need transport across the Wilds that will not draw attention to us. I could fly us back to Amaroth, but we fear attack. We hoped that you could send some wolves to aid us."

"I will send out a message right away. You shall have your wolves. I wish I could join you, but it would take far too long. Besides I am needed here. Finris keeps close quarters with Avana. They plan to march to the Tiered Mountain. They are afraid the dwarves are in danger. Meanwhile, I am in charge of protecting Amaroth," Fallon explained.

Aohdan answered, "Thank you, friend. I am both gladdened and frightened by your words. We shall be on the lookout for the wolves you send."

With those words he broke his connection to Fallon and returned to the group.

"I spoke to Fallon and bring both good and bad tidings," Aohdan said.

Andrew groused, "Well, get on with it! We haven't got all day."

Aohdan allowed a small smile to cross his face at the cranky Ranger as he told of Fallon's news.

Valanter agreed with the plan. "Avana has done well to strengthen the Guard of Amaroth. Her troops will greatly aid Halfor if he is attacked. Besides, it is better to draw Killkari's attention to the Tiered Mountain than Amaroth. It is more defendable from dragon fire than the city."

Aohdan shuddered. Visions of Amaroth on fire raced through his head. It was one thing to be attacked by goblins and Ice Trolls, but quite another to face off with an army of dragons. His mind was brought back to the conversation with Caleb's words.

"We should expect the wolves to reach us within the next day depending on how close they are," he said.

"The elves have prepared your packs," Valanter answered. "You should head for the edge of the forest with all haste. Speed is your friend."

Caleb nodded. "Indeed. We thank you for your hospitality and aid, Valanter. We are indebted to you."

Valanter waved away his thanks. "If you succeed in defeating Killkari, it is the elves who will be indebted to you. We do not wish to fight in another war."

With warm goodbyes, the travelers bid Valanter farewell. Bentaris and Nedanael accompanied them as they traveled through the forest. Aohdan kept the heartstone in a leather bag hung round his neck. He and the others noticed how the forest seemed to follow him.

Strange animals from the depths of the forest paralleled them. A dangerous pack of orange-and-black-striped Thlaycine wolf cats trailed the group. The normally ferocious predators padded quietly along, never offering so much as a growl. The hummingbirds and butterflies congregated over them alighting on Aohdan any time they stopped to rest. Then there were the trees. They creaked and groaned as the heartstone passed by them, bending their branches low to touch Aohdan.

Before his transformation, Aohdan would have been alarmed by the forest. Yet now he only felt quiet confidence. He was grateful that his companions also took everything in stride. All of them had seen their share of strange and magical things in recent days.

They reached the edge of the Greenwood as the sun was beginning to set in the west. The group settled down under the trees to wait for the wolves to arrive. The light faded away and the stars began to glitter in their starry fields. But even as the quiet of darkness settled over the Wilds, the forest behind them came to life in even greater force than before.

The trees congregated around them, swaying though there was no breeze. The animals of the Greenwood howled, screeched, and yammered. Aohdan felt like every beast in the wood was mourning the leaving of the heartstone. Dozens of pairs of eyes gleamed from the depths of the forest. Bats circled and swooped above their heads. Nearby, a spotted panther sat next to a regal stag with antlers that glinted silver in the starlight. A tawny owl hooted softly on a branch above them.

"The Greenwood is troubled," Bentaris said as he took in the raucous chorus emanating from the forest.

Andrew harrumphed and rolled his eyes. "What gave you that idea?"

"Are you sure that is all right for me to take the heartstone?" Aohdan asked as he listened to the Greenwood.

"You must take the heartstone," Nedanael answered. "Killkari is a bringer of destruction. Eventually his fires would touch the forest. It is better to be upset than destroyed."

Before Aohdan could reply, a distant howl rose up from the empty stretch of the Wilds that rolled away from them.

"The wolves are coming," Caleb said with a smile. Then he threw back his head and let out a bone chilling howl of his own. The wolves responded to him, their voices rising and falling in an eerie song.

The companions now waited wordlessly for the wolves to approach. Soon they saw their silver forms floating over the dark expanse of the Wilds. Caleb approached them first.

"We thank you, wolves, for lending us your aid." Then he let out a series of low growls and snarls, speaking in the wolves' own tongue.

"We are glad to carry you, wolf friend," the lead wolf rasped out. His voice scraped over the words as if he was unused to using them. "I am Josiah, and the pack members with me are Lara, Baruk, and Essa. Come, there are goblins on the move. We should cover as much ground as we can."

Caleb nodded. "Let us bid our friends farewell and then we shall be on our way."

He turned from the wolves and back to the group. The travelers bade a sad farewell to the elves. Aohdan noted that there were tears in the eyes of Nedanael and Caleb as they embraced and said goodbye.

"I am not young anymore, old friend," Caleb said to Nedanael. "We have had some fine adventures with sword making. But I fear you will not see me again. I know my ancestors are long lived, but I feel age creeping over me. I think that this will be my last great excursion."

Aohdan's own heart twisted as he listened to his grandfather's words. He knew that Caleb was much spryer than a normal man of his age, but to hear that he was beginning to slow was still hard to take.

Nedanael replied, "If it is your last, then it has been a remarkable one. I am honored that you, Avana, and now your grandson all carry swords that were forged in my fires. If you ever wish to settle again in the Greenwood, the elves would welcome you."

Bentaris added, "You have wandered for many years, Caleb. We will mourn that your wandering is over but rejoice that you can finally rest."

With one last farewell, Caleb left the elves and led the way to the wolves. He swung himself onto the back of Josiah. Aohdan watched Caleb closely as he pulled himself onto Lara. He noticed for the first time that his grandfather's movements were not as fluid as they used to be, and he was a fraction slower than Aohdan remembered.

He wondered for the first time if this was the real reason why Avana had wanted to lead their expedition. His mother was a keen observer. Aohdan was sure she had begun to notice her father slowing down and he was surprised that he hadn't noticed it himself when they set out, but he had been completely focused on Saoirse. His thoughts were broken by the rough voice of Lara from beneath him.

"Fallon speaks highly of you. I hope that I can bear you as well as he has," she said.

Aohdan replied with a quiet laugh. "I'm glad to hear he has something good to say about me. I'm grateful that any of you are willing to carry us across the Wilds. I know your people are a proud race."

"Peril to the pack is of greater concern than our pride. Evil stalks us. It is better for us to help you stop it before it becomes too strong," Lara said.

They were interrupted by a growl from Josiah. "It is time. Hold fast, for we are going to run!" With a howl he sprang away, Caleb crouched over his back.

The other three wolves followed suit, and they raced away into the night.

Chapter 25

THE WOLVES LOPED OVER THE GROUND, eating up the leagues with determination. The pace was grueling. Their stops were for their riders more than for themselves. Josiah deemed that at best it would be five full days of traveling. And that was dependent on the riders. The wolves could travel farther without food or rest than their human counterparts.

Then, at dawn of the fourth day, they encountered trouble. They intercepted a dozen goblin scouts. The wind had been carrying the goblins' scent in the opposite direction. So the wolves were just as surprised as the goblins when they nearly collided with the foul creatures. Snarls and shouts went up. It didn't take long for them to dispatch the goblins, but they were greatly disturbed by the meeting.

The goblins had all been armed with bright silver. And they were still traveling though daylight was streaming over the horizon. Goblins hated the sun and very little would cause them to brave it. Worst of all it was obvious that the creatures had been part of a larger group what with the little food they had carried with them.

This threw the wolves into a greater hurry, though now they traveled with more caution. Their worst fears came to pass that afternoon. The wolves scented a great horde of goblins dead ahead of them. It was going to take precious time to skirt around them without being discovered. They debated on whether to wait for cover of darkness but decided against it as sunlight was still an asset against the creatures.

Their pace now slowed. They wolves slunk forward, using all of their senses to keep watch. Aohdan added his own magic to the search. The goblins were not far away and he guessed there were about three hundred or so of them. Aohdan was dismayed to find that they were heading in the same direction that they wanted to travel. More than once the wolves were forced to stop and wait while goblin scouts passed close by.

Then raucous cries rang out from behind them as the goblins discovered the pawprints of the wolves. Now it was time to throw caution to the wind. It was only a matter of time before the goblins came upon the travelers themselves.

The wolves began a deadly sprint knowing it would be a race. And a race it was. Aohdan clutched Lara's thick fur as she ran full out beneath him. Out of the corner of his eye he could see a swarm of goblins coming up over the hill on their right. Behind he could still hear the war cries of the goblins who had now spotted them.

A shower of arrows hissed over them. Aohdan turned in surprise when he heard a yelp of pain go up from Baruk's throat. An arrow had sunk into his haunch, but he powered on. At first, Aohdan was filled with confusion. Goblin arrows could not pierce the hide of a Northern wolf, but then he remembered the scouts they had met earlier. They had been armed with bright silver. *The arrows must be tipped with the metal,* he reasoned.

Putting aside his thoughts, Aohdan focused on the arrow in Baruk. He wasn't sure that he could help the wolf with so many distractions, but he felt he had to try. He imagined the arrow working its way out of the muscle. Then the torn tissue healing over. Concentrating on this image he felt the heartstone begin to glow with warmth through the bag that bounced against his throat. Aohdan glanced over at Baruk and was delighted to see the arrow slide from his hindquarter.

Another barrage of arrows fell around them. Aohdan's thoughts now turned to protecting the group. He envisioned an invisible shield covering them, similar to the one that he used to protect his mind. He smiled to himself when the next round of arrows bounced back harmlessly off his invisible protection.

The goblins were enraged at being thwarted while the wolves raced on grateful for the protection. It was a near thing as the goblins closed in from the side and behind them. Aohdan could feel Lara's ribs heaving as she took great breaths, lungs expanding. They barely burst past the angry goblins, and still the wolves ran on as if the very wings of a dragon carried them.

Finally the wolves stopped at a small stream. Their red tongues lolled as they panted, sides rising and falling rapidly. Wolf and rider alike drank deeply. The riders found that their limbs were shaky from clinging to their mounts on their wild run. Searching with his mind, Aohdan looked behind them only to find that the goblins were still in hot pursuit of them.

"The goblins are coming," he said to the group.

Killian said, "We must go on then."

"Not without a bite of food first," Andrew muttered. "We won't last long at this rate without a quick meal."

Essa spoke up. "We need a moment's rest anyway." So saying, she lay down beside the stream and closed her eyes.

The other wolves followed suit while their riders began pulling food from their rucksacks. They ate handfuls of dried fruit and meat that the elves had packed for them.

"I do not care for the way the goblins are pursuing us. A normal goblin horde of that size would have given up and gone on with their route," Caleb said as he chewed on a piece of fruit.

Andrew nodded. "It's more than us escaping them. They are driving us."

"Yes, to something unpleasant," Caleb replied.

"I'd warrant there's another host of goblins stationed outside of Amaroth," Killian said with a wry look.

Aohdan listened silently to their conversation. At their words, he let his mind go out ahead of them. He found the city and then searched around it. It didn't take him long to discover that Killian and the others were correct. Another two or three hundred goblins had camped out some distance from Amaroth.

He told the others of his findings. "You're correct. There is another host of goblins ready to ambush us ahead."

They looked round at one another wondering what to do.

Killian broke the silence. "We have to go on. There's nothing else for it. We cannot reach the hidden fortress without being resupplied."

"Agreed," Caleb said. "We should rest now like the wolves."

"I will keep watch," Aohdan volunteered. "The heartstone gives me extra strength. I am not as worn as the rest of you."

Killian eyed him with the concern but did not protest. The three sprawled out on the grass and closed their eyes grateful for a moment of respite. Aohdan sat and surveyed the peaceful scene. It was a stark contrast to the harsh reality of the goblins still pursuing them.

His thoughts wandered to Killkari. *Where had the dragon possibly acquired a heartstone? How powerful was Killkari in wielding it?* He clearly was showing signs of growing stronger.

Aohdan let a heavy sigh escape him. He knew that it was up to him to spy on Killkari and eventually confront him. But part of him was still afraid. He'd woken his dragon and magic such a short time ago. Though Nokoa had deemed him ready, he couldn't shake the images in his head. Killkari attacking Saoirse in the mountains and again on the edge of the Greenwood. Saoirse battered and chained. *How could he defeat this pure evil?* Aohdan looked around him again.

He smiled as he did so. He would defeat Killkari with help. That was the only way it would happen.

Quiet confidence filled him with this knowledge. With his mind at peace, Aohdan let the others rest for a few minutes longer before urging them to get up. The travelers and the wolves rose. They took one last drink from the stream before continuing on. The wolves ran with a renewed vigor.

Now their flight was going to be a marathon. A measure of who could last the longest, it was still a day's journey to Amaroth. The wolves kept a steady pace as the sun faded away to darkness in the west. The wolves would run all night and it was up to their riders to keep themselves awake enough to not fall off.

By the next morning Aohdan could feel his strength fading. They had stopped only once during the night and he had again volunteered to keep watch. His actions had allowed the group to rest more fully thus enabling the wolves to put more distance between themselves and the goblins chasing them.

Though he had given them a lead, he would soon need a rest of his own. Aohdan also knew that the wolves would need water. He was relieved when Josiah eventually led them to a hidden pool. Aohdan stumbled off Lara, his eyes straining to keep open. Now it was his turn to rest. He didn't even bother to pull off his pack. He flopped back into the grass and let his eyes fall shut.

Aohdan awoke to the cold nudge of Lara's nose. He rubbed his eyes with the back of his hand. Groaning, he stood up. The others were already mounted.

"We let you sleep as long as possible," Killian said.

"Thank you. I needed it," he replied as he swung onto Lara.

Aohdan could tell he physically felt renewed from the rest, but his mind was still fuzzy. Pulling his canteen around he took a quick swig of water. The drink helped to clear the fog. Replacing the canteen he said, "I'm ready." Then they were off again.

Chapter 26

NOW THAT HIS MIND WAS CLEAR, Aohdan looked ahead to try and gauge where the goblin force was between them and Amaroth. The goblins were closer than he would have liked. He told the others. Then he contacted his mother.

"Mother," he said, reaching out to Avana.

He felt her react to him in surprise, but she recovered herself quickly. "You too, Aohdan? Though I should not be surprised. Cynthia hinted that you should learn to shift. But I am prattling needlessly. What is it?" Avana asked.

"We are almost to Amaroth, but a goblin host stands between us and the city. Behind us we are being pursued by another horde. We could use some help."

"Help you shall have! We have been keeping watch on the goblins near Amaroth. I did not know that there was another host farther out, but we had suspicions," Avana said.

Aohdan smiled to himself. "It will be good to see you, Mother."

"I will be glad to see you safe. I will send Zellnar to aid you. He knows to take great care for the goblins carry bright silver. But I'm guessing you already know that."

Aohdan replied, "First hand, unfortunately. We are all well though."

"Good. I will not detain you any longer." With those words, Avana cut off the connection.

The odds against them were much evened out. He relayed the news of Zellnar to the others who met the tidings with smiles. Only a few hours later, they were delighted to see the form of a dragon wheeling overhead. The dragon shadowed them as they continued their journey toward Amaroth.

They were drawing near the city when Aohdan noticed Zellnar was flying decidedly lower. Suddenly the dragon went into a steep dive over the hill in front of them. They all heard the roar that came from the dragon's throat and the accompanying hoarse cries from goblins.

Loosing their swords, the riders plunged over the hilltop. In the shallow valley below them Zellnar was wreaking havoc on the goblins. However, the goblin archers were retaliating. The arrows bounced harmlessly off his hard scales but were able to pierce his wings.

Unfortunately, wolves and riders had been spotted as they rode farther into the depression. Aohdan quickly threw up a shield around them against the arrows that now sought them. Several dozen goblins charged the travelers. The wolves snarled and snapped, flinging goblins aside as they ran through their ranks.

In Aohdan's hands, Illista gleamed a dangerous blue. What goblins Lara did not kill, were promptly dispatched by Aohdan. They broke through the goblin lines and headed for the next hilltop. There they were met with a terrible surprise.

A deep bellow echoed over the valley and three monstrous Ice Trolls charged over the hill. Their blueish gray skin glinted in the sunlight. Black horns, akin to that of a bull, sprouted from their heads and were polished to deadly points. They wore hideous black armor with the skulls of their victims swinging from their belts. Aohdan sensed the deep chill of fear that ran through the wolves. Ice Trolls were their mortal enemy. He berated himself for not sensing their presence, but his frustration was short lived as the Trolls attacked.

Each Troll carried a heavy spiked club in one hand, while in the other a short sword covered in the runes of evil spells. With a fierce growl, Josiah launched himself at the lead Troll. Caleb swung his sword Ristfaeth as the wolf sprang, slashing the Troll from shoulder to hip. The Troll fell dead beneath Josiah's paws. Seeing their comrade fall infuriated the remaining Ice Trolls.

One flung his heavy club at Lara. The wolf leaped away, but the handle of the club managed to catch her hind legs sending her and Aohdan tumbling. Lara rolled once and was instantly back on her feet, fur bristling, teeth bared. Aohdan's first thought was of the heartstone. As he scrambled to his feet he was relieved to still find the pouch still safely secured.

He barely made it up before the Ice Troll was battering him with its sword. Illista threw blue sparks with each blow that it deflected. In a fury, Lara attacked the Troll from behind sinking her teeth deep into the Troll's shoulder. Roaring in pain, the Troll frantically tried to grab hold of the wolf.

Aohdan was quick to take the advantage Lara had given him. With a sweep of his blade he hamstrung the Troll, bringing the vile creature to its knees. The Troll swung its sword indiscriminately, forcing Lara to let go. Flinging back its head the Troll attempted to impale the wolf on its horns. A tip caught the wolf along her side and cut a bright ribbon of red down her snowy flank.

This was the Troll's downfall. Its neck was exposed and Illista came biting down in retribution. The Ice Troll's head toppled from its body as Aohdan ran to the injured Lara. The others had killed the last Ice Troll. Behind them Zellnar kept the remaining goblins at bay.

A scarlet stain soaked the white fur of the wolf and she shuddered when Aohdan touched her side. Immediately, he began to heal the wound. Soon, Lara's bloody fur was the only sign she had been injured. Though healed, Aohdan knew she was weakened from the loss of blood.

"Thank you for your bravery," he said to her. "Are you well enough to carry me or shall I shift?"

Lara gave him a thoughtful look. "Thank you for healing me. It is not far now. I will bear you till the end."

So Aohdan pulled himself onto her back and they resumed their journey. Zellnar followed after them. Aohdan could sense the dragon was in pain from the many arrows that had pierced his wings. He knew he could heal Zellnar's injuries, but there were so many it would take too long in their present situation. Now he needed to focus on making sure there were no more surprises before they reached Amaroth.

When the walls of Amaroth came into sight, wolves and travelers alike let out a yell of celebration. They reached the city as the last horn of the day sounded the closing of the gates for the night. They were greeted heartily by the guards clad in the red and gold of Amaroth.

The wolves departed from them at the gate, preferring the Wilds to the city. The riders thanked the wolves and Aohdan felt a stab of sadness as they went their separate ways. Once inside the walls, they found the city to be a flurry of activity. Soldiers marched along the streets while citizens scurried from the markets carrying food to stock up for a possible siege.

They heard the clatter of hooves and a dozen mounted soldiers approached. Behind them, astride the great wolf Chieftain Finris, came Avana.

"You have returned!" she cried out, jumping from Finris and rushing to them. Avana threw her arms around her husband, burying her face in his neck. Killian held her tightly. Releasing Killian, she hugged Aohdan, Caleb, and Andrew in turn.

"You are a welcome sight," Killian said, "But we are worn from our journey. I'm afraid we must rest before we can properly tell you anything."

Avana nodded. "I understand. It is enough that you are back safely."

Finris now joined them, and he focused on Aohdan. "You have

changed, O son of my daughter. Your story will be interesting indeed."

The weary travelers were escorted with honor back to the Guard compound. True to her word Avana did not ask for their full story. She was content to wait for the morning. Instead she arranged for a lavish meal to be set out for them. Aohdan ate hungrily, but soon found he could not keep his eyes open. He retired to his room and let sleep take him.

When Aohdan woke the next day he realized two things: first, that it was late morning, and second, that he was still terribly hungry. He made his way to the dining room to find that his mother and father were already there. Killian was telling Avana the full tale. Aohdan devoured the side of ham and warm bread that was brought to him. He mostly listened as Killian spoke, but added details where he thought necessary.

After learning the news of the hidden fortress, Avana leaned back in her chair thoughtfully. She addressed Aohdan. "You will have to go yourself, won't you." It was a statement, not a question.

"Yes. I wish to take only a few others with me, but I fear it will turn into a battle," Aohdan replied.

Avana nodded. "I think that is the best option. We don't know what we are up against so a frontal assault could be disastrous."

"Are you still planning on marching to the Tiered Mountain?" Killian asked.

"We leave at the end of the week. Halfor has been under attack from both goblins and a gold dragon. Presumably the same one that attacked you," Avana said.

Concern flooded Aohdan. "You do not fear that you leave Amaroth vulnerable?"

"Zellnar and the majority of the wolves will protect the city. I will not be taking the entire army. Halfor is our friend and he needs our help. Besides, we have a secret weapon."

"A secret weapon?" Aohdan asked.

Avana raised an eyebrow and grinned. "We have Cynthia on our side."

Killian laughed. "She will give the goblins a hard time should they decide to attack in force."

Aohdan felt a smile creep over him. "That is a most excellent point."

"I know you will want to head out as soon as possible, but I would advise you to try and rest first," Avana said with a worried gaze at her son. "You may be imbued with extra strength from the heartstone you carry, but I fear you will need to be at your best to fight Killkari."

Aohdan sighed. "My heart wishes to leave today, but my head tells me that you are right."

"Rest is always the hardest," Killian said, shaking his head. "I too would like to continue on. My heart worries that we will find ourselves short on time."

"It is not time that worries me but responsibility. I have learned to shift for a reason. Is it to draw the forces of Killkari away from you or should I go with you directly?" Avana mulled out loud.

Aohdan and Killian did not have an answer for her. Aohdan knew that his mother would be an asset to infiltrating the hidden fortress. She was legendary in her ability to access impossible strongholds. However, he did not want the army of Amaroth to feel abandoned by the royal family.

He was surprised when his mother stood up and threw the cup sitting before her across the room in a fit of frustration.

"Ruling is such a bother. I have no interest in political games. Fighting is in my blood and here I sit, hiding behind the army of Amaroth," Avana stormed.

Killian stood up to placate his wife. "You are not hiding. You are out among the Guard every day. You train them yourself. You have stepped up to the task of ruling with a heart for Amaroth."

Aohdan added, "Perhaps it is time to let the Guard see that you believe in the training you have given them. They are loyal, dedicated fighters. Make them feel that they are ready for a mission alone while you have other priorities."

Avana looked between her son and her husband. "You are both right, I suppose. I need an adventure. Staying behind while you were gone was miserable."

"That sounds like you will be joining me," Aohdan said, letting a smile cross his face.

Avana squared her shoulders. "Yes, I have made up my mind. It's been some years since we've gone on a journey as a family. It's high time we did so!"

Chapter 27

AFTER A WHIRLWIND OF PREPARATION AND traveling, Aohdan found himself in his family home on the Tiered Mountain. They had marched with half of the Amaroth army to the aid of King Halfor. The dwarves were involved in dog fight skirmishes with the goblins. To make matters worse, the attacks by the gold dragon made fighting above ground nearly impossible.

Aohdan and Avana had kept the Amaroth army safe by covering their movements in a heavy shroud of fog as they traveled. They had stayed on high alert for the entire journey, but had made it successfully without incident.

Halfor and his son Prince Halever had objected strongly to the idea of attempting to infiltrate the hidden fortress.

"What will happen to Amaroth if you fail?" he asked.

"Caleb will rule," Avana told him. "Besides, it is my responsibility to protect my people. They are in grave danger from Killkari."

Eventually, Halfor and Halever had given in though they still did not like the idea.

According to the map given to them by the elves, they would reach the hidden fortress in two days' travel from the Tiered Mountain. This close proximity was why the dwarves were the obvious choice for Killkari to attack first.

They decided that they would take only a small group with them. Andrew and Blane from their own guard, while two dwarf soldiers from Halfor's personal guard would bring them to seven members. They were to leave early the next morning.

Aohdan stood in the lush garden that Killian had made for Avana. He looked out over the mountainside and wished that Saoirse was with him. Reaching out with his mind he contacted her.

"Saoirse…Saoirse," he called out to her.

"Aohdan! It is good to hear from you again," she replied.

Aohdan could tell that she was much better than she had been before. He felt the release of a burden he hadn't even realized he was carrying. "Saoirse, we are coming to rescue you and stop Killkari."

"You will be none too soon. Killkari appears to be gaining mastery over the ability to control whole fleets of dragons at once. I believe he will be launching a full scale attack soon," Saoirse said, her voice full of concern.

"We leave first thing in the morning. It is a two-day journey on foot. We dare not draw attention to ourselves by flying."

Saoirse replied, "I am heartened by your news. I will try to pass the word along to the other prisoners to be ready when the time comes."

"Thank you. If it comes to a fight, we will need all the help we can get," Aohdan said. He paused for a moment, then changed the subject. "I wish you were here. You would love the Tiered Mountain."

He projected to Saoirse a picture of the lovely garden and of the surrounding mountainside.

"It is lovely indeed. But you will be showing it to me in person soon. I believe in you," Saoirse said with confidence.

"I miss you," Aohdan thought. He hadn't realized he had mindspoke the words when Saoirse hesitantly responded to him.

"I…I miss you too."

An ache he wasn't sure how to express pressed into Aohdan's heart. He felt the feeling reciprocated in Saoirse. He wanted to desperately come clean to her and tell her the truth, but it didn't seem right to do so through mindspeaking. So he decided to end the conversation.

"I will see you soon. We will make the utmost haste. Goodbye till then."

"Goodbye. I will be waiting anxiously."

Aohdan spent the rest of the day prowling around the dwarf kingdom. He was unsurprised when his mother joined him in his pacing. Mother and son walked in companionable silence. Both were clearing their minds for the journey ahead.

That night they ate together as a family in their mountain home. For the first time, Aohdan stopped to consider that this might be the last time they did so. This was not some quick goblin skirmish or dealing with a wandering band of brigands; this could be all out war. To add to the seriousness, if they were unsuccessful, Saoirse would, in all likelihood, be killed.

These revelations brought a steely resolve to Aohdan. He was going to do everything in his power to succeed, no matter the cost. His parents had always taught him to do the right thing, even in the face of adversity. Now he had an opportunity to step out of their shadows and stand up against evil *with* his parents.

Morning came with a flash and a deep growling rumble. Rain poured down on the travelers from a black sky. Lightning arced and sizzled above them. Deafening thunder-claps shook the forest as they trekked over the mountain. The storm was natural cover, though it made hiking most unpleasant.

The rain continued on throughout the day. The more rain that fell, the more treacherous the going became. Avana led them on firm paths where fewer loose rocks slipped beneath their feet and they kept to the high ground for fear of flash flooding. Still, the mud caked on their boots and legs making the trek dangerous.

When they camped for the night, the rain was still coming down. They could make no fire for fear of being spotted, so dinner was a sorry affair. They quickly downed the dried food they had packed with a few swigs of water from their canteens. Few words were spoken. No one felt like talking. Better to curl up in your bedroll and sleep than to try and carry on a conversation in the rain.

They rotated watch through the night. To everyone's relief the rain quit at dawn. They ate another cold meal before starting again. Aohdan felt the warm delight of the sun's rays as they traveled onward, following the elvish map. Seeing the sun above them gave Aohdan and the others a boost in morale. Avana now led them with greater care, but her pace had quickened.

Aohdan knew his mother was anxious to get a decent view of the fortress while there was still daylight left. Then they could decide how to get inside. As they drew closer, Avana seemed to reach an invisible point where everything about their trek changed. She slowed them down to almost a snail's pace. Instead of the straight line approach she had taken before, now they zig-zagged and backtracked.

They left a confusing trail in their wake. What couldn't be obscured or swept away was nearly impossible to interpret. Avana knew her craft. She could disappear before Aohdan's eyes only to return a few minutes later in a completely different place. They began to dodge goblin patrols, raising everyone's senses to high alert.

It wasn't long before they finally spotted the hidden fortress. Avana brought them up to a rocky outcrop hidden by the trees, affording them an unobtrusive view of the ancient stronghold. They lay on the rocks, peeking over the edge.

The fortress blended in perfectly with the surrounding mountainside its stone walls created from naturally occurring rock formations. Cunning builders made the window slits in the wall to look like depressions in the rock. A sheer drop off to the east, made the fortress impossible to attack from that side.

Unless you can fly, thought Aohdan to himself.

A narrow winding track ran up through the trees to the front gate. Between the forest and the stronghold the ground was riddled with deep crevasses. Crossing these would prove to be extremely difficult. The track was the only practical way to reach the fortress. Guarding the gate was a rust-colored dragon. It stayed so still that if Aohdan hadn't known better he would have thought it a statue. A burbling, quick-running stream wound its way from the fortress over the pockmarked ground.

"This should be interesting," Andrew muttered.

Killian let out a soft snort. "Having second thoughts?"

"Only about breakfast," Andrew retorted.

Aohdan couldn't help the smile that he felt creeping over him. The others also let out quiet snickers at the exchange. Only Avana seemed unaffected by the soft banter.

"That's how we'll get in," she said, so low that Aohdan barely heard her.

Killian tilted his head toward his wife. "What was that?"

"That's how we'll get in," she repeated. "There's a culvert letting the stream out of the fortress."

Andrew grunted. "It will be covered with a heavy grate."

"Not to mention we will probably have to swim," Blane added.

Avana gave them both a disapproving glare. "I know. But from what I can see we don't have many options. It will take days for us to cross the ground with those crevasses. And even if we flew, we would be easily spotted on the east face."

"I agree. The culvert is probably our best bet." Killian nodded.

"I think my sword could cut through the grate," Aohdan said. "It's hardened with dragon fire and unless the metal of the grate is made of bright silver, I don't think it will be a problem."

Orvis, one of the dwarves, said, "How are we going to make it up-stream? Dwarves can swim, but we are not built for it."

"That is certainly a concern," Andrew grumbled.

A moment of silence reigned. Each person lost in thought of how to circumnavigate their problem.

"What if Aohdan and I swim as dragons? The rest of you could hang onto us. It would hopefully prevent anyone from being swept away," Avana theorized.

Aohdan said, "That could work. I don't think it would wear us out terribly like trying to swim in our human form."

"Then let's try it," Avana said. "Unless anyone has a better idea?" She looked around.

No one volunteered anything else.

"Alright. We will make our first attempt when full dark has come," she stated.

Chapter 28

THE VAST EXPANSE OF BLACK VELVET sky stretched above them as the infiltrators ghosted to the edge of the noisy stream. Aohdan and Avana both shifted in the woods. They shrank down to a size that would make them hard to spot while swimming. Aohdan put a spell over the heartstone pouch to let it grow and shrink with him. Killian carried Illista for him.

The two dragons slipped into the river. The found that they could touch the bottom of the fast moving stream. The water was cold though. The dragons were not affected, but the humans and dwarves spluttered softly when they waded in. Soon their teeth were chattering and they shivered incessantly as they clung to the dragons.

"C…c…can…you…you…magic us…some…some heat?" Andrew asked as he clutched one of Aohdan's back spines.

"I think so," Aohdan mind-spoke in return. Trying to heat someone up hadn't been part of his training with Nokoa. This would be an experiment. Aohdan focused on his internal body heat. He imagined it increasing, then spreading out through his body. When it reached Andrew and the two dwarves hanging tightly onto him, he envisioned pushing the heat through their bodies as an extension of his own.

It worked. His passengers quickly ceased their shaking. Aohdan passed on what he had done to his mother, who immediately did the same thing. With everyone comfortable, they were able to make faster time upstream. The current grew fiercer as they drew closer to the fortress.

Aohdan knew that he and Avana were safe, but he worried for the dwarves and men. With only their heads above water, they had to fight against the current to hang onto the dragons. One benefit to the turbulence was the noise that muffled any inadvertent sounds. The strange caravan cut through the water, appearing as shadows in the darkness.

Aohdan was grateful for the sharp channel walls on either side of the stream that helped to hide them as they drew near the fortress. His nerves were singing when they finally reached the culvert. He let his passengers transfer themselves to Avana before shifting. Bracing himself for the shock of cold water, he changed back to human form.

But it wasn't the cold that proved to be a problem. When he changed he was nearly swept away. He barely managed to grab onto the bars of the grate in time. Cutting through the bars would be more difficult than he had thought. Gritting his teeth he reached out for Illista from his father.

Killian handed him the sword. It was going to be very tricky hanging onto the sword while keeping himself from being swept downstream. Aohdan gave an experimental hack at the bars of the grate. To his relief, Illista cut right through. He continued his awkward cutting, but in his current position there was little else he could do. Slowly he was able to open up a hole in the grate.

Once he had a sizable opening, he shifted back to his dragon form. He was relieved to no longer have to struggle against the water. He squeezed through the hole he had made, followed by Avana and the riders. They swam through the tunnel to the other end. Aohdan carefully peeked out, surveying the surroundings.

The steep banks of the stream flattened out in the courtyard. To Aohdan's surprise, the courtyard was largely deserted. A few goblins lounged lazily at their post, but otherwise there was no sign of life.

Across the yard there appeared to be another level of the fortress with a second wall towering up, blocking their path. The stream also flowed beneath this wall.

Aohdan grimaced internally. The men and dwarves were losing strength. The distance wasn't far from their hiding place to the next wall, but he knew that everyone was ready to be out of the water. Silently he mindspoke the images of what lay ahead. He sensed the grimness that settled over the passengers as they prepared themselves to continue their swim.

It would be harder to hide in the water without the steep banks for protection, but Aohdan was confident they could make it to the next wall without being spotted. They swam forward again. The dragons made every effort to be unobtrusive as they went on. Aohdan felt the sense of relief that passed through everyone when they made it to the second culvert.

But like good soldiers there was also an undercurrent of concern for the lack of enemies they had yet seen. Aohdan cut through the second grate quicker, being prepared this time for the challenges. The tunnel of this culvert was considerably longer than the first. Blackness consumed them in a disorienting cloud. Only the pull of the current gave them any sense of direction.

Suddenly, Aohdan realized that Saoirse was near. He could sense her somewhere above him. Reaching out for her with his mind he found that she and other prisoners were chained to the mountainside just as he had remembered. The number of those chained had grown. What had been only a dozen men and women with a few dragons, had now grown to twice the number of humans and about fifteen dragons.

Aohdan knew Saoirse had also sensed his presence, but he was afraid to reach out to her any more than he already had. Nokoa had warned him that other mind-speakers could tell when someone was searching with magic. With the *Elestari* under Killkari's control, he did not want to risk anyone noticing his intrusion.

What he had been able to discern though was important. They were close to the end of the tunnel. And from what he could tell, the vast majority of the *Elestari* army Killkari had created was stationed further inside the mountain. The prisoners were kept outdoors on the side of the mountain where they could be easily watched. Rescuing them was going to prove very difficult.

He relayed this information to the others. There was a mix of reactions, but they were determined. Just as Aohdan had seen, they soon reached the end of the culvert. Keeping to the shadows they looked out into the yard. To their right a small copse of trees grew next to a pool of water that had been dammed up from the stream. Aohdan guessed that long ago it had been used for bathing and washing clothes. It would afford them the cover they needed to regroup and plan their next move.

To their left the yard opened up and was dotted with the forms of sleeping dragons and goblins. A large doorway leading deeper into the mountain was guarded by a dozen goblins and two dragons. Though they were on alert, Aohdan doubted they would be looking toward the pool.

Still, it was tricky business getting everyone out of the water without being spotted. Man and dwarf alike started to shiver as soon as they were away from the warmth of the dragons. They were also tired. They were not nearly as worn as they would have been if they'd swum the whole way on their own, but their strength was taxed.

Aodhan felt the heartstone humming around his neck. He wondered if he could revive everyone with it. After he returned to his human form, he cautiously pulled the heartstone from its pouch. The moment it touched his skin a wave of well-being and power swept over him. Though he knew what to expect, it still took Aohdan a moment to bring his senses back under control.

He was afraid to touch anyone with the stone outright, so he decided to simply try skin to skin contact with himself as he held the stone. Aohdan walked among the company taking the hand of each member. He started with Andrew and was gratified to see his energy and life restored to him. He finished with his mother. Avana was in much better shape than the rest, but he didn't think it would hurt to boost her strength. When he touched her hand there was a crackle of energy.

For a moment he could have sworn that they both had a reddish glow surrounding them, but it faded so quickly he thought his eyes were deceiving him. Yet he knew it must have occurred for he found Avana staring at him, her eyes huge in the darkness.

Neither was sure what had just happened. But there was no time to wonder. The group gathered round in a circle to quietly discuss their next move.

"I think we should split up," Aohdan said. "I need to get to Killkari and the best way for me to do so is to go alone. The rest of you can free the prisoners."

He had expected resistance to his idea, but instead heads nodded around him.

"It will be dangerous for you, but you will be much less likely to be spotted that way," Avana stated.

Andrew added, "Besides if you are able to break Killkari's control, it's probably a good idea if we can give direction to the *Elestari*. They will need leadership of some sort. If we can get Saoirse free, she can help bring them together into a cohesive force to either escape or fight against Killkari."

"You think Killkari will keep fighting even after losing the heartstone?" Aohdan questioned.

Andrew shrugged. "He may or may not, but I know that the goblins surely will. They will fight if they think they have an advantage. Which they do with the bright silver."

"The bright silver will certainly be a problem," Avana said. "The *Elestari* will be vulnerable to it. And for that matter, so will we." Her eyes flicked to Aohdan.

Aohdan sighed. "It will be dangerous no matter what. I will be off then. Night won't last forever."

With a nod to his father and a squeeze of his hand from his mother, Aohdan disappeared into the night.

Chapter 29

AOHDAN GHOSTED TO THE WALL. HE found a small, unguarded door that he could slip through. Finding himself in a large pantry, he was surprised to find that it was full of food. There must be more *Elestari* in human form than he had realized. He guessed that it was easier to house a fortress full of humans than dragons. Now that he was inside the inner fortress he began to feel a low, humming vibration coming from the heartstone reacting to something. It had to be the other heartstone.

Following the humming guidance of the heartstone, Aohdan wound his way through a maze of passages. More than once he was forced to duck off into a side hallway or room as goblin and *Elestari* guards marched past. During one of these side excursions he found himself in a barracks full of sleeping *Elestari*. There had to be at least fifty people crammed into the small space. A spike of adrenaline rushed through Aohdan as he slowed his breathing in an attempt to be as quiet as possible.

When the guards had marched past the door, Aohdan slipped back into the hallway, nerves singing. Soon he found himself in a great hall. Torch light flickered red on the walls while tables and chairs were scattered around the room in disarray. The far end of the hall was dark, unlit by any torch. The heartstone Aohdan carried was now humming with such intensity, he feared someone would hear it. Judging by its energy, Killkari's stone had to be in this room.

The hall appeared to be deserted, but Aohdan knew that looks were deceiving. He stayed in the shadows, slowly inching his way forward. As his eyes adjusted to the poor lighting he recognized the outline of a large dragon curled up and hidden by the darkness. It was Killkari. There was no mistaking the black dragon.

As Aohdan drew nearer, he realized that Killkari was sleeping on top of a large mound of raw brightsilver. Aohdan carefully surveyed the scene, hoping to catch a glimpse of the heartstone. When he finally saw it, his heart sank. Underneath the front claws of Killkari, he saw the soft, red, glowing light of a heartstone.

How was he supposed to reach it without waking him? No good ideas came to mind. Killkari would sense any magic that he could try. There was nothing else to do but sneak up to the sleeping dragon. Once decided, Aohdan let go his nerves. He focused completely on his goal.

Silent as death, he stole toward Killkari. Soon he found himself standing in front of the massive dragon. Face to face with Killkari, Aohdan felt a surge of rage and hate for the evil dragon. For a moment he nearly lost his head. Killkari was vulnerable. He could easily kill him as he slept. There was nothing to stop Aohdan from slaying Killkari and taking both heartstones.

Aohdan would be the most powerful being in all of Arda. He would rule as no one had before him. All would bow to him and serve him. He could eliminate the goblins and bring safety once and for all to Amaroth. His name would be forever remembered.

As these thoughts ran through his head, a picture started to form in the back of his mind. The faces of his parents and Saoirse grew clearer as he focused on them. Aohdan let this picture grow as he fought against the strong desire for power and revenge. Pushing aside his anger, he carefully took out the heartstone he carried.

When Aohdan pulled out the heartstone, Killkari shifted as if responding to the new power that had suddenly been revealed.

Aohdan froze. Agonizing seconds passed before he started to move again. With his free hand he quietly unsheathed his sword. He didn't know what would happen when he put the two heartstones together, but he wanted to be ready for anything.

Killkari's stone lay nestled between his talons. A tiny sliver of stone stuck out. Ever so slowly Aohdan reached out with the heartstone he carried. With a soft click, the two heartstones touched.

The effect was instantaneous. A flare of unexpected power washed through Aohdan only to be immediately sucked away leaving him with a huge sense of loss. The two stones glowed a brilliant red for a few moments then turned black. Aohdan found that he was no longer able to touch them. In fact they seemed to be burning him. He yanked his hand away at the same time Killkari pulled his taloned paw back.

Killkari let out a tortured howl, "WHAT HAVE YOU DONE!"

The dragon reeled back, just as Aohdan himself stumbled away. Both were keenly feeling the loss of their heartstones. The stones themselves, still black as night, stayed stuck together and rolled off to one side on the floor.

Killkari was the first to regain his senses. Letting out an earsplitting roar that turned into a scream, he pounced on the heartstones only to be repelled by them. Aohdan was leaning against a table trying to pull himself together after the loss of power. Killkari now turned his anger on Aohdan.

Growling so deeply he shook the floor, Killkari stalked toward the prince. "Foul human! You are one of them. An *Elestari*, I can smell it. Why would you destroy the source of your power? We could have ruled together."

Aohdan stepped away from the table and held Illista in ready position. "You are a liar, Killkari. You would never share power with anyone else."

A sibilant laugh emanated from the dragon. "You're right. I wouldn't. But now you have made me lose the chance at that power. And for that you will PAY!"

The black dragon reared back and let loose a stream of fire at Aohdan. Aohdan brought Illista up against the blaze. The sword drank up the dragon fire, filling the blade with a bright blue glow. With a yell, Aohdan ran forward pushing the dragon fire back at Killkari.

Killkari jumped away in surprise. No one he had encountered had been able to challenge him like this before. With a frustrated yowl the dragon leaped at Aohdan. Meeting him head on, Aohdan sunk Illista deep into Killkari's leg and rolled aside as they dragon landed in the spot where he had just been.

Blood spurted from the wound as Killkari turned awkwardly around to face his adversary. The hall was too small for him to fly, putting him at a disadvantage. Again, he charged Aohdan and was met with the sharp bite of Illista. Then he tried a new tactic. Killkari began to wantonly spew flame. The tables and chairs spread throughout the room ignited.

Aohdan knew he was in trouble. He was vulnerable in human form to the flames. He could put a fireproof spell around himself, but the air in the room would quickly turn to smoke making it difficult to breathe and there was nothing he could do about that. If he shifted to dragon form there would be little room to maneuver.

He would have to get out. But the heartstones were still unaccounted for. Killkari chased him, trying to drive him into the fire as he looked for the heartstones. He spotted them laying on the floor beneath a burning chair. Aohdan kicked the chair in the direction of Killkari who let out a snort of derision.

Hoping that it would protect him, Aohdan yanked the leather pouch from around his neck and used it to grasp the heartstones. It worked. He looked around for a way out as he did so. Just behind Killkari he could see the doorway he had come in from. Clutching the stones in one hand he ran straight at Killkari. To his surprise the dragon retreated before him, leery of being cut again by his sword.

Aiming for Killkari's wing, he brought a long slash through the thin membrane, causing Killkari to flail about wildly nearly taking Aohdan down with his tail. Aohdan dodged the angry dragon and sprinted through the door and out into the hall. He was followed by a hot blast of dragon fire.

Chapter 30

WHILE AOHDAN WAS TRAVELING THROUGH THE inner fortress, the others were sneaking to the top of the wall where the prisoners were being kept. Avana led the group while Andrew took up the rear. They managed to get past the guards but were forced to stop when they reached the final ascent. There was only one set of steps to go up and they were heavily guarded by goblins. There was very little chance of them being able to kill all the goblins without making a great deal of noise.

"This is where I excel, my friends," Avana whispered. "Give me the rope, Killian. I will scale the wall and drop down the rope for the rest of you when I reach the top."

Wordlessly Killian handed her the rope he had stowed away in his pack. Avana coiled it across her body and shifted Stelenacht to her back. Once prepared, Avana started her climb. There was very little to hang onto, but she had years of experience. The others watched anxiously beneath her as she cautiously made her way upwards.

When she neared the top she slowed her pace. She listened for the sounds of footsteps or breathing. Hearing nothing, she climbed the last few inches and ever so slowly pulled herself up onto the top of the wall. Immediately, she rolled into the shadows and froze. She assessed the situation.

Avana could see two goblin guards standing about thirty paces or so from where she lay. Beyond them the dark outlines of dragons and humans made strange shapes against the craggy mountain backdrop. Drawing herself into a crouch, Avana stalked forward. It would be difficult to kill both goblins at once without making any noise. But she knew that she would never be able to get the others up without first taking care of the guards.

Pulling out her saxe knives she crept up behind the goblins. Quick as a snake, she rose up behind them and slit the throat of the closest guard. The second turned in surprise as his comrade begin to fall. Avana plunged her other knife between the ribs of the second guard. Then swinging round with the first saxe, she cut his throat before he could cry out. She silently searched the guards and found a heavy set of keys.

With the two guards taken care of and keys in hand, Avana stole back to the edge of the wall. She tied one end of the rope to a heavy metal ring that was attached to the ground clearly meant for manacling prisoners. The other end she tossed over to those waiting below. The rest of the group quickly made their way up to join her.

Avana couldn't cover the tiny sense of shame she felt when they saw her spattered in goblin blood. She knew they were all used to battle, but somehow it didn't seem to fit with her idea of what a queen should look like. She knew her husband had felt her insecurity through their bond, because he reached for her hand. Taking it in his, he caressed her knuckles, though they were covered in blood.

Smiling in the darkness, Avana let go of her fears. It had been ages since she had let anything like this bother her. She was not going to allow them to compromise her now. Taking the lead, Avana sneaked toward the prisoners. She kept a sharp eye out for the silver shape of Saoirse.

The closest prisoner was a very large dragon. In the darkness Avana wasn't sure what color it was. Perhaps a dark purple, she guessed. Afraid of frightening it with her voice, Avana placed her hand on the dragon's side trying to put thoughts of friendship at the forefront of her mind.

The dragon jumped at the intrusion. Avana encountered a wall around its mind so strong she feared that she wouldn't even be able to communicate with the dragon. It had buried itself so deeply within its mind.

"Please hear me!" she cried out. "I am a friend. I'm here to free you!" She sent a flood of images at the dragon.

Twice more she repeated her words with no response. Without warning she found herself under attack from the dragon's mind. Her first instinct was to fight back. But she knew that would not prove her innocence so she let the strange dragon dig through her head.

It didn't take long for the dragon to retreat in confusion. "You speak the truth," it rumbled. "I am called Dax. If you free me, I can help you with the other *Elestari* so they won't make a ruckus."

"We would greatly value your help, Dax," Avana replied.

Coming back to herself she pulled out the set of keys she had taken from the guards. Using them she unlocked Dax's chains. With a groan he shifted back to human form. He looked to be a man in his early fifties. His freeing and transformation had already been noticed by the other dragons who had been chained closest to him.

They raised their heads and eyed their would-be rescuers in a wordless cry for help. Avana hurried from dragon to dragon unlocking their chains. Dax went with her passing on his silent message of freedom to each *Elestari*. Most shifted back to human form, but a few opted to stay as dragons.

They had freed nearly a dozen dragons when Avana saw Saoirse. She ran to the silver dragon with tears in her eyes. Avana had already grown to love Saoirse like she was her own daughter. To see her chained to the rocks was a terrible sight.

"Saoirse!" she whispered, coming alongside the silver dragon.

Saoirse's violet eyes sprang open, and the relief in them was so evident that Avana had to pause for a moment to keep her emotions in check. She quickly freed Saoirse from her chains. The silver dragon shifted to her human form. Avana threw her arms around Saoirse and the two women wept.

Avana handed the keys to Dax as she let Saoirse cry against her shoulder. Killian joined them, adding his steady presence to comfort Saoirse. As they stood together, the whole world seemed to shift. The very air around them felt like it had changed.

"The heartstones," Saoirse said.

"Their power is gone," Avana added.

Dax stood over them. "The spell is broken. We must leave now while we can."

Letting go of Saoirse and Killian, Avana nodded. "Yes, gather your people. They will need guidance. But I will wait for my son. He may need help."

"Your son broke the spell?" Dax said in astonishment.

Killian answered, "That was what he set out to do. Clearly we no longer feel the effects of its power so he must have succeeded."

"Which means he is in the gravest danger," Saoirse said. "Killkari will try and destroy him."

"And so are our people. Killkari forged an alliance with several other dragons to aid him in his conquest. They are outcasts among dragon kind like Killkari himself. We will have them to deal with, and to top it off there are the goblins," Dax spoke quickly.

Avana asked, "Will the *Elestari* fight back?"

Dax shot a sad glance at Saoirse. "Not as many as I would wish. We have strived for peace for so many years. Most will simply want to flee. Though they have courage and will defend themselves in a pinch."

"I think this counts as a pinch," Killian stated wryly.

Dax shrugged in frustration. "But they may not see it like that. Those of us who were kept chained here were the *Elestari* that Killkari could not bend even under the strongest spell. We are the strongest fighters among our people. The worst part is that the mountainside is crawling with goblins. The hosts have been assembling for days now."

Avana looked at the crowd of freed prisoners that had swelled around them. There were no more than thirty of them. Their numbers were not enough to take on an entire army of goblins.

She sighed. "Will they at least shift to dragon form? That will get everyone away the quickest. We will lead everyone to the Tiered Mountain. That is where King Halfor and our army are making a stand against the goblins."

"Yes. I think they will. They will want to get away from here as fast as possible," Dax replied.

"Good. Then let us begin. Can you get your people split up into two groups? Some to fight and the rest to lead the enslaved?"

Dax nodded and spoke quietly to the *Elestari* gathered there. Saoirse said, "You know where I will be, Avana."

Avana let a smile cross her face. "Yes. You will be with me. We will fight to reach Aohdan."

"Not without me you won't," Killian said indignantly. "I will be right there with you."

Avana felt her smile grow. "Of course, my love. It seems to be our lot to fight evil."

Killian pulled her close to him. "We are warriors. It is in our blood."

Memories of past battles flew through Avana's mind. They had faced great peril together and survived. She had no intention of changing that this night.

Chapter 31

ALL WHO COULD, SHIFTED, INCLUDING AVANA and Saoirse. Killian carried Stelenacht for Avana. She crouched down and he climbed onto her back. Andrew rode on Saoirse, while Blane and the dwarves also took a dragon. Without a sound the dragons leapt into the sky. They circled for a moment looking down on the open yards below them.

Chaos was starting to break out. The *Elestari* dragons that had once been under Killkari's control, like the golden dragon Markus standing guard, were now attacking the goblins. Dax swooped down to bring sense to the confusion. He broadcasted the message of what had gained their freedom with mindspeak. The dragons immediately responded to him.

Most flew and joined the group while a few stayed with Dax, shifting to human form to go and lead the rest of the *Elestari* out of the fortress. They ran to the same small side door that Aohdan had passed through earlier.

As they did so, a large red dragon came rocketing from the main doors that led into the heart of the fortress. It roared angrily. Right away Avana knew this was no *Elestari*. The red dragon launched itself into the sky seeking to destroy all in its path. Behind it came a bronze dragon, followed by another red. They made straight for the invaders.

Letting out a roar, Avana headed for the lead dragon. The dragons met with a screech, biting and clawing at one another. Avana tried her best to keep Killian from falling as she brawled with the rogue dragon. Out of the corner of her eye she saw Saoirse diving toward the large doors where the dragons had come from. Avana silently cheered her on. She too wanted to go after Aohdan, but right now she had other priorities.

Saoirse found herself heading into a large dark hallway. She couldn't fly here, but she could fit at full size. On her back Andrew clutched tightly to her spines. The echoing growl of a dragon ahead of her spurred her onward. Her connection with Aohdan told her she was close to him. She heard footsteps.

Aohdan came racing down the hallway toward her. In one hand he carried a sword that flickered with a bright blue light while in the other he had an odd-shaped bundle. He stopped dead when he saw her.

"SAOIRSE!" he cried out. Another angry bellow came rolling down the hallway.

"We must hurry!" Aohdan regained his senses and ran to Saoirse. "Killkari is coming. We cannot battle him inside this place."

He reached her side and stopped again. Hastily he ripped off a piece of his tunic and wrapped it around the strange object that he carried. With great care, he put it in a leather pouch. Saoirse crouched down and allowed Aohdan to scramble onto her back and join Andrew.

"Here, Andrew," Aohdan said, offering the pouch to his mentor. "Guard this with your life."

Andrew took the bundle. "If that's what I think it is, then you have no need to remind me."

A fire of joy filled Saoirse at finally being reunited with Aohdan, and Andrew's banter only increased it. She knew Aohdan felt the same way. Saoirse turned around and galloped back out the way she had come. She was none too soon. Killkari came barreling around the corner spouting flame.

When they reached the entrance, Saoirse leapt into the air. She powered upwards flying higher and higher. Not far from them, Avana and the *Elestari* battled the rogue dragons.

"Saoirse," Aohdan spoke to her. "I'm going to shift."

Saoirse responded with a thrum of acknowledgement. Though she knew it was coming, her heart still somersaulted when she felt Aohdan let go of her. For a long moment he was free-falling away from her. Then he was a huge obsidian dragon, wings snapped out against the wind.

His shift had distracted her from watching the doorway for Killkari. The evil dragon almost took her by surprise as he came flying up from below her. Saoirse sensed his presence and dodged out of the way just in time. Backpedaling with her wings she banked hard to come back after Killkari.

Aohdan beat her to him. He crashed into Killkari with a thundering roar. Claws and fangs ripped at scales and sinew. Then they broke apart. Now it was Saoirse's chance to attack. She dived at Killkari making use of Andrew on her back who now wielded Illista.

At the last moment she adjusted her dive to avoid Killkari, instead giving Andrew a chance to bring Illista down across Killkari's back. In Andrew's hands, the sword no longer glowed with power the way it did for Aohdan, but it still was sharp as any other blade.

As Saoirse and Andrew swept away from Killkari, Aohdan attacked again. This time they stayed locked together spinning and flailing in the sky. Aohdan had a low hold on Killkari's throat, but the evil dragon had bitten deeply into his shoulder damaging a wing muscle.

Circling, Saoirse looked for an opening. Andrew too was searching for the right moment for them to jump in. The two black dragons spun in the sky. For a brief moment, Killkari's back was toward Saoirse and Andrew. Shooting forward she took the opportunity. She raked her claws across Killkari's back and right wing.

Yowling in pain, Killkari released Aohdan and turned on Saoirse. Striking out with his tail, he managed to knock her off balance. She wavered in the air, flapping furiously. Hissing in fury Killkari came after her. He scored her hindquarter and back with his claws, causing Andrew to duck. Then as she twisted back toward him to defend herself, he snapped and bit down on the base of her neck. Saoirse knew it was a shallow bite, otherwise she would already by dead. Still it caused a flare of fear to run through her.

Killkari bit down harder in an effort to kill her. Taking advantage of the situation, Aohdan latched onto Killkari's wing with a terrible crunch. From the sound Saoirse knew that Aohdan had broken the evil dragon's wing. But she was now afraid to fight. If she moved the wrong way, Killkari could change his grip and snap her neck.

Then she remembered Andrew. He was not sitting idly by on her back. He had clambered forward toward the great head of Killkari. Sword in hand he drew closer and closer. Abruptly he jumped from Saoirse onto the broad back of Killkari and plunged Illista deep into the chest of the evil dragon.

Killkari spasmed, releasing Saoirse and throwing Andrew from his back. He writhed in the air spewing blood and flames. Then the life left him, and he fell to the ground destroying part of the fortress with a terrible crash.

Saoirse managed to catch Andrew in her talons, gently setting him onto Aohdan's back. The joint sense of relief that overwhelmed the three could not be stated with words. Seeing Killkari's demise took the fight out of the rogue dragons. One by one they turned tail and flew away.

As the adrenaline of battle wore off Saoirse began to keenly feel her wounds. She let herself drift to the ground followed by Aohdan and Andrew. She shifted back to human form when she landed. Aohdan too shifted. He took Illista and the heartstones back from Andrew, then turned to her.

He threw his arms around her pulling her in close to him. She felt the power flow from him as he healed her wounds. He smelled of smoke and blood, but she didn't care. This was what she had wanted for days. She buried her face in his chest as he stroked her hair.

"I love you, Saoirse," he said in his deep voice. "I was so afraid that I had lost you."

He tilted her face upwards and she stared into his bright blue eyes. Then he leaned in and kissed her. Saoirse kissed him back. Through their bond she could feel the outpouring of love Aohdan had for her. It promised that he would never leave her. She was everything to him. His heart longed to make her his forever.

"I love you too," Saoirse mindspoke, showing him that she felt the same way he did.

In response, Aohdan broke their kiss and spun her around. Then he kissed her again. She felt his giddiness to her answer. Behind them Andrew let out a loud cough bringing them back to reality.

"It's about time," he said gruffly, but his eyes sparked with merriment.

"How long have you known, Andrew?" Saoirse demanded, pretending to be in a huff.

"Longer than you," he shot back with a grin.

Saoirse felt a blush creep over her cheeks, but she didn't care. Her heart and head were finally at peace with one another. Her people were free. Killkari was dead. The goblins would still cause trouble, but for now the greatest danger was past.

Chapter 32

THE ATTACK ON THE TIERED MOUNTAIN was short lived. With the aid of the *Elestari* willing to fight, Halfor's army along with Amaroth's warriors quickly routed the goblins. Fighting against bright silver weapons caused more wounds for the *Elestari*, but facing nearly thirty irate dragons proved too much for the goblin hordes.

Saoirse stood leaning her head on Aohdan's shoulder in his family garden overlooking the mountainside. She felt complete. The *Elestari* were recovering from their captivity. For the first time in hundreds of years they were mingling freely with other races. The fears of the outside world that had paralyzed them for so long had begun to disappear.

She wrapped her arms around Aohdan and sighed. He held her close. Saoirse could hear the steady beat of his heart. It was the best sound in the world, she decided. He kissed the top of her head and peeled her away from him. She looked up at him in puzzlement.

"There is something that we haven't yet addressed," he told her, a note of gravity in his voice.

Reaching to his throat he touched the pouch that carried the two heartstones. He pulled the cord over his head and set the small bag down onto a rock on the ground.

"What are we going to do with them?" Aohdan asked her. "I've tried to pull them apart and each time they repulse me. I just can't do it."

Saoirse regarded the blackened heartstones thoughtfully. "What if I tried with you? Perhaps two can pull them apart."

Aohdan nodded. Gingerly they each touched a stone. Saoirse felt a blast of burning power that she tried to wrestle against. For a moment she was able to keep her grip on the stone, but soon it grew too much. She yanked her hand away at the same time Aohdan pulled his own hand back.

"That was better," Aohdan said.

Saoirse panted. "Better? I don't want to know what your other tries were like if this was better."

"Let me get Mother and Father. I think you're on to something, Saoirse." Aohdan left her still trying to calm her racing heart while he went to bring his parents out to the garden.

By the time the family had returned, Saoirse's heart had finally returned to its normal speed. She wasn't excited to tackle the heartstones again, but she knew they had to try. This time Aohdan and Avana each held onto their swords as an added conduit for the magic to run through.

On the count of three, the foursome touched the heartstones all at once. Again Saoirse felt the fierce blast of power, but this time something was different. Instead of fighting them, the stones seemed to be testing them, trying to find their motives. Saoirse hardened her resolve to pull the heartstones apart. She had no interest in power, only to put things back to right.

In response, the heartstones came apart with a bright flash of red light. The four touching the stones went flying backwards from the force of the magic. Saoirse lay on her back blinking in astonishment for a moment. Pulling herself upright she saw the others were also scrambling to their feet.

Aohdan held one of the heartstones while Killian had the other. Surprise shot through Saoirse that Killian was able to handle a heartstone. Then she remembered the memories Aohdan had shared with her of the strange affinity Killian had to the sister stone in Illista's pommel. For whatever reason, Killian could take the power of the heartstone.

She watched as Aohdan carefully put his heartstone back into the leather pouch. Killian pulled a handkerchief out of his pocket and wrapped the other heartstone up in it.

"Well that was exciting," Avana said as she dusted herself off.

Aohdan nodded. "That's for sure. Now I can fulfill my promise and return the heartstone to the elves."

"What do you think we should do with this one?" Killian asked.

They stopped and pondered his question. "Do you think Halfor would take it?" Avana said slowly. "I don't want it anywhere near Amaroth. I do not wish to guard it."

Killian gazed at her thoughtfully. "Yes, I think he would."

Aohdan added, "Somehow that feels right. The dwarf kingdom will be better off for it, and they can protect the stone."

"Then I will take it to Halfor," Killian said, tucking the heartstone into his pocket. He turned and left the garden, followed by Avana.

Saoirse let out a huge breath. "I'm glad that's settled."

"Me too," Aohdan replied, watching his parents leave. He turned his gaze back to Saoirse. She saw his eyes flicker with something she wasn't sure how to read.

"Will you travel with me back to the elven realm?" he asked.

"Of course. My last trip got a bit interrupted," Saoirse shot him a smile.

Aohdan took her hand in his. "What about other adventures? Would you go with me if I asked you?"

She laughed. "Yes. If it is in my power to do so, I will go with you."

"What if it's a dangerous journey?" he pressed.

"Then I will still go," Saoirse replied.

"Why would you go with me?" Aohdan continued.

Saoirse tilted her head, trying to figure out what Aohdan was getting at. "Well, I would go because I love you."

A hint of a smile had begun to play over Aohdan's lips at her words. "And what if I asked you on a different sort of adventure?"

"I'd still go along," she answered.

"What if I asked you to go on the adventure of marriage with me?" Aohdan queried.

Saoirse felt her stomach flip at his words. Her heart sang. "Then I would say yes."

"Then in that case, Saoirse, will you marry me?" Aohdan asked, his blue eyes shining.

"Yes. Yes, I will, Aohdan. Yes, I will."

THE END

Acknowledgements

Writing a book is a team effort. Thank you to all who have believed in me, especially my family and friends who have encouraged me to continue on my writing journey. I am so grateful for that love and support. My family are my biggest cheerleaders, and this book would not be possible without them.

I also want to thank my lovely editor Alice Osborn for her support and kind words. She has kept me on track and made my work look better than it deserves. Thank you to Sarah Flood Bauman for an eye catching book cover. People really do judge books by the cover! Great job! Thank you to my interior designer Karina Granda. You have made this book just as beautiful on the inside as it is on the outside.

To all my readers out there, thank you for reading this book. I am so grateful for every person who picks up this story. I hope you have enjoyed it!

And most of all, I want to give God all the glory, for He is the One who gives me inspiration to write.

Fac Recte Nihil Timere
Do Right, Fear Nothing

About the Author

CAITLIN HODNEFIELD has been writing stories since she was a little girl. She loves reading and all things outdoors. Hunting, fishing, and horseback riding are her main passions. If you can't find her inside with a good book, she is probably out riding her horse or sneaking in the woods with her bow. Caitlin can occasionally be bribed into other activities with her favorite snack, popcorn, homegrown by her husband. She is a jill of all trades and has tried her hand at a little bit of everything in the job department. Caitlin would love to meet a real dragon someday and live in a hobbit hole with her husband.

Made in United States
North Haven, CT
24 July 2022

21723290R00159